LURE

BLOOD BROTHERS
BOOK TWO

HEATHER LONG

LURE

Of all the dreams I'd ever chased, the last thing I expected was for a nightmare to be the one that came true.

I'm no stranger to survival. I've always acted a lot tougher than I am, but I'm a big believer in fake it until you make it. But even I couldn't imagine the relentless pursuit of my former kidnappers, and the only thing standing in their way are four calculating and dangerous men.

Each time I think I've found some measure of relief, a new danger threatens to suffocate me. It's not just about who I can trust anymore. No, everyone has an agenda—even me. Why else would I find myself attracted to the men who are keeping me prisoner?

More unsettling, these handsome, complicated men with fire in their eyes that burns hot and cold, do not appear to be in any hurry to let me go. It's not up to them. It can't be.

Not when I need answers. Not when I need to find my sister. Not when every moment that passes is an eternity that pushes her farther and farther away from me. I refuse to bow to anyone or anything.

I'd rather end up a casualty of the hunt than be kept hostage "for my own good" no matter how sexy my jailers are. In this twisted tableau of danger, desire, and deceit, I will take any risk to find her no matter what it costs me.

if your talent is unthinkable chaos, this book is for you

SERIES SO FAR

Burn

Lure

Own

FOREWORD

Dear Reader,

Welcome to the second of five books in the Blood Brothers series. This is a series that should be read in order so if you have not read Burn, please pause and begin there. If you are curious about where the Blood Brothers story came from, I shared some background on that in the foreword of Burn.

Previously in Blood Brothers, model Grace Black found herself kidnapped by a human trafficking operation. While there, she endured assaults, but cooperated while she looked for a way out. When another group attacked the one that had her, she was kidnapped again. This time, she woke on a truck with others being transported to somewhere. When the truck was stopped and they were tacitly rescued, she is introduced to the team that will take them all home.

Two members, Lunchbox and Alphabet escort her to her place in New York. She spends most of it worried about her twin sister Amorette who is also missing. Or so she believes. The guys drop her off at her place but keep watch.

When a team shows up to reacquire her, they take out the team and help her escape.

After rendezvousing with their team, the guys urge her to rest. Then one of the team members—Voodoo—takes her on to the next destination. He is also checking to see if she is being tracked. Bones, the group leader, made this call because he recognized the interest Alphabet and Lunchbox had in her.

After avoiding another hit team, Voodoo takes Grace to a clinic and a physician who locates the tracker in her back and removes it. Emotionally spent and deeply upset, she is beginning to collapse under her own trauma. Voodoo helps to distract her and they have sex.

Bones rejoins them the following day and he's annoyed. They are pursued by another group, that they then have to eliminate. Finally, they reach Alphabet and Lunchbox at a small airport. Together, the guys take her to their place in Montana. They aren't giving her a lot of answers and she's struggling.

She attempts an "escape" and they have to get her down. She and Bones clash frequently. Alphabet's dog Goblin is a source of great comfort for her. When a mission is moved up, the group leaves for Mexico with Grace in tow. Though they keep her at a distance from the action, she encounters an attacker in the barn at their remote location and only Alphabet is still present. She can't scream to warn him.

That brings us to now.

Please be aware this book contains content with dark themes and intense situations intended for mature audiences only, including but not limited to: sexual assault, dubious consent, physical violence, emotional and mental abuse, as well as kidnapping, stalking, manipulation, and other potentially triggering topics.

And now, as always, the housekeeping notes:

For those of you who have never read a why choose, or reverse harem before, first let me thank you for picking this up and giving it a shot. Second, the heroine will not make a choice in this book or any other between the guys in her life. It may take her a while to reach that conclusion, but it's the journey that drives it. There are many ways to frame this kind of relationship, currently why choose fits it very well.

I'll see you on the flip side.

xoxo

Heather

CHAPTER

ONE

ALPHABET

The door to the barn was partially open, and lent more evidence to Gracie being in there. Goblin remained on point next to me. His whole body seemed to vibrate with tension. I flattened my hand.

"Goblin, *bewaken*," I said in Dutch. Goblin's hackles went up and the low tonal growl he responded with told me he was ready. The smell of copper and dirt in the air aggravated me, irritating my nose. If it smelled that bad to me it had to be worse inside.

A flash of Gracie being hurt *again* flashed across my mind. I shuttled it aside and stuffed it into a compartment where it couldn't distract me. Find her, secure her, clear the scene and *then* I could deal with the rest.

The faint drag to my right foot had me making sure I stepped carefully. No way whoever was in there didn't know I was here. Goblin paced me, his aggressive posture didn't have him lunging forward. Not yet, he wouldn't until I gave him the command.

Not wanting to get my head blown off, I crouched as I slid around the door. Duck walking was a bitch, but I ignored my body's complaints. The interior of the barn was all shadows and motes of dust. The lack of a breeze said the only way to disturb that much into the air was activity.

Goblin snapped his head to the left even as a thump of sound reached me. It took less than three seconds to assess the situation playing out in the gloom. A match struck fire to my temper at the man holding Gracie aloft with a fat hand over her mouth. He shook her like a rag doll. The thump was her head hitting the two by four stud.

"*Loop*," I said, snapping my left hand forward. Goblin lunged. He crossed the distance between me and the assailant in mere seconds. He hit the man on the calf and sank his teeth in.

I was already moving as the man let out a shout, his yowl of pain was only a momentary beat of savage satisfaction before he tried to lash out at Goblin. The Staffy avoided the blow and attacked the other leg. The vicious bites penetrated the denim, adding the stain of fresh copper to the air.

To try and fend off Goblin, he had to release Gracie. She dropped, collapsing to the dirt floor like someone had sliced all her strings. Goblin drove the son of a bitch back and right toward me.

"Goblin, *erop*," I ordered and Goblin released the bastard and darted back toward Gracie to protect her. The command pulled the man around to face me. Big dude, but I'd fought bigger.

I ducked the back swing of the guy's meaty paw and slammed my left fist into his kidney as he stumbled past me, then slapped him across his face with the side of my pistol. A knife flashed in his hand and it sliced through the fabric of my shirt, but no pain followed its path.

Despite his behemoth of a size, he was far more spry than I expected. He caught me in the side of the head with a blow from his fist. I twisted, catching his arm with the knife and putting it in a hold. Even as he locked a hand on the wrist of my gun hand.

Yeah, I wasn't going to fire wildly with Gracie and Goblin right there. Our assailant lacked a firearm, and I wasn't letting him have mine. The pressure he put on my wrist was brutal, but I didn't let go of the gun and I kept it pointed away Gracie and Goblin.

The beast of a man let out a growl that vibrated up from his chest. With bared teeth he tried to slam his head into mine. I stumbled back a step, avoiding the strike, and it pulled him off balance. Then I snapped my head forward and slammed it into his nose.

Nose had cartilage, and it didn't hurt as much to strike it with my forehead. But it definitely hurt him. He let out a shriek of pain as blood sprayed from his nose. It covered me but it also caused him to let go of my wrist and he dropped his knife.

He staggered back a few steps, putting a hand up to his bloodied face. The blow had definitely given me a headache, but I really didn't give a shit about that at the moment.

If anything, I wanted to pistol whip him with the Glock until he couldn't move.

Then I wanted to tie him down, and remove all of his digits, one at a time, then his extremities. Answers would be nice. His pain would be better. Sadly, we didn't have that kind of time.

The few scattered seconds between my head butt and his releasing me were far too fleeting. He recovered quicker than I would have liked and he crashed into me, hitting me at the midsection and sending me crashing back through some old boards into what was probably an old stall.

Heavy fucker knocked the breath out of me as we landed. The gun was sliding out of my hand and rather than let him grab it, I sent it skittering into the darkness away from us. He swore in Spanish, but between the nasal obstruction from his bloodied nose and the spittle flying from his lips, I didn't understand him.

It wasn't important, cause he had the knife again, but I got my legs up between us as he reared back and then slammed both feet into his gut. He let out a harsh grunt as I shoved the air out of him. It didn't send him back far enough and he struck with the knife, slamming it right into my right calf and then into the top of my foot.

Ignoring it, I swung my left leg and this one clocked him right in the ear with my foot. He staggered to the side. No more games. No more playing with him. I pulled a knife from the sheath on my belt and I made it to my feet before he made it to his.

The bloodied mess of his face in the shadows, with all the dust flying that had been stirred up by our fight, gave him a gruesome appearance. As much as I wanted to question him, or at least tear him apart strip by strip, we didn't have time for this shit.

Gracie didn't have time for this.

I didn't waste any more time playing with him. Grip firm on the combat knife, I slammed it through his throat from the side, piercing both carotid arteries. Shock rippled across the man's face. I twisted the blade, severing the trachea and the vocal cords as I sliced down.

When I pulled the knife out, blood squirted from the injuries. He slapped his meaty hands against his throat like he could staunch the bleeding. His wet gurgling gasps filled the silence as he staggered. Cutting a person's throat was never a silent or swift way to die—not like they tried to show it in the movies.

He had enough time to recognize he was going to die. To feel the fear leach into his blood as it sprayed out of his body. To want to fight to stay in the land of the living. Fight or flight kicked in, the furious pumping of his heart desperate to get blood to his brain would only serve to shove the blood out of him faster.

Three steps.

He made it all of three desperate steps as he staggered before he went to his knees.

Thirty seconds was an eternity when you couldn't get air or stop the bleeding, when the world began to blink in and out as it faded. It was long enough for the very real fear to punch through the adrenaline.

I gripped his hair and yanked his head back as I stared down at him. "Burn in hell," I told him. "Enjoy the downtime, because when I get there—I'm going to make it much worse."

His mouth moved, the gasps of air punching more blood and bubbles from him, but no sound. He made it to almost forty-five seconds before his struggle ceased and he collapsed. I stared down at him. Slick with his blood, I gave it another ten seconds to make sure his chest didn't rise or fall and that the gasping sounds truly ended.

Then, and only then, did I retrieve my gun. I cut a look over to where Goblin stood guard over Gracie. The good boy hadn't left her. Not even once, his whole body seemed to tremble though. It was a lot to ask him to stay out of the fight, but if I'd lost—I needed to make sure she was safe.

I cleaned the knife off on the guy's pant leg as best I could so I didn't sheathe a bloodied knife. I'd have to clean it later regardless. Then searched the guy for ID. All I found were some keys for what looked like a four-wheeler. That would explain why we didn't hear him arrive.

Asshole.

Phone out, I shoved the guy over and took his picture, then I got closeups of his hand. It wasn't perfect, but I could use it to simulate prints and then I'd run them. Leaving him for the trash he was, I crossed over to Gracie and Goblin. My right leg protested and I was feeling the blows and the bruises.

"Goblin, *vrij*." The release command had his tail wagging as Goblin glanced between me and Gracie. He let out a little whimpering noise and nudged her face. She didn't react, but her chest rose and fell. I wiped my bloodied fingers on my jeans to try and clean them as much as possible before I pressed them to her throat.

Pulse.

A little uneven, but definitely there.

With care, I searched the back of her head. There was a lump and when I pulled my hand away, there was fresh blood on my fingers. I glanced over at the corpse. Too bad I couldn't kill him twice.

"Let's get her out of here," I told Goblin. She needed medical treatment. The girl had taken way too many blows over the past few days. I didn't doubt she'd had at least one concussion before. This would be another.

She weighed next to nothing as I lifted her. The blood on my clothes easily transferred to hers. With a grimace, I braced her against me. There was nothing to be done for it. I needed to get Gracie and our gear packed up and out of here.

It took me a minute to get her back to the house, I left Goblin guarding her as I retreated for the ancient van they'd left parked in the shed behind the barn. We'd only used it to get across the border. That wasn't how we planned to return.

For now, it worked to evacuate us as swiftly as possible. It took me twenty minutes to load the gear and equipment in. I had three messages from the guys, but I ignored them all. I could answer once I had her on the road.

Each time I returned to the house, I checked on her. She was still out, but her breathing had steadied, as had her pulse. There were fresh red marks on her face and her throat.

Every glimpse of them just fired my temper hotter. Once I had everything in the van, I grabbed her bag and threw it in there, then I carried her out with Goblin following. I sent him to pee and then he hopped inside with her. I did one last sweep before I climbed in.

The engine gurgled to life and let out a backfire as we pulled out. Tired slammed into me in waves, but I ignored it and the vibrations of my phone until I'd put a solid couple of miles between us, the house, and the body.

It took effort to not glance back at her. I'd secured her to the bench seat with the ancient seat belts and Goblin lay on the floor right in front of her. Once I made it out to a paved road, I was able to accelerate.

The phone ceased its fits, and I had to call them when we'd gone far enough.

"What happened?" Bones demanded when he answered.

"We had one attacker. No idea who he was. Gracie is down. Assailant is dead. We're on the road. I'm also covered in blood, so we need at least one stop and medical before we head anywhere else."

CHAPTER

TWO

GRACE

The scent of oil, gas fumes, and something far more noxious...

"Damn, Goblin," Alphabet grumbled. "What the hell are we feeding you, my dude?"

I'd never been so damn happy to hear his voice. The van, we were in the van. I cracked my eyes open, but squeezed them shut almost immediately. It was dark, but the light from the dashboard stabbed me right through the eye like an icepick.

My stomach chose that moment to roll as I burped something distinctly hot and unpleasant. I hated vomiting more than this so I did my best to try and quell the all-out rebellion in my gut.

Goblin licked my face, the roughness of his tongue grounding me in the present. I raised a hand to rest it against the side of his head. He went from nuzzling gentle kisses to licking me from chin to eyebrows. It was almost funny, except it was making the pounding inside my skull worse.

Didn't stop me from laughing, or at least attempting to laugh. The pain, however, the sound generated made me groan.

"Hey, Gracie," Alphabet said from ahead of me. "How you doing?"

There was a ten-thousand-dollar question. Kidnapped. Attacked. Assaulted. Kidnapped again. Chained to a wall. Assaulted again? Maybe. Then freed—sorta. Treated. Taken home. Another kidnapping. Attempt that time. Then away with the guys only to be chased, shot at, attacked *again*, and then...

"I don't know," I finally admitted. It was all too much. Each time I tried to sort through it all, the thundering inside my skull took on a jackhammer like quality. It pounded apart the thoughts before I could cobble them together and scattered the debris like so much rock dust.

Goblin let out a little whining sound, but at least he wasn't licking me anymore. Though he leaned heavily against my shoulder and I kind of wanted to cuddle him.

"Hang on dude," Alphabet said. "Finding us a spot right now."

A spot for what? Belatedly, the fact the vehicle was slowing down registered. Goblin leaned into me as our inertia carried us forward. I didn't go far though, there were straps over my legs and my arms.

After the van came to a stop, Alphabet threw the driver's side door open and I made the mistake of cracking my eyelids apart. The muddy light from the dim overhead was like a blow right between the eyes.

"Hold tight, Gracie," Alphabet said. Then the door next

to me slid open. The rattle and grind of metal on metal was pure torture. The cacophony just seemed to echo inside my head adding to the hell and agony pulverizing my thoughts. "Goblin, come."

The puppy left me with a wag of his tail. At least I could register that as it brushed over my hand. Putting my hands down, I tried to push upward, but the seatbelts were kind of in the way.

"Hang on." Alphabet was there and the snap of the buckles releasing seemed ridiculously loud inside the van.

Warm air teased my skin. The smell of corn chips, a hint of syrup, and a dusting of cloves and cedar, with something spicier. The competing scents were not helping my stomach.

"Let me do the work," he said, half-lifting me from the seat and I grimaced.

My head did not like the movement. The smell was even worse, it was like rusty metal or something. The cloying odor clung to my nostrils and coated my throat. My stomach rolled, and the sensation of throbbing right behind my eyes made me groan.

"I'm going to throw up," I warned him.

"I got you," he promised, then I was mostly upright and turned so my back was to his chest. Oh, look, there was dirt and clumps of grass in front of me.

The sick burned its way up. Vomiting produced nothing but bile and acid. The act, however, hurt my throat as much coming up as it did add to the thunder in my head. Panting, I leaned over the arm that Alphabet kept around my midsection.

Probably a good thing or I would have fallen. My breath came in short little pants. I needed to lift my head cause leaning just seemed to add to the pressure on my forehead.

"Worst. Hangover. Ever." No sooner did the complaint pass my lips than I frowned. I hadn't gotten drunk. I hadn't even been at a party. The present threaded its way past all the pummeling in my skull to offer me a series of unpleasant reminders.

Right.

Not drunk. Not even a little tipsy.

We were in Mexico. At least, I was pretty sure we were. The dry air around us and the darkened landscape offered zero clues. We'd been in a little safehouse, a rustic farmhouse with rattling air conditioning and few amenities.

The guys had been out and Bones was a dick. So I took a walk and then...

"There was a guy." It was taking a minute to sort through all the disparate pieces and fit them into place. Some were chipped and a little broken, but I had most of it. The giant man with his fat hands and...

"The guy is dead," Alphabet said, the ease in his voice grounding the panic bubbling in my already beleaguered stomach. "You were out when I got there. Did he do anything I need to know about?"

Did he do anything...?

He'd tried to throttle me. The tightness of his grip on my throat and face seemed to have been permanently imprinted there.

"Just—I don't know. You were out there calling me." That little piece just jostled loose. The guy had been gripping my throat and then he hit my head on the wall. I lifted my hand and touched my fingers to the skin at my neck like I could still feel the guy.

My feet were getting steadier. The dry air wasn't cold, but it seemed chillier against my overheated skin. When I tugged a little at Alphabet, he eased his arm from around my midsection.

"Take it easy," he warned. "I don't want you falling."

"Ditto," I murmured. I needed to move, to get away from the furnace he seemed to create pressed up against me. The slide of his hand over my abdomen to my hip was light and not remotely invasive.

That was something.

I was so over people grabbing me. Just...

Tears burned in my eyes and I shook my head—a mistake—and squeezed my eyes shut to make them go away.

"Careful," Alphabet cautioned again after my first wobbling steps.

"Where are we?" I focused on that rather than what could have happened or did happen, shutting all of that away in the same box I'd been stuffing everything else. It was going to burst sooner or later, but I couldn't afford to fall completely apart.

Not yet.

I will, I promised myself. *Later.*

Ruthlessly suppressing everything wasn't healthy, blah, blah, blah. But I needed to be aware of what was happening and the emotional fallout was going to make all this other trauma look like a walk in the park. So yeah, for now, shutting that shit down was the way to go.

"Honestly," Alphabet said with a long sigh. "Not really sure. I mean, we're halfway between where we were and a town called *La Seguridad.*" Tiredness marked the words.

I frowned, adding that new snippet of information to the other bits and pieces. Hands on my hips, I continued to pace away slowly.

"Here," Alphabet suddenly appeared next to me, bottle of water in hand.

That looked frigging amazing. It was also cold and I rinsed my mouth with the first couple of sips then spit it out before I took a longer drink. Closing my eyes, I pressed the bottle to my cheek.

"Thank you," I whispered.

"I'm sorry," Alphabet said by way of answer, and it took a moment for those three syllables to sink in. Twisting, I finally looked at him.

It was still an almost impossible dark out here, but the muddy little light from inside the van offered a suggestion of illumination. But Alphabet stood between me and the van so it made "seeing" him a challenge.

"For what?" I grimaced. Honestly, he could be apologizing for just about anything really. Holding me captive. Not letting me call or go see about my sister. Maybe the fact that boney boy was a dick. The possibilities were a little wide and varied.

A damp nose brushed against my hand and I glanced down to find Goblin had rejoined us. Another bump of his head to my palm, I gave him a gentle scratch between the eyes.

"For you getting hurt on my watch." Alphabet turned away. "Shouldn't have happened."

"It's not your fault." I ran my fingers through my hair, carefully aware of the tenderness along the back of my skull. There was definitely a lump and the hair had matted some. I pulled my hand back and stared at my fingers. I couldn't tell if there was blood on them.

"I said you would be safe with us," Alphabet said as he continued to the back of the van. He popped open one of the doors and the muddy light there hit him. The dark stain on his shirt extended down to his jeans and across his neck.

The rusty smell hit me again when the breeze shifted. Alphabet peeled the shirt off of himself. The way it stuck to him as he dragged it upwards and seemed to fight letting go made me grimace.

"Are you okay?"

"I'm fine, Gracie," he said without looking at me. He dropped the shirt to the ground with a plop and my stomach rolled. With the light on him, the stain on the shirt had also smeared his chest.

It was blood.

He was covered in blood.

Goblin let out a low whine and it jerked my attention downward.

"Take a deep breath," Alphabet said. "We're both alive and the threat has been dealt with."

I crouched to pet Goblin rather than waver on my feet. I was already fighting to keep from getting sick again. The water helped and the air helped, but...

Alphabet had wipes in his hands and he was cleaning himself up. "Good girl," he said, shooting me a look. "Just give me a sec and you won't have to smell or see it. Then we can get you cleaned up too. How's the head?"

"Still hurts," I admitted, sliding past the idea that I needed to clean up too, especially since my back was sticky. "Hurts a lot."

"Keep hydrating," Alphabet advised as he studied his arms before wiping them down again. He glanced over at me. "Sit on the ground if you need it or sit in the back of the van. I don't want you to fall or pass out."

I'd have argued that I wasn't likely to pass out, but somehow, I didn't have it in me to pick the fight. With

Goblin planted next to me, I took a seat on the hard packed earth. The dog leaned into me, his tongue lolling in that happy grin he wore.

With a sigh, I glanced back at Alphabet as I took another swallow of water. He wore a gun strapped to his hip. I somehow doubted he planned to change his jeans out here. Hopefully, they weren't as bloody.

I avoided looking at his crotch as I swept my gaze lower and then froze. "Oh my god…"

"What?" He was two strides away from the van and the gun that had been holstered was now in his hand. He swept the area with a look before he focused on me. Even Goblin had gone still and alert next to me. "What did you see?"

"You have a knife in your leg—and your foot." I gawked at him. There was no mistaking the hilt that jutted upwards from his boot and lower shin. How the hell was he even walking around like… "I don't really know first aid, but we need to do something."

There was a brief pause as Alphabet glanced down at his leg and then back at me. "Oh. That's not a problem." His faint smile held no amusement or comfort. "I thought something was really wrong."

He slid the gun away with a sigh, then made a flat hand motion and Goblin went back to panting and relaxed against me.

"*Not* a problem?" I stared at him. "You have a *knife* in your foot." Yes, my head was killing me but was he *insane*?

"Easy, Gracie," Alphabet said, making that same flat hand gesture even as his voice took on a soothing note. "Come here."

"Why?" Instantly suspicious, I put the cap back on the water bottle.

"I'd say trust me, but I know we've lost a few steps

there. So just come here and I'll show you why it's not a problem."

He was going to show me why…

Maybe I'd just taken one too many blows over the past few days, or the latest concussion had knocked something loose in my brain. Pushing up from the ground, I rose carefully.

Hand extended, he took a step toward me and I had to repress a shudder at the fact he was putting weight on that leg. Still, I took a beat to make sure I wasn't going to fall on my face before I headed toward him.

Goblin trotted next to me, seemingly unconcerned. Once I made it to the back of the van, Alphabet backed up a couple of steps and motioned to me to sit. At my bland stare, he gazed back—waiting.

Right, if I wanted to know, I had to cooperate. "I don't know if I mentioned this before, but I'm really not good with orders."

"You're not?" He even managed to sound scandalized. "Total shocker, Gracie-girl." I rolled my eyes and sat.

"Ass."

"Sometimes," he said, and this time there was a real hint of humor in his smile. "Now, take a breath. The knife is fine and I kind of forgot it was there."

How the hell did you *forget* something like that?

He braced his foot on the back of the open van next to me. Yes, it gave me a *wonderful* up close and personal view of the hilt of the blade, the bloody smears on the handle and the fact that his jeans did have blood on them—only none near his lower leg or foot.

"Gonna yank it out," he warned me about two seconds before he jerked the blade out. It took some effort for him to get it out and there had to have been four or five inches of steel embedded in him.

No blood sprayed.

He didn't make a sound.

And the knife was out.

"Like I said, not a problem," Alphabet said. When I lifted my gaze to him, he set the knife aside and then rolled up his pant leg to reveal the prosthetic beneath. "See?"

CHAPTER

THREE

Staring at his prosthetic was probably rude as fuck so I focused on the area around us, not that I could see much. The darkness was deep, but when the light behind went out it was like the night took on a texture of its own. Above, there were so many stars.

"Keep drinking the water," Alphabet advised as he tugged on a clean shirt. The sound of his zipper pulled my attention back to him. "Just getting changed," he said, not looking at me. Or maybe he was. The velvet night outlined him. He was a darker shadow amidst the others, but maybe it was the memory of the light from the car made his blonder hair seem almost like a halo.

Or maybe my brain was just making shit up.

I opened my mouth to offer to help, but then closed it again and leaned my head against the side of the van and stared at the sky again. In school, there were pictures in books about the stars and they showed up in the movies.

But this was...

"It's something else, isn't it?" he asked.

"I've always lived in cities," I admitted. "Traveled to cities. Lived close to cities."

"Sometimes, the best part of deployment was where it took us—took me. First time I saw anything like this, I was in a high desert in the mountains. Cold enough to freeze your nuts off, but we couldn't use a fire. Not that I would have traded the view for the warmth."

"Do they go away with any light pollution?" That was the word right. The throb of the headache had taken on a steady cadence. It wasn't quite killing me anymore, but I wouldn't mind if it went away.

How many concussions was too many? It had to be a concussion, right?

"Not totally," he said and there was something soothing about his voice in the dark. Goblin was nearby, I could hear the soft huffs of his panting. The smell of metallic rust and sweat still coated my nose but then a breeze would come to brush it away. "It does take away from some of it. It's best on a night with no moon."

That made sense.

"Drink, Gracie." The gentleness in his tone softened the order to a request. Thankfully, he didn't continue to press me. Course, I also unscrewed the top of the water bottle and took a drink.

His movements disturbed the air so I could kind of follow him getting dressed again. While I didn't comment, a part of me wondered how hard it was to get dressed, or undressed for that matter, with the prosthetic.

Also, how far up did it go? What had happened to his leg? Clearly, he'd been injured. I wasn't a total idiot even if my brain actually hurt at the moment. They were all former military, they had to be. Or close to it.

"How did you get the name Alphabet?" The question slipped out in the darkness. I'd already asked Voodoo what his real name was and he hadn't answered me. Or maybe he had and that answer was none of my business.

"My name is a bitch sometimes," Alphabet admitted. "I always have to spell it for people. It became a running joke... so—Alphabet."

I took another long drink of the water. He popped open the wipes. The faint scent of the scentless teased me. Nothing was truly scentless.

"I'm going to guess you like it better than the other?" I mean, it was still a question but when men in their what? Mid-thirties? Went by nicknames permanently, they had to like them, right?

"Eh," he said and I could almost hear the smile that kissed the words. "It's not bad. And I don't have to spell it."

A snort escaped me. "I mean... I guess you could always sing it if someone does ask."

The silence that greeted my statement had me swallowing my own humor with another long gulp of water. I'd almost finished all of it and my stomach wasn't rolling anymore. Good sign, right?

He huffed, then let out a real chuckle. "Sing it." I could almost picture him shaking his head. "You know what, Gracie. Maybe I will next time."

That made me grin all over again. There was the sound of plastic rustling, probably sacking up his filthy clothes. The smell was much better so I'd take it.

"Now, for the hard question," Alphabet said and I had to fight the urge to roll my eyes.

"Because everything else that's happened has been so easy and gentle."

"True," he mused. "But you're a big girl. You can handle it."

Yes, I probably could. Or I could fake it. Either way... "What's the hard question?"

"Do you want to change? I'll be honest, I was more worried about getting you away and making sure you didn't have any open wounds than I was worried about your clothes. But I also didn't realize how sticky some of that shit still was on me when I put you into the van and got you out."

I made a face. "Would you mind looking at my back for me? I really don't want anyone's blood on me." Not even my own.

"I don't mind at all." A simple, straightforward answer. I screwed the cap back on the empty bottle. "Light coming on." Instead of the overhead which I expected, he had a flashlight in his hand pointed at his boots.

It was much brighter than I expected, but also whiter than the muddy light from the overhead. Weird, the things you noticed. I pushed up from where I sat on the lip of the back and turned away.

The light threw my shadow against the door and past it. Goblin was right there, panting. It wasn't that warm out here but maybe he was tired. "Should we give him water?"

"Yep," Alphabet answered. "We will. Going to touch your back, okay?"

"Okay."

Instead of touching me directly though, he pulled the sticky shirt away from my back and my stomach rolled. A shudder rippled through me and then there was a hand on my shoulder.

"Breathe," he ordered. This time it was not a request. "It's mostly sweat, I would imagine. But there is some blood. So, your bag is right there... let's get you out something clean and..."

The light swept lower, over my leggings.

"Your butt looks fine, and your legs. So I don't think you got any there. Shoes are good." He swept the light upwards again. "Touching your head, okay?"

Despite the no-nonsense tone, he waited for my response.

"Yes, I found a lump. But I don't think it was bleeding."

"Well, that's something." He moved a little closer, then his hand was in my hair, gentle as a butterfly's wings while his fingertips traced over my scalp. "Definitely a lump. I'm pretty sure you have a concussion."

"I kind of guessed."

"You're going to be fine," he continued as though there were zero other options.

"Or what?" The tease fell out of me. "Going to sing me the ABCs?"

His snort pulled a real, if reluctant smile to my lips. "I might save that for when you do something really bad." As fast as the humor appeared, it vanished. "We'll save that for later though. Right now, let's get you cleaned up and get Goblin some water and we'll get back on the road."

"Can't wait." If he could fake enthusiasm. So could I.

Changing meant taking the shirt off in front of him. Not that I cared.

"I can turn around if you want." It was a nice offer.

"It's just a body, AB," I told him. "And if you don't mind doing me one more favor, I'd like it if you could make sure to wipe any of the blood off me."

"AB?" He repeated the letters in order. "Giving me another nickname, Gracie?"

"If you hate it..."

"I don't," he said quickly. "It's kind of nice. Okay, let's get you cleaned up. Once we've got signal again, I'll tag Voodoo about the pain relievers you can have for that headache."

Changing me took almost no time at all. I did my best to not think about any dampness I touched as I stripped the shirt off. He used the light and a wipe to clean up my back then he sighed.

"Gracie..."

"It's on the bra too, isn't it?"

"Sorry." The funny thing was, he sounded absolutely sincere.

"I'll live." I reached behind me and undid the snaps then shrugged it off. It fell on the ground and I left it there. He finished wiping down my back. The wipe itself was cool and it left goosebumps in its wake as the breeze hit. He cleaned away all the traces of the earlier attack.

If only everything could be washed away as easily.

"All done. Do you need me to get you a bra?" He handed me a fresh wipe. I'd already pulled out a t-shirt, but I made sure my hands were as clean as I could get them.

"No, thank you. One upside to my tits. I don't bounce that much." I tugged the shirt on. It was dark too. Even the perceived sensation of something on my skin had me shuddering.

When I would have reached for the bra, Alphabet touched my arm lightly. "I'll get it, put it in the bag with my stuff. Go back up front and get some more water for us and for Goblin?"

I tried not to let my relief show, because yeah, the last thing I wanted to do was touch the items again. Frankly, we could burn them. I wasn't sure you could get that much blood out in the wash. Especially not what was on him.

"On it." The water cooler was tucked under the back bench seat. Weird van, but someone had restocked it. So I opened a bottle and filled the bowl hanging off the pack on the front passenger seat. Goblin trotted over as I set it down and he slurped down the water.

I opened a bottle for Alphabet as he closed the back-doors then came up to where we were. Once he was in arms reach, he shut the flashlight off again. It took a moment for my eyes to adjust and I found myself staring upward again. The scattering of stars across the sky were really beautiful.

"Do they look different from different parts of the world?"

"I don't think so," he answered in an equally quiet voice. Only the sound of Goblin lapping up his water filled the air around us. "I guess it might look different depending on the time of the year, but I never really noticed it. Just... like looking at them."

I did too. There was something peaceful about them. They were all so far away and seemed small, but we were the small ones really. "Think this is what it would be like to have a time machine?"

His soft snort made the corners of my lips twitch. "Maybe. Their light could have taken thousands of years to get here. We could be seeing those stars and the Milky Way how it appeared when dinosaurs roamed the Earth."

"That's—unsettling."

"But cool," he intoned, then took a long drink of his water. "Still got Goblin's bottle?" I passed it to him without question. He crouched and emptied the rest of the bottle out for the dog. "What do you think?"

"About how long it took the light to get here?"

"Sure," he answered. Maybe he hadn't meant that.

"I don't know what to think. Not really. I mean they're

gorgeous and looking up at this now... I never want to move from here. I want to see this forever, but that's not how time works or life for that matter."

"True, but if you like the stars, Gracie. We will find you more stars. There's a couple of good spots at base where we get some excellent views of them. If you want, I'll show you when we're back."

"AB?"

"Don't ask me to let you go, Gracie. Not yet. Not while you're not safe." The length of his sigh wore at me. "I know you weren't safe back there and that's on me. But I'm not letting that happen again. Once we get this solved, find out the threat and eliminate it... then you can go home."

"We don't even know what the threat is," I said. "Other than human traffickers, I can't imagine that's a short list. Then there's Amorette..."

"I haven't forgotten her." Nothing about his words sounded like a lie. But a good lie wouldn't. That's what made them a good lie. "Like I said earlier, you need to learn to trust us. Trust takes time."

"Even if I tell you no and say just drop me off somewhere, that's not an option, is it?" I'd ask every single one of them if I had to.

"You already know the answer." He crouched again and came up with Goblin's bowl. "Want to ride in the front with me now that you're awake?"

"Sure," I said. What other answer was there? Sit in the back and sulk like a child? I mean, the idea had merit, but at the moment, my head hurt too damn much for that.

With a light nudge, he moved me aside and removed the pack from the passenger seat. He moved to the back and stored it, then got Goblin up into the back at his command. The panel door slid shut after him.

I stared up at the stars while he got us ready. They really were beautiful. I'd never cared for camping when we were growing up. Maybe I needed to add that to my list of hobbies.

Am would probably laugh, then worry I needed therapy if I brought it up. The idea of her laugh made me smile. Definitely needed to tease her with it now. Just to find out.

I missed her.

The driver's side door slammed shut. It was time to go. Lowering my gaze, I stared out into the darkness. This felt like a weird metaphor for my life. There were bright, unexpected moments, but everything else was shrouded in darkness.

Alphabet didn't hurry me along. I gave myself one last look at the stars, then I climbed into the passenger seat and pulled on the seat belt.

"So what are the rules?" I asked, summoning up some humor.

"For?" Alphabet asked as he got the van started.

"For the music. Driver controls it or do I get some say?"

CHAPTER

FOUR

It was almost one in the morning and I hadn't heard from the guys for more than two hours. Going radio silent wasn't unusual. They were all more than capable of looking after themselves, but there was an itch in between my shoulder blades that seemed to increase with every minute that passed.

Gracie waking up helped allay at least one of my worries. Though, I kept one eye on her too. Her speech hadn't been slurred earlier, but it had been *slow*. I couldn't imagine her head felt great.

Another reason I remained intensely aware of the passage of time. I wanted Voodoo to give me some direction on what meds she could have. We had a whole damn kit in the back, though I was leery of giving her anything without consultation.

A glance at my watch told me I was still heading in a rough northwest direction. We'd crossed into Mexico via New Mexico, our route out would take us via California.

There were a couple of spots we had friends that could grease the wheels.

If we had to go overland, we'd do that too. I'd rather avoid having to take her on foot though. She didn't need to push it. Her breathing didn't sound labored and she wasn't complaining about any chest pain. If she'd complained of either, I'd have asked to check her ribs.

"The stations here are shit," she muttered after her umpteenth attempt to find one we could even tune in. So far the closest we'd come was a news station. We'd listened for all of about five minutes before the signal dropped again.

"It's the reception," I said by way of apology. "There's no bluetooth in here or I'd offer to play something from my phone." As it was, if we tried to just listen to my phone it wouldn't be loud enough over the rattle of the ancient van.

The vehicle was great for traveling incognito but it definitely lacked any amenities. Not something we normally worried about. Gracie deserved better. Another glance at my watch told me that only five minutes had passed since my prior check.

Impatience crept through me. I debated trying to call them but that would break with protocol. Then again, our protocols didn't take Gracie into account. Putting a pin in that, I made a mental note to update our protocols. We needed better ones.

"Are you okay?" The soft question punctured the bubble of worry around me. Goblin had left the bench in the back to come up to sit on the open space between us. His soft wuff was a reminder he was there.

"I will be," I told Gracie rather than lie to her. "As much as I want to tell you that there is nothing to worry about, it wouldn't be fair to mislead you."

"Well, I kind of figured we had things to worry about. I mean…" She lifted a hand to motion to herself with a kind of wry smile. "I know that I look like I have all of this handled, but not sure I'm doing that great either."

"Head still hurt?"

"I'll live," she said in a kind of droll voice that I didn't care for. "I'd say I've had worse, but pretty sure that wouldn't be true either. As epically shit weeks go, this has to be in the top five, probably top three. Maybe top two."

"You have something that tops this?" Did I really want to know? To be fair, I could think of a few incidents in my own life that seemed worse than her past week or two, but that was comparing apples and oranges. I'd signed up for my shit.

She definitely *hadn't*.

"The week my mom died," she said and all the air went out the teasing jokes I'd been trying to think of to alleviate the mood. "We knew it was coming, didn't make it any less hard."

Turning her head to look out the window again, she sighed.

"I'm sorry," I said, because what else could I offer? "It's just you and your sister, right?" I'd been putting together a lot of info on her, but I hadn't finished the deep dive. There was an older brother—deceased—as well as the deceased mother. Nothing on the father. Just absent.

The majority of the background came from her sister and herself. On the surface, Gracie lived a very public life. Yet, comparing what was available publicly about her with what I'd put together interacting with her… There was just so much more to her than the public face she let the rest of the world see.

The woman in the van with me was not the woman

portrayed in the gossip columns and articles. If anything, she seemed so much more real and down to earth.

"Yes," Grace answered with the longest, most profound sigh. "Hopefully, anyway."

I frowned. "Gracie..."

"Don't promise me we will find her. Don't ask me to keep trusting you when you can't even promise to let me go. You need your illusions and lies. I need mine." The flatness in her words chilled me. We had asked her exactly that. *I* had, not even all that long ago.

"I want to find her for you," I offered.

"Okay," she said. "I'd like to find her period, so I guess that will have to be enough for now."

Aggravation exploded through me. I opened and closed my mouth several times. A huff of a sigh dragged my attention downward briefly. Goblin had his head on her thigh and she was stroking him. I got the need for self-soothing and hated myself even more for being another factor in the reason she needed it.

Jerking my attention back to the empty road ahead, I scowled. The lack of highway lights, speed limit signs—signs of any kind really—and places to stop said more about our remoteness than anything else.

Where the fuck were the guys? We needed to get back to base, and I needed to find her sister and prove to Gracie that we could keep our goddamn promises.

White knuckling the steering wheel while I tried to focus on sniper breathing to wrestle my temper back under control helped. Not much, but some. Then like a gift, my phone rang.

Finally.

I snatched it up, and answered with one stroke of my thumb over the screen. "Alphabet."

"We've hit a few complications." Bones' steady voice didn't do much for my nerves.

"Not enough of them," Lunchbox snapped. "Or we wouldn't have problems."

"How many and how far?" I scanned the area automatically. I saw no other headlights and I hadn't for more than an hour. If I had to intercept them, we might be too far to do much good.

"We're twenty minutes out," Bones answered as though Lunchbox hadn't issued a single comment. "Maybe thirty if the tracker is off."

I doubted it. Part of why I hadn't checked their location earlier, Grace was more important in that moment and I didn't want to know if they were in trouble. Not until I was in a position to do something about it.

Twenty to thirty minutes, that gave me time to find a good spot. "How many? And do you have a plan?"

"Well, the plan was to lose them a few hours ago." The conversational tone peppered with Lunchbox's derisive snort actually made me smile. The fact that Voodoo wasn't saying anything didn't bode well. Then again, he tended to avoid our arguments with Bones, preferring to deal with him directly.

"They are apparently not taking no for an answer, however. That leaves us with the options of digging in and eliminating or pulling them into the trap."

I was the trap.

"Understood. Numbers?" Since he'd skipped that part.

"Ten or twelve," Lunchbox said before Bones could. "Pretty sure we hit a couple of them, but they are spread out over three vehicles—"

The report of a gunshot echoed in the background.

"Nine or eleven," Voodoo tossed in. "Also a motorcycle, but he keeps dropping back. Sneaky little shit."

"Got it. Line them up," I said. "I'll send a message when I'm in position." I hung up and stared ahead then glanced to the area around us. It was just all dark emptiness around us.

"What's wrong?" Grace asked.

There was zero point in lying to her.

"We are going to have problematic company and I need to find a place to deal with it." Sooner rather than later.

"More tossing bombs on them kind of problematic company?" The direct question almost made me smile.

"Close, but not letting them get that close." I glanced down at my phone then ahead again. The silence dragged taut between us.

"Can I help?" The unexpected offer left me in a quandary. She could, but she shouldn't have to. "I mean I don't really know anything about mixing up chemicals or anything..."

The laugh that escaped was more disbelief than humor. "We don't have the stuff for that on board."

"Oh," she said, with a long exhale of relief. "Good. I suck at throwing things."

I snorted. Not how I remembered it, particularly since she'd nailed Bones but good. Still, a conversation for another time. "Are you good to look at a phone while we're moving?"

"Yes," she said.

I unlocked the screen and tabbed open the map. "We're the red dot, they will be the blue dot. You should also be able to see the landscape, tell me if there are any good hills or rises—something with a vantage point." Then I handed over my phone.

Her silence wasn't promising, but I let her scan the screen. Goblin had settled back on the floor. Good boy had relaxed so maybe she had too. There was tension knotting in my gut and bleeding into my veins.

"It's pretty flat." The frown she had to be wearing reflected in her voice. "How high do you need?"

"Not that high, just a place to get the van out of sight and where I can..." Goddammit.

"Where you can target them?" Her fearless attitude humbled me. This was not a thing she needed to be dealing with.

"If I tell you, I make you an accessory." That seemed a reasonable point.

"If I find the location for the ambush, I'm already an accessory." Apparently, she had the skills for absolutely sinking my battleship.

"Then yes, where I can target them. We need to clean up any pursuers so we can get back to base." At this point, I didn't care if the damn job was done or not. We could refund the fucking money. Nothing was worth putting Gracie at this kind of risk.

"Right. I see something that looks like it might be a little hillier, the ground is bumpy. Maybe." Wasn't much but we didn't need much.

"How far?"

"Um..."

"Press your finger to the area and drop a flag on it, then hit the arrow."

"Oh, that's easier. It says a little over thirty minutes at ninety kilometers an hour."

"That would make it forty-five kilometers. Actual distance?" The van was gonna rattle like fuck when I pushed it, but we could push it.

"Says it's closer to thirty-seven kilometers, at least to the center of the flag, if I move the flag to the edge…" She went quiet for a long moment. "Oh, that's much better, that's less than thirty kilometers."

Right. "Hit the arrow again, and then go, then tab over to the phone log and call back the last number that called me."

The GPS offered me instructions, including telling me we would be on our current road for a lot longer than we needed to be before we turned north.

Grace didn't argue or ask more questions, but she held up the phone which rang once on speaker. Bones answered after the ring.

"You have something?"

"Dropping you a pin. Meet me there. Don't take any detours."

I wanted to get Gracie back to base. Finished, I motioned to Gracie to end the call and she hung up.

"That felt good." The savage satisfaction in her voice made me laugh.

"Hanging up on Bones?"

"Yes." She didn't even pretend she didn't enjoy it. "He's a dick."

I could argue the point, but I didn't. Right now, I preferred the boost to her mood. Selfishly, I'd like it to last a little longer.

"Do me another favor?" I said. "Climb in the back and call Goblin up onto the seat and thread his harness on so he's buckled in."

"Okay." She handed me my phone back before she unbuckled, then climbed back there. Goblin, the good boy, did as he was told and she got him buckled in, then he laid down. "You want me back here buckled in or up there?"

Not smiling was a challenge. "Up here is fine, but definitely buckled in." She didn't make me wait, returning to her seat and then pulling the seatbelt across her chest. I wasn't sure if these buses came with these kinds of harnesses or if someone had upgraded them.

I also didn't care.

"Hold tight," I said. "This ride is about to get bumpy."

Then I did a hard turn off the highway and onto the hard packed earth. The arid land might crumble in places, but it was as sturdy as any dirt road. It also shaved time off the drive. A lot of time.

The sound of the van rattling climbed and if I didn't trust our contact, I'd worry about it falling apart with the way it vibrated. As it was, Grace let out a sharp laugh—whether it was in disbelief or shock, who knew, but I did like hearing it.

She said something, but I missed it. "What?"

"I said," she shouted. "You're crazy."

I grinned. "Yes, Gracie-girl, I am."

Then I pushed the accelerator to the floor.

CHAPTER

FIVE

Between the violent shaking of the van as Alphabet raced across the desert, coupled with the vibrations rattling my body, I was kind of surprised it didn't make my head hurt worse. Honestly, it had, for a bit, but the noise and the bouncing seemed to drown out the ache. Weird.

Or maybe not. It wasn't like I hadn't done plenty of shoots with a hangover. Sometimes, you just had to rely on the music and the laughter to boost your endorphins. Granted, a race over inhospitable landscape in an ancient Volkswagen Bus van that reminded me of the Scooby Doo Mystery Machine had never been on my bucket list.

But hey, here we were.

I tightened my grip on the oh shit handle as the van bounced into a dip and then up again. This was not the vehicle we needed to catch air in. Alphabet's sudden laugh reached me and I whipped my head to look at him. The wide grin on his face was wildly infectious and I found myself smiling in response.

Until he looked at me.

"Eyes on the—" I ordered, glancing forward. "Dirt or whatever."

A fresh bark of laughter escaped him. "Don't worry, Gracie-girl, we're almost there."

That shouldn't be comforting, yet my grin felt just this side of feral as I held on tight. I stole a look at the map on the phone. The distance had been shaved considerably. What had been thirty-ish minutes had been trimmed to under five now.

If I'd thought it had been remote before, it had nothing on this. There were rises ahead. Dark rocks jutting upward like dark fingers reaching for the sky. Despite the starry sky, I wasn't sure how I could make out any of these details. The next hard bounce had my teeth clacking together.

That definitely didn't help the headache. Light spilled over the side of one rock, giving it a red, ruddy appearance. *Like it had been stained with blood...*

The moon was on the horizon, where it hadn't been before. Half-full, it offered so much light to turn the inky blackness into a more velvet blue-black. We were already slowing down from the juddering pace. I was going to feel those vibrations in my soul permanently.

It couldn't have been more than fifteen minutes since he took us off-roading. I reached for the phone where he had it set. We were almost to the flagged location. And I was right... It hadn't been more than fifteen minutes. It had been twelve.

"Gonna find a place to set up. I'm going to need you to stay in the van, Gracie-girl."

"I hate that." The answer escaped me almost automatically and he shot me a glance. At least I could hear myself think again. The thud of my headache was still there and it seemed to throb into my teeth. "I get it, I'm not some super bad-ass spy-mercenary-action hero chick, but I'm not some helpless damsel either."

We were amongst the huge rocks when he finally stopped the van and cut a look toward me. Lips pursed, he studied me.

"Before you say anything..." I said, pointing a finger at him. "The vehicle isn't always safe *either*." Granted, he hadn't been there when Voodoo, Bones, and I had been forced off the road and down that hill, but it was a fact.

Instead of arguing, Alphabet smashed his lips flat as he stared forward. I could almost see him arguing with himself. That was better than arguing with me, so I wouldn't complain. I glanced at the phone. The blue dot was getting closer to us. But it was coming from a different angle.

Hopefully, they were on the road and not taking our shortcut. "Not sure how far away they are, but they are headed to us."

"If you go with me and Goblin, you do *exactly* what I tell you, when I tell you, no questions or arguments."

"Okay." I could agree with that. Because it also meant I wouldn't be stuck here in the van wondering what the hell was going on or risking getting hit again. The barn was safe the first time we wandered out to it at the safe house. I had no idea where that man came from or who he was or why he'd attacked me.

Honestly, I wasn't sure why any of this had targeted me or if they had targeted Am and I'd been swept up into it. The sickening realization had been there in the pit of my stomach since the nightmare began—none of this was an accident.

If that was true, then it was a solid chance that Am was *definitely* missing. The cold dread of that reality struck like a sucker punch to the gut. Tears burned in my eyes and I forgot how to breathe.

A whine from the backseat had Alphabet twisting toward me. "Hey…"

I swallowed around the hard lump in my throat and blinked furiously. I didn't want to cry. I didn't want to *feel* any of this. Am *had* to be okay. If it was me living in denial, then I would invest in a vacation home here. I was going to hold on until my fingernails were gone and I didn't have the strength for it anymore.

"I'm okay," I lied. "I mean, I'm not, but I will be. What do you need me to do?" The last thing I wanted to do was talk about any of this. Not about what happened or why or who…

Alphabet touched my chin with light fingers and I shifted my gaze to meet his. The contact was barely there, another illusion of connection but one I leaned into this time, instead of away.

"I will be okay," I told him. "I promise. We don't have time for me to be anything else."

He studied me and I hoped he found whatever he was looking for, because I couldn't fake it anymore than I already had. Not when we had a whole other threat on its way to us.

"We're going to talk about this again," he said in a voice that was almost too soft. It held more force than when he'd yelled earlier.

"Later," I murmured, needing him to agree. But would he? "If you insist."

"I do," he said, with a nod. "For now, unbuckle Goblin and let him out." He swept a look down me. "It's going to be chilly out there, grab a jacket from the back and a knit cap."

He was agreeing and an unreasonable amount of gratitude spilled through me. "Okay."

With that, he let me go, shut off the van and climbed out. He wasn't kidding about the cooler air. Goosebumps decorated my skin as I released my own seatbelt then climbed into the back to free Goblin.

The dog gave me an open mouth grin before he licked me from chin to eyeball. It was ridiculous and made me laugh. "You're welcome," I told him before I slid open the side door. Goblin hopped right out without needing me to say a word.

Even without a breeze, the sweat on me seemed to make it colder. I hadn't even realized I had been sweating. I closed the side door before I circled to the back. Alphabet had a huge case in his hand and he passed me a jacket and a knit cap. I put them on then took the next bag he handed me.

"Let's go."

True to my word, I didn't ask anything as I followed him up the rise to where the rocks continued to stretch toward the sky. It didn't seem like we were that much higher, and we weren't—from the van. Apparently, we'd come up an incline or to the top of an incline.

Goblin paused to piss on a rock before he trotted after us. The walk was up a bit more of a gentle sloping hill. Or maybe not so gentle, it made the backs of my legs protest. Once we got to a spot where we could see the desert spread out below us or as much as we could with the light of the moon, he set down his case.

"Get down, flat to your belly."

"Where do you want the bag?" I mean, he'd said no questions, but then he gave me the bag.

He faced me and lifted the strap off my shoulder with a faint smile. "I have it."

I nodded once then dropped to lay on my belly. The rock was definitely cold and hard. Alphabet didn't say anything, just unlocked the case and flipped it open. There was a gun inside... a *really* big gun.

He set his phone on the ground next to me so I could see the screen too. We were still the red dot, I assumed, and that blue dot was definitely getting closer. Goblin came to sit next to me while Alphabet assembled the gun.

I didn't know what it was, but it was damn impressive. A dozen questions formed and died on my tongue. Maybe we could revisit those later too. Still, once he had the gun together, he set it up on some kind of stand that kept the barrel up while he laid down and put his eye to the scope.

The silence grew deeper now that the shivers of metal scraping on metal as he put the pieces together faded. Then he unzipped the bag, splitting the quiet. He passed me a pair of binoculars and then pulled out a huge cartridge that he plugged into the gun itself.

With a sharp clack of the slide bolt, he had loaded a bullet. There was no mistaking that sound. I swallowed again. "Use the binoculars, let me know the minute you see a vehicle heading this way. They should be close enough to spot by now."

Happy to pull my attention from his monster weapon, I put the binoculars to my eyes and then snickered. His monster weapon.

Oh my god, Grace. Shut up.

"What's funny?"

"Absolutely nothing," I said, sobering immediately. Because it shouldn't be funny. Voodoo was definitely packing and it wouldn't surprise me if Alphabet was.

Shut. Up. Brain.

As inappropriate and insane as those thoughts were, they buoyed my mood. How much crazier could my life get? Binoculars up, I frowned because the world wasn't dark through them. If anything, it was—

"Oh, these are night vision." That was cool.

Alphabet chuckled then said something in what sounded like Dutch. I didn't speak that as well as I did German. Hmm, maybe a new language to learn. But rather than ask, I focused.

I caught the dust of their movement first. "Got them."

"Tell me how many and what the configuration is..."

Didn't he—*No questions, Grace.*

"SUV, large in the front, followed by two more, one is an SUV, the other looks like a bigger car. There's something smaller too..."

Flashes of white popped into and out of view. I backed my head up a little then frowned again. Some flashes of white came from the SUV in the front.

Gunfire.

It was gunfire.

How had they made it all this way shooting at each other? The SUV in the front kept pulling away and the one behind it kept trying to catch up. There were more flashes and the cars behind it dropped back.

That was how.

"Okay, there's also a motorcycle, SUV and a big car, I don't know what kind it is."

"That's fine," Alphabet said in a comforting voice. "Hit the right button on the binoculars, it's going to start giving you numbers. Focus on the closest vehicle *behind* the first SUV."

That made sense. The first SUV was our guys, I would guess. Lines appeared in my view, then green numbers began to flicker, once I had the feel for it, I shifted the view to the vehicles behind the SUV.

They were definitely getting closer.

I rattled off the first series of numbers. Then said, "They are getting lower. Do I need to count it down?"

"You can," Alphabet said.

I didn't make it two numbers before the gun next to me fired. The report of it was *loud* and I jerked, but not before I saw an explosion hit the back tire of the vehicle I'd been tracking. Another sharp report and a second explosion hit the vehicle and it was suddenly tumbling.

"Second vehicle." The command in the snap of his voice had me reversing my attention back to the chase unfolding below. The quake in my hands made focusing harder. Then Goblin laid down next to me and pressed into my side. It wasn't a lot but it helped.

Mouth dry, I finally got the second car in my sight and gave him the numbers. He did something, I could practically feel the movement next to me, but I didn't want to look away. This time, I made it four numbers before he fired and there was no missing the way the engine hood blew upward and back toward the car or that it swerved wildly before it too started rolling.

Another report from the gun and there was a bright flash of white from the under carriage as it kept flipping and then the whole car exploded. I could imagine the heat billowing out from it. The motorcycle vanished in the conflagration because there was a sudden bright flash a half mile back. The SUV had gone up too.

My heart slammed against my ribs almost painfully and my skin was tight. "Looking for the motorcycle."

"Deep breaths, Gracie-girl," Alphabet said in that same lulling tone he'd used earlier. "We have time."

Did we? It didn't feel like it. The shaking seemed to intensify. I was shuddering harder than the van had when we'd been flooring it across the landscape. Sweat trickled between my shoulder blades and I was boiling despite the cold rock below me.

Where was it? Had it actually been taken out with the others? No, I didn't see it, but would I—there.

"Got him. He's off road." Then I gave him the numbers.

"Sneaky little bastard," Alphabet murmured. "Isn't he?" Then before I could answer, he added, "Fire in the hole."

I almost didn't jump this time when he fired. Almost. And maybe I was a glutton for punishment, because I didn't look away. The back tire on the motorcycle went up in flames and the vehicle pitched forward, sending the rider flying.

He was also on fire.

I saw everything before I closed my eyes and lowered the binoculars. Goblin scooted up along my side and whined. Turning, I rubbed the top of his head and let him lick me. The tears I'd fought earlier escaped, and my heart raced so fast, I thought I was going to throw up.

"You did good, Gracie-girl," Alphabet said in that low silken tone. He also ran a hand over the top of my head. Okay, maybe he was petting me and Goblin both. "Real good."

CHAPTER
SIX

VOODOO

I pulled the covers over her bare arm. The exhaustion she'd been fighting since we hooked up with her and Alphabet knocked her out. The paleness under her tan seemed to stand out even more than after the accident that sent us tumbling down the hill.

Alphabet had been sketchy on the details—well, we all had been—and she hadn't volunteered any. We needed a debriefing and we needed it yesterday. I'd still wanted to do a full assessment of her injuries. The bruises on her throat had been darkening all day as we traveled.

You could almost make out the shape of the hand that had been there. Alphabet had already eliminated the target, but he shouldn't have been allowed to get that close to her in the first place. Her lashes fluttered up once. Thankfully, there was no surprise in her eyes when she focused on me.

"Shh," I murmured. "Just keeping watch."

A yawn had her stretching her jaw. The faint pop just

told me how tired she was. "You have to go talk about stuff..." The mumbled words made me smile.

Lifting a length of dark hair away from her face, I tucked it behind her ear. "Go to sleep, Firecracker. No one is going to hurt you again."

"Can't promise that," she told me even as she turned away. "No one can."

The empty acceptance in her voice pissed me off. Clamping down on the temper, I blew out a long breath.

"Sleep. I'll be here when you wake up." I hadn't intended to stay here, she deserved her privacy if she wanted it. But nightmares were often a byproduct of trauma. I'd rather be on hand if something went sideways and not try to clean up after it.

"Fine," she huffed before another yawn cracked her jaw. "Tired..."

I didn't answer because I didn't want to give her a reason to keep fighting the sleep I'd thought had already swept her under. Only when her breathing deepened, then evened out did I make myself walk away.

Despite the fact I'd done it earlier, I did another check of the exits—particularly the windows. They were secured and we'd already added another set of alarms at the top. Just because we couldn't fit through them didn't mean someone else couldn't.

She highlighted a weak spot for us. Never let it be said we didn't learn when opportunity presented itself. I pulled the blackout drapes closed over the blinds. There was a soft light on in the back of the bathroom. Enough to let her see the room, not so much it would bother her.

It had to be enough for now.

I needed to add some listening equipment in here. I'd talk to Alphabet. If we set it to a certain decibel level, it could activate if she was in trouble. That would still respect her privacy.

Until then, I'd just crash in here. The bed was big enough for both of us, but there was also a chair and I could sleep on the carpet. The floors in here offered palatial comfort compared to some of the places I'd had to sleep.

Lunchbox straightened from where he leaned against the wall as I closed the door behind me. Concern reflected in his eyes. "How...?"

"She's sleeping, hopefully she stays that way. Let's get the debrief done. I want to be back up here before she wakes up or a bad dream does."

Mouth flattening, he glanced past me to the door. Sorry, brother. I already called dibs for the night. You could try to get it tomorrow. Not that I was remotely apologetic for my choices. Nor voicing it aloud for him.

"Did she tell you..."

I shook my head once as he followed me to the stairs. The absolute lack of sound below was almost as telling as the worry carved into Lunchbox's expression. Lunchbox and Bones could easily have briefed Alphabet without me. The only thing they would have waited on was his debrief for us.

That said, Lunchbox waited and the quiet? Yeah, no one was talking. The cold glare Bones and Alphabet favored each other with had made the air crackle with all the tension popping. As long as Grace was awake and with us, they shut that shit down.

Now that she was in bed?

The gloves were going to come off. No one was in the kitchen or living area. That made sense. Debriefs when we have a guest should be in a more secure location. Alphabet's office was the next obvious location.

"I'm grabbing coffee," Lunchbox told me before he diverted to the kitchen. Since he didn't correct my course, I assumed I was on the right track.

The door to Alphabet's office was open and Goblin was parked right at Alphabet's side, his body a literal barrier between Alphabet and Bones. The snap of wordless insults had been replaced by a stonier silence.

Alphabet's attention was on his computer screen and his fingers flew. There was a picture of a man up and some details. Bones, on the other hand, sat there like a judge waiting to pass a sentence. His relaxed pose was a facade, because none of that emotion translated to his expression.

They both cut looks to me when I walked in. Right. "You two ready to kiss and make up or should I go get you gloves and let you settle it in the ring?"

It wasn't often we had differences we could only solve by actually fighting it out. Didn't mean we couldn't or wouldn't if necessary. We definitely had in the past. Bones gave me an impatient look. He didn't scrap with Alphabet. Ever.

His mistake.

Lunchbox and I had both sparred with him. I'd also used his prosthetic against him because it only strengthened his defenses *and* proved how normal he was. For Bones, he rarely scrapped with Lunchbox either. To be fair, Lunchbox tended to be the most even-tempered of us.

Me? Not so much, and if Bones needed to work some of that aggression off, I would cheerfully take him on. I cracked my knuckles. Frankly, I would enjoy it, particularly after his bullshit tone with Grace.

That girl did not deserve his ire. I didn't give a fuck what she'd said or *why* she'd said it. The mission had been a cluster fuck from the beginning and that was on *us*, not *her*.

"Coffee," Lunchbox announced as he returned. The man carried a full damn tray with coffee, an extra carafe probably full and piping hot, along with sandwiches. "And food. Alphabet, you need to eat."

"I'm fine," Alphabet said without glancing up from the screen. "Let's just get on with this, I have work to do."

"We," I said, when Lunchbox and Bones didn't respond to him but glared at each other. Putting a hand on Alphabet's shoulder, I glanced down at him when he shifted his annoyed gaze to me. "We will get the work done. We will deal with whoever this asshole is…"

Not that it seemed a leap to think this was the asshole who found the safe house. So many questions. I memorized the man's face for future reference. I could *feel* the harsh sigh that Alphabet released before he hit two keys and the screen went dark.

Letting him go, I gave him the space to rise and join us. The office might not be the best room for this discussion, but there were whiteboards and a video wall available if we needed it.

To be honest, I'd always thought it was a little sci-fi and overkill, but when he detailed all the things he needed to make this the perfect base of operations? These were some of his top items…

Making it happen was a no brainer. It was just a matter of sourcing the right items. Fortunately, I was good at my job. "Let's keep the debrief short and to the point. We *all*," I stressed that last word with a look at each of them before continuing, "have concerns. We *all* have issues with the mission. We *all* have issues with how it played out. For now, let's keep our focus on what happened, when it happened, and what we did to resolve it in the moment. We can save the rest for the planning for the next stage."

"*If* there's a next stage," Alphabet said as he rose. His movements were definitely stiff and he favored his right leg. I didn't think he'd rested enough to be back at work already, but he was an adult.

"Are you suggesting there won't be?" Bones asked, giving me a narrow-eyed look before transferring his attention to Alphabet.

"Not suggesting shit," he muttered before easing down into one of the chairs. We had four of them in here and it was set up like a mini round table of sorts. Despite the size of the office, it did make it feel crowded in here. "We need to revisit protocols and anything on our docket for as long as Gracie is with us."

"I second that," I said before picking up one of the coffee cups and taking a long drink, dark and strong enough to clean the pipes in the drain. Fuck, that was good. I took the seat closer to Bones. Running interference with the captain was something I did well.

"I don't think we're relying on Robert's Rules of Order," Bones said, his tone dryer than the desert.

"Maybe we should," Lunchbox piled on. "As someone keeps reminding us, we're not on active duty and don't have to follow military command parameters." He moved a cup of coffee closer to Alphabet and a sandwich. Then he took a second sandwich off the side and put it—plate and all—on the ground for Goblin.

The dog checked with Alphabet first who eyed the food, then Lunchbox, then the dog. "*Vrij*," he murmured. "Take it easy buddy, we're safe."

That should not feel like such a damn concession, but the Staffy went from on guard to relaxed, tail wagging, in seconds. Then he immediately started on his own meal. No one said anything as Lunchbox took a seat. Then I wasn't the only one staring at Alphabet until he picked up the food.

We tried to bully Grace into eating something, but she'd steadfastly refused before she consented to a protein shake and water. Not ideal, but better than nothing. Honestly, as tired as she was, probably a good idea she hadn't tried to force herself.

After Alphabet took a bite, Bones claimed his own coffee cup. "We can revisit how we take jobs," he said. "Vet the criteria and the checklists. That's an acceptable use of resources and man hours. As for protocols? Make a list of which ones you find problematic, we'll take those on later this week. For once, I agree with Voodoo, we need to sharpen our focus tonight and then let everyone get some rest."

By everyone, I seriously doubted he meant himself. A problem I would deal with later.

"Fine, let's debrief then." Alphabet was positively spoiling for a fight. "How was our location compromised?"

"Unknown," I answered before Bones could. "Our first sign of an issue was the arrival of the crew at the factory location. According to the calendars you'd mapped, and backed by our observation, that target should have been empty and easily demolished."

Sending all of their people in, no matter how abrupt, created a logistical nightmare. It didn't help that they had sweeper teams on the move.

"Second issue occurred when a sweeper team uncovered Lunchbox's position. It didn't leave us with a lot of options." Particularly because the men weren't welcoming in the slightest.

"It was fast elimination," Lunchbox said with a shrug after he finished his bite. "While they might have been former military, they weren't that trained or in for that long."

I didn't laugh but the level of insult in Lunchbox's voice was amusing.

"Once they were down, we were on a clock." I motioned to him to keep eating and then glanced at Bones. Because this was when we'd had to make calls.

"If they tracked us—they had to have picked us up near one of the locations." Bones kept it clinical and detached. "We never took the same route to the safe house twice. We're always careful. Lunchbox handled the majority of the driving."

"I avoided tails," he said like it was a fact carved into stone. I didn't argue with him. We'd all been looking... "I don't know how they found the house." That was a source of serious irritation.

Not only had our security been compromised, but Grace had been hurt. Neither were acceptable outcomes.

"It could have nothing to do with any of us or the job," Alphabet said. "I'm far from done with my investigation, but the man who attacked her in the barn doesn't appear to be linked to this particular cartel or any of the other gangs in the area."

The silence that struck after that hit like a sledgehammer.

Bones frowned. "It was bad luck that the man picked that house and that barn?"

"Bad luck, shitty security—whatever you want to call it." Alphabet stared at Bones steadily. "She got hurt, on my watch. If I hadn't gone out there when I did..."

"We don't need to fight over speculation. There's no point in the what-if game," Bones said, waving off all the words Alphabet hadn't said. She could have died and he'd have been in the house and utterly unaware until the mission ended or Goblin alerted.

Goblin *hadn't* alerted. So maybe the guy had been hiding in the barn? Too many questions, not enough answers.

"Well, if she'd been in the house instead of walking off some prick's comments, she wouldn't have been in that situation," Alphabet said, ice slicing over the words. "So let's fight over that."

"No," Bones said as he rose and Lunchbox hit his feet not even a split-second later. While he didn't crowd the captain, he put himself firmly between Bones and the door. "We're not doing this," Bones continued, ignoring Lunchbox's choice apparently. "All three of you are compromised where she is concerned. The last place she needed to be was on a call where we were freely discussing the possible elimination of several noncombatants."

"We can't just pretend she isn't present." A logical argument on Lunchbox's part. Calm and cool even. "If we take her on missions, she's involved."

"I can assure you, we won't be taking her on any future assignments."

I didn't roll my eyes, but that dismissive tone he'd adopted wasn't doing him any favors. "Guys," I said before Lunchbox swung with the fist he currently clenched. "Table this part for tomorrow. I only have one question, then Bones and I need to talk."

That snared all of their attention. Fine. I could take the heat. Their silence was as good as agreement so I went with it.

"Why was Grace on that hill with you and why was she a part of the targeting?" We'd heard all of it. I thought Lunchbox was going to explode at her soft voice reciting the numbers. All expression erased from Bones' already chilly demeanor as he switched his attention from me to Alphabet.

"I made a call," Alphabet said, an element of remorse in his tone. "Maybe not the best one, but the only one I could in that moment."

"Why?" I repeated the question, because he had clearly made a call. What I wanted to know was what prompted it.

"Because when I tried to leave her in the van, she said it wasn't safe in the car..."

Something she'd learned with me and Bones.

"She was afraid," Alphabet continued. "She was also *tired* of being afraid. If she needed some control and I could give it to her? Then fuck it. I was giving it to her. Especially after everything that went down."

He practically dared us to disagree with him. Frankly, I couldn't tell if he really wanted us to point out the flaws or offer him some absolution for doing it in the first place.

Maybe both.

I nodded once, then rose. "Get some sleep. Both of you and yes, it is an order. We'll revisit the chain of command after some serious rack time. I will keep watch over Grace tonight so take something if you need it."

I took my coffee and motioned for Bones to lead the way. The rest of this conversation could be handled by us—for now. Despite me expecting an argument from them, Lunchbox and Alphabet surprised me by saying nothing and not preventing our exit.

"Where do you want to do this?" I asked Bones. "Downstairs or our barn?"

Our barn was also empty, but it would put us away from the house.

"Downstairs," Bones said. "I don't want to compromise security."

Fine by me. Once we were down there, I stripped off my shirt and set the coffee aside before I began to wrap my hands. The gym down here had everything we could need for rehabbing or staying in shape.

"I'm not fighting you," Bones said with a sigh.

"Okay," I told him as I pivoted to face him. "Stand there while I beat the shit out of you. That works for me too."

CHAPTER
SEVEN

"I'm not fighting you." The fact I had to repeat it should have told him everything he needed to know. Not that Voodoo paid a damn bit of attention to me.

"I heard you the first time," he said, flexing his hands in the wraps. "My answer is the same. Now get your ass over here. If you don't burn off some of that aggression, you and Alphabet *are* going to come to blows."

The fuck we would. "I'm neither a child nor a man under your command." If I needed to remind him that I outranked him, this would go even worse.

"We're also retired," Voodoo said with the faintest of smirks. "You get to call the shots only when we *let* you call them."

Throwing my own words back at me was dirty pool.

"So, any more chicken-shit excuses to duck this beating you deserve?"

Chicken-shit...

I glared at him. "You want a fight."

"You're damn right I do. So get your ass over here." Hostility edged every single word. It was as much a request for help as it was a demand for action.

The problem, however, lay in the fact... "I don't think I can hold back." My temper had been fraying in the pitched silence, with both of my hands wrapped around its throat to strangle the life out of it.

"Then don't." He gave me the barest of shrugs.

"Bryant..." I exhaled.

"After," he said, the crack in the pair of syllables offering zero negotiation room. "Let's go. You need to purge."

I needed something, but lashing out at my team was not an acceptable way to handle my temper. Fuck...

Yelling at civilians wasn't either.

Rolling my head from side to side, I soaked in the sound of the crack. It might have relieved some of the tension, but really, it just highlighted how stiff and unyielding I'd become.

"Fuck it," I muttered, then moved away to strip off my own shirt. I toed off my shoes. His were already gone. We were both in jeans, not ideal, but then we weren't going for finesse or points.

The only concession I made was to wrap my hands. Frankly, bare-knuckle brawling would feel too goddamn good. As much as I craved the pain, I needed to maintain some semblance of control.

Once I was ready, I faced one of my oldest friends. The patience in his expression and the ease in his stance decried the very real irritation he'd demonstrated earlier. I'd pissed him off. This was how we resolved it—for the most part.

"Bryant... Don't let me hurt you."

With a roll of his eyes, Voodoo just jerked his head to the

"ring" we used for sparring. It didn't actually have ropes, but the padding on the floor was thicker. Made movement more of a challenge than you might think. The walls closest to it were also padded. Training didn't mean breaking.

His eagerness didn't overcome strategy or experience and Voodoo never turned his back on me. Nor did he lunge forward. No, he was playing the long game. In forcing me to go to him, it let him choose how we engaged. Irritation scraped along the inside of my skin.

It would serve him right if I made him come to me. Which of us was the most stubborn?

Someday, we might find out.

As it was, I packed away the annoyance his tactics provoked. The fact he knew to do this was a testament not only to how well he knew me, but also how much I needed this fight.

"I really fucking hate it when you're right," I said before surging across the mat. I expected him to dodge and evade, so I was already lunging to the left and leaping over his leg even as he tried to sweep mine from beneath me.

What usually followed was a combo of hits. But he changed the playbook and caught me in the jaw with a backhand. The metallic tang of copper flooded my mouth. It was a wakeup call, sharpening my focus.

Instead of leaving me to chase him, Voodoo closed the distance and delivered three sharp blows to my side and one to my kidney before I caught his arm. Mother fucker had been training.

Turning his arm around, I yanked him off his feet. But he didn't just let me control the fall. He shoved himself right into me, forcing me to release him. His arms were around me and we hit the mats together.

It was hard to get him in a grappling hold. Slippery bastard kept getting away from me. The fourth time he broke the hold, he caught me in the jaw with his forehead. Blood exploded through my mouth and seemed to drench my temper in kerosene.

I drove my left into his abdomen twice even as I tumbled us back and over. I got my foot up and then I shoved him off me. Rebounding to my feet, I blocked his right, then his left, then his right again.

Old combo, bad call.

I let him through on the next left, because it opened up his right. The moment he swung, I let the impact push me away. Not far, though, because I wanted this opportunity. A series of swift combo, hammer blows had him gasping as I drove him back across the mats.

Three times I landed blows to his kidney. His elbow caught me right in the back of the head. It sent me stumbling forward right into the mat-covered wall. The blow to the face wasn't painful but it did knock the haze off.

I staggered back to find him on the far side, watching me with narrowed eyes and raised fists. Blood decorated his wraps and I didn't have to look at mine to know they were likely spotted and soaking as well.

Air came in hard little pants. The haze over my vision, however, cracked, then splintered before it shattered.

Fuck.

This wasn't just me being annoyed. This was... fractured training. I was letting my temper win. This would get someone killed.

"I hate when plans derail," I admitted aloud. "I hate it even more that it was my call that left Alphabet and the client—"

"Grace," Voodoo said, not letting me dismiss her to a category. "Her name is Grace."

I wiped the blood from my face with the back of my hand and stared at him. "Fine, it was my call to leave Alphabet and Grace at the safe house. That put them well out of reach when shit went sideways."

"Alphabet's a big boy," Voodoo said, clearly unimpressed with my reasoning. "He's also more than capable of taking down an opponent, which I remind you, he did. He also has Goblin and Goblin is more than capable of taking down his fair share."

Leaning my head back, I tried to get the pounding in my temples to slow down. "It's not the point."

"Actually, it *is* the point. Alphabet isn't an invalid or incapable. If he suspected more of an issue, he would have been the first one to say something."

Fine, I could admit it. He had a point.

"The real issue isn't just that someone showed up at the safe house, it's that they got their hands on Grace. That could have gone a hell of a lot worse."

"She shouldn't have been outside while he was on ops."

"No, she shouldn't," Voodoo said with a shrug. "*You* made a choice when you snapped at her. Not sure where the fuck you thought she was going to go, but it is what it is."

"So you think everything is my fault." Though it wasn't a question, it definitely came out far surlier than intended.

"Does it matter what I think?" Like me, Voodoo had gotten his breathing regulated. The longer we stood here, the more in control I felt. Still, he wasn't backing down yet.

Good. I didn't want him to back down. "No," I said. It really didn't matter.

"Because you're going to blame yourself regardless." As much as he shrugged off the words, it wasn't that easy.

"People get hurt when I don't account for the variables. We have a plan for a reason." Risk assessment. Contingencies. Deployment. We engaged in all of it and we planned out our strategy.

"Absolutely. As much as we try to plan, as much as we build in contingencies, sometimes shit just goes sideways."

Unacceptable. I shook my head. "Let's get back to this." I didn't want to debate this with him. We would never agree. The last time I'd had a plan go that sideways, Doc had gotten burned and Alphabet lost part of his leg.

Mistakes hurt *everyone*.

"You thinking again?" Voodoo challenged me and I shot him a bland look. "Good," he said. "It's about time. You're down to me by four points."

"Bullshit," I snapped back at him but it was with more laughter than irritation this time.

"Put your money where your mouth is K, let's do this."

"Dick."

"Yep." He didn't deny it.

This time, when we clashed, it held a lot more finesse and control. I still ate the mat more than once and I put him down an equal number of times. At the end of another hour, soaked in sweat and stinking of it, I didn't argue when he called a halt to it.

Instead, I just laid flat on my back to get my breathing under control. The whole exercise worked to sand down all the jagged edges.

"Grabbing a shower, then I'm heading to Grace's room," Voodoo told me. I debated calling him on it. The fact he wanted to be in there as much as he felt like he should be was another problem.

Not one he wanted to listen to me on right now.

"You should do the same," he said. He'd pulled the wraps off his hands, and he was in worse shape than I was from the sweating.

He was also going to have a hell of a black eye. I'd feel bad, but he damn near broke my nose. So I figured that made us even.

"I'll be fine," I told him, shoving up from the floor as he headed toward the exit. "And tomorrow…"

I didn't have to look at him, he'd stopped at those two words.

"I'll talk to her tomorrow. Explain things to her." Probably should have done it before now, but we hadn't had the time.

"Or…" Voodoo elongated that syllable and I turned to find him staring at me. "We *all* discuss it with her. We also *listen* to her and not just give her orders."

I snorted. "We don't agree," I reminded him.

"I know," Voodoo said with a smile. The faint kind that said he knew he'd already won the argument, but was doing me a solid and not gloating about it. "That's what will make it so interesting."

Then he was gone and I took the time to pull the wraps off my own hands. Everything ached. But it ached in a good way. The bruises were mine and I'd damn well earned them. The tightness in my gut was gone, the sick worry that left me unsettled and second guessing everything was also absent.

The job had been simple. Deal with the Rojas operation. They were more a ring than a cartel. The job called for us to eliminate their processing houses and if possible, burn the stashes with it.

More than a warning shot across the bow, the move

was designed to hurt them. Mentally, physically, but most importantly, financially. We'd failed on two fronts. We'd have to go back. Unfinished business was not something I planned to leave in our wake.

It wasn't until I'd gotten up to my own room and stood under the hot spray to wash off the sweat that it hit me what questions we hadn't asked. What question *I* hadn't asked.

Someone had betrayed us. That meant it could have been the client themselves—hiring us to what? Get taken out? Create a reputation? Improve one? One way or another, the Rojas had been alerted to our arrival. They'd shifted operations, abruptly. They'd also caught us on our way out, sending heavy pursuit and firepower to eliminate us.

A stretch, maybe. But the tenacity in their pursuit didn't smell like an accident or just stubbornness. The farther we went, the more likely they were going to be the ones led into a massacre—which was exactly what happened.

So why do it?

Because they were following orders.

Wiping a hand over my face and then up over my hair, I glared at the wall. That left one other question. The man at the safe house? Dumb luck? Or sent there on purpose? I turned that info over as I showered.

Instead of going to bed when I was done, I dressed and headed back downstairs. The house was quiet, security engaged. I didn't stick my head in to check on Grace. Voodoo had that job.

After brewing a fresh thermos of coffee, I carried it into my office and locked myself in. I wanted some answers *before* they were up, that meant reaching out to contacts in the Network.

They were going to love hearing from me.

CHAPTER

EIGHT

GRACE

"**G**race! We're going to be late!" Amorette threw a sock at me. "You look fine."

"But I want to look better than fine!" It was an old argument, and I was doing it more to yank her chain than anything else.

"I'm sorry," Am deadpanned.

I paused and twisted to look at her while I tied my hair up into a ponytail with a scrunchy. "For what?"

"You're stuck looking like me." Not even a twitch of her lips betrayed her even if merriment danced in her eyes.

A laugh snorted out of me before I could stop it and Am grinned. Still, I couldn't resist tweaking her just a little. I glanced at the mirror and affected a sigh... "What do you think of a nose job?"

I barely dodged the decorative pillow she grabbed from the chair by the door and flung at me. Laughing, Am shook her head. "Let's go, brat."

She pivoted on her heel and strode out of my room. I was still *laughing as I grabbed my purse and strung it over my chest before I snagged my backpack. I was only four steps behind her, but Am was already outside.*

"Are you trying out for track?" I called as I hurried after her. I rushed through the front door and then stumbled to a halt. This wasn't...

Turning in a slow circle, I stared at the cemetery. We didn't come here often and we never came alone. At least, I never did. When I would have shifted my backpack, I couldn't find the straps.

It was gone.

So was my purse.

My shoes were absent too.

Instead of being dressed for school, I was in a simple sundress. The air was warm and the grass was soft beneath my feet. There was a bee buzzing lazily around some fresh flowers that had been delivered to a grave. More than a few of them had similar bouquets. A lot of families made their way out here over the holiday weekend.

We'd come for her birthday and for Mother's Day. It wasn't either, so why had I headed out here again? I walked over the hill and then down past where the dogwoods stood to the stone we'd erected for Maman. A smaller one sat to the left of Mom's—it was the gravestone for Louis. The stone to the right was new. No one should be that close to them...

Dread ballooned in my gut and I flexed my toes against the grass, digging my heels in to stop moving. It failed, though, I kept moving as though someone dragged me toward the graves. I couldn't turn away, or stop, and when the force finally released me, I landed on my knees.

The third headstone was right there. I could see part of it above where my hands were planted against the earth. I didn't want to look up. I couldn't.

No.

But like my feet that wouldn't obey me before, I couldn't stop my chin from lifting or my eyes from raising.

Amorette Monet Black.

No. No. No. No.

Beloved daughter and sister.

Agony robbed me of any breath.

Always together, never apart, joined as one heart.

No. No...

"No!" I jerked upright, one arm outstretched. Loss dug its jagged fingers into my heart and threatened to rip it right out of my chest. The room seemed to swim in shadows around me illuminated only by the faintest of glows from around the edge of the blinds and the heavy curtains.

Reality swam around me. This wasn't a cemetery. It was a bedroom—the one at Base. The one Bones had dumped me in that first day. I swallowed. Or I tried to, but it was hard to dry swallow the lump in my throat. I couldn't get my breath back. Jerking my gaze around, I barely resisted a scream at the suggestion of movement to my left.

The rabbiting of my pulse added to the thunder behind my eyes. With care, Voodoo sat forward. His expression gradually grew more visible as my eyes adjusted to the dusk in the room.

"You with me?" The quiet question grounded me in the present.

"Is this real?" The question slipped out before I could stop it. I'd just been in a cemetery. The heat from the sun. The grass under my feet. The air—it had been so real. None of that was present in the room we were in, but was the room we were in real?

Or was this another nightmare?

"Need me to pinch you?" The question held not one ounce of judgment or teasing. "I can stand up and go open those blinds too—give you more light. Or we can just turn the lamp on." At the last he motioned to the lamp on the nightstand closest to me. "Whatever you need."

A harsh laugh exploded out of me. "Whatever I need." Those words really didn't mean anything anymore. Especially if I had no idea what I needed. How could I? I raised a hand to my face. The trembling, though, gave me pause. It was like my heart was going too fast and I couldn't control the shaking,

"Whatever you need," Voodoo repeated, the stress he put on the syllables demanded that I believe him. Closing my eyes, I tried to regulate my breathing but it wasn't happening. The panic was right there, an acrid taste on my tongue and an untamed wildness under my skin.

"Not sure that would help, if I even knew what it was."

"Okay," Voodoo said, as though he accepted me at my word. "Tell me what you can then."

What I could? That had me opening my eyes again. He hadn't moved from where he sat. He leaned forward still, hands spread but everything else about him was still. His—

"What happened to your face?" I didn't think it had been that bruised when we joined up with them the day before. Had it? It had been hard to focus on any of them after seeing those vehicles explode. But I didn't remember serious injuries.

"Therapy," he answered easily.

"What kind of therapy gives you a black eye?"

A flicker of a grin graced his face and it stretched the cut on his bottom lip, distorting his smile.

"The passive-aggressive kind."

"The—" I blinked.

"How is it passive *and* aggressive?" He canted his head as though offering me an invitation to play.

"The aggressive part, I get," I admitted before shoving the blankets back. I didn't even remember getting in bed the night before. I'd been so damn tired when we got back here. Voodoo had gone to pick me up—maybe? I turned that mental image over in my head, it sounded right but maybe it wasn't him? Had one of the other guys tried to carry me up here?

It was all a mess of tangled emotions and images. I was so damn tired. Rubbing a hand over my face, I grimaced at the bruise on my jaw. While not a huge one, it still stretched to my neck and added to my sore throat.

"Not sure where the passive comes in?" The question reminded me I'd already responded to him, partially.

"No, not really," I admitted and then swung my legs out to stand. The t-shirt I was wearing hit me below mid-thigh. I liked big shirts. Folding my arms to chase away the sense of a chill, I headed for the bathroom. Every step seemed to identify a new bruise. Every muscle ached and I swore something felt pulled in my ass.

"I'm going to stand up, Firecracker," Voodoo said. I paused in the doorway to the bathroom, then glanced at him over my shoulder. It meant half-twisting, cause the pull on my neck was really aggravating.

While looking at him, I flicked on the light and then studied his expression in the illumination. He waited until my gaze was on him again and I nodded before he stood. "So what is the passive part of it?"

"The other guy stands there and takes it until he figures out that if he doesn't fight back, I am going to kick his ass. Then he can get out some aggression too." Simple as pie his tone and manner declared, as though kicking the crap out of someone was "normal" behavior.

Honestly? Not what I expected. One hand braced on the doorframe, I considered asking him who. At least with the light on, I could see the damage he'd done to himself. A good solid half of his face was mottled and bruised. "That looks like it hurts."

"I'll live," he told me with a wink. "Not going to ask me whose ass I kicked?"

"Haven't decided," I admitted. "If you said AB—I mean Alphabet, I might have to get mad at you."

"So only for him?" He didn't comment on me calling Alphabet A-B.

"Maybe. I really need to pee." I pushed into the bathroom and started to nudge the door closed, but then paused to find him halfway to the bathroom but paused by the bed as though still giving me space. "I admit—I almost hope you say Boney Boy. So don't tell me yet. I kind of want to savor that image."

Petty?

Yes.

I pushed the door closed and headed for the toilet. The lights in the bathroom made the bruises on my throat really stand out. I tried to ignore them for now. I still had a cut on my back that was mostly healed. Bruises littered my arms and legs. Little ones. Big ones. But the one on my throat?

It had the look of a grotesque hand necklace. That sent a cascade of images shuddering through me. The man in the barn. The sudden charge. The grip of his fingers and the way he lifted my whole body. Suppressing another violent shiver, I made myself go to the toilet. If I was going to make myself sick...

Fortunately, I didn't. I took the time to wash my hands

and face after I pee'd, then I brushed my teeth. I was tempted to shower, but I had showered after we got in. It hadn't been a long one, but it had been thorough. I'd braided my hair rather than wait for it to dry. Leaving it, I pulled the door open to find the bedroom much brighter.

Voodoo had opened the curtains and the blinds to let the sunlight in to warm the room. The bed had been made, and there were clothes laid out at the foot of the bed. I opened my mouth to say something when I saw the blanket now folded up on the hope chest at the foot of the bed and the two framed photos.

They were the only items I'd been able to grab from my apartment. I hadn't seen them since we left the house in Pennsylvania or wherever that place was. The plummeting feeling held me captive as I headed over to pick up the photo of me and Amorette. It was like a talisman to remind me she was real, not some figment of my imagination.

"It was time you got those back," Voodoo said, a hint of apology creeping through the words. "I've had them since we got here."

"I thought I lost them," I admitted. Sinking down to sit on the hope chest while tracing my fingers over Am's expression. I missed her so damn much. "I didn't have time to get anything else and then we had to leave the car..."

"I know," he said, facing me. "It got overlooked because we were a little busy. We're going to fix that, Firecracker. We're going to fix a lot of things."

Meeting his gaze, I raised my eyebrows. "Can you even make that promise?" He hadn't been able to keep the last one.

"It's not a promise," he admitted. "It's an oath."

I guess that answered that. Still, I hugged the photo to my chest. "I want to believe you."

"No you don't," he countered, calling me on it. "You want to want to believe me. But we need to re-earn some of that trust. That's next on the list. So, when you're ready, we're going downstairs and we're going to let Lunchbox feed you, then we'll check on Alphabet and we're going to do a real debrief. For you and for us."

"What does a real debrief entail?" I really couldn't shake the suspicion even if I would like to believe I could believe him.

"Get dressed, and I'll show you. Easier to understand, and to trust, if you can experience it yourself."

Meeting Am's gaze in the picture, I turned the idea over in my head then lifted my attention back to Voodoo. *Knowledge is power.* I could practically hear her remind me. Truthfully? What choice did I have right now?

"Who did you have therapy with?"

Voodoo grinned. "Boney boy."

I didn't cheer.

Much.

LUNCHBOX

We needed to do a supply run for fresh fruits and vegetables. Cold storage was full with meat and fish options. Dry storage was too. Frankly, if we didn't like fresh foods, we could probably hunker down up here for another ten years.

Okay, maybe five. But if we continued to hunt that would easily supplement what we had. Shaking that off, I finished mixing up the eggs for omelets. I'd diced mushrooms, onions, spinach, and tomatoes. Three different kinds of shredded cheese along with bacon crumbles and ham.

There was more bacon going for the guys. They tended to eat a lot after an op. While this one had gone FUBAR, it had still been an op and no one ate well when we were on the move.

A shuffle of steps against the wood had me glancing toward the stairs. The clicking of Goblin's claws alerted me to who it was before Alphabet came into view. I whistled once and Goblin bounded toward the door. Disengaging the alarm, I opened the door and left it open for the dog.

I stepped out onto the back deck to study the area and scan it. Wildlife wandered through regularly. Satisfied, I headed back in. Alphabet looked like shit.

"Trouble sleeping?" It would make sense. Of the four of us, he seemed to have the most trouble unwinding after a mission. As easy going as he was, it wasn't easy for him to decompress.

"I dunno," Alphabet admitted as he rolled his head from side to side. The cracking of his vertebrae was loud in the quiet of the kitchen. He was at the coffee pot and filling his oversized mug. We all had them. Hence, why I started the morning with two huge pots and a third carafe that I'd set aside for Gracie.

I checked my watch. "You want me to get your omelet going or coffee first?"

"Coffee first." Then he paused to take a deep drink and I could totally respect the profound moment of relief on his expression as he leaned his head back and closed his eyes.

While coffee couldn't fix everything, it sure made life a little fucking easier. We needed to grab easier with both hands every chance we got. Leaving him to his coffee, I got Goblin's breakfast ready.

By the time he trotted back in, his food and a little treat were in his bowl and he had fresh water. The dog paused next to Alphabet first, always checking on him. When the man murmured something, Goblin thumped his tail against the cabinets and Alphabet's leg before he trotted to the bowl.

A door closed upstairs, and I wasn't the only one turning my attention to what—or should I say *who* was up.

A soft hum of feminine laughter drifted down toward us and some of the tension cording my muscles unlocked.

From the moment we hooked back up with Alphabet and Gracie, she'd been *off*. Pale, eyes hollow, and a kind of violent trembling hovered around her even if she herself wasn't shaking.

Shock.

Trauma.

Fear.

All three ignited my temper as it had Voodoo's and, despite all his attempts at coldness, Bones' as well. He could try to rationalize it all he wanted, Bones had been *angry* at her condition. That anger had focused on Alphabet. While Alphabet's?

Yeah, he'd been pissed at Bones. We all were. This clusterfuck was going to keep getting worse if we didn't address it. Hair braided back away from her face seemed to highlight all the fragility in her fine-boned features.

At the same time, some of the softness in her seemed to have been whittled away. She was—hollow? No, that wasn't the right word. Voodoo sported fresh bruises, but his gaze was watchful as he moved next to her on their way down the stairs.

He managed to hover without actually invading her space. It was impressive.

"Coffee?" Alphabet offered as she reached the last step.

She paused, flicking a glance from Alphabet to me then back again. What the hell had happened in those hours we were gone? The feisty woman seemed stretched far too thin, almost washed out? Frustration edged over my nerves. Was this the attack? Bones being snappy? The shooting? What?

Blowing out a breath, she seemed to gather her composure before a faint smile softened her lips. "I would like that, thank you."

"I'll get it," Voodoo said, giving her a gentle wave toward the table. "Go sit down so Lunchbox can feed you."

"Actually..." That single word froze all three of us. "That's brewed coffee. Do you have anything to do espresso? Or maybe steam some oat milk? Or regular milk if you have it?"

Voodoo swung his gaze from her to me just as Alphabet did.

"We do," I said. "Let me go grab it. Have a regular cup for now? Might take me a minute."

I didn't wait for her response, just headed to the door for the basement and dry storage. In addition to the gym and the safe room, we also had longer term storage down there. The pantry upstairs was big, but when you laid in stock like we did, better to have more space—not less.

It took me a good eight minutes to track down the espresso machine. Doc had given it to us. Mostly as a joke, but the note he'd attached to it when it arrived at our private mail box had been pretty rude. Damn funny, but rude.

Since you're out and no longer need to pickle your livers. Discover real coffee.

Asshole. I grinned when I pulled the unopened box out from behind three stacked boxes of baked beans. I stared at the oversized cans. Who the hell ordered that many beans?

Problem for another day.

The soft sounds of her speaking drifted toward me as I climbed the stairs from the basement. All three of them were in the kitchen. She'd taken a seat and had a steaming mug in front of her. Instead of drinking, however, she was sitting sideways and petting Goblin.

The dog had his head tucked against her lap, eyes half-closed in bliss. I could respect the hustle. Alphabet eyed the box on my shoulder.

"I forgot he sent us that." A snort of laughter escaped him. "Such a dick move."

"Eh," Voodoo said. "He likes froo-froo coffee. Despite the bullshit he'll put up with and drink."

"So do you," I reminded Voodoo. He loved a good coffeehouse. If we had time and there was one near a job, he'd make a point of checking out their offerings. Probably cause he grew up in the PNW where everyone had coffee in their blood.

I grinned at my own joke, even as I tracked the flickering smile that touched Grace's lips as she glanced between us. The uncertainty there cut at me. The fiery, feisty nature she'd had on display in New York seemed conspicuous in its absence. The combination of darkness in her crystal blue eyes and the ashen hue in her face was even far more disturbing than the lack of attitude.

This was the same woman who'd picked up the universal remote and thrown it at Bones' head just as she'd thrown everything she could reach in her own living room at the attackers in her place. That woman had been so vital, alive, and ferocious. Voodoo shoulder-checked me after I set the box down.

It yanked my attention off Gracie and onto him. I raised my brows. "Problem?" I pitched my voice low, trusting he was close enough to hear me.

"Was going to ask you the same thing," Voodoo said, pinning me with a hard look. "Stop staring at her."

I frowned, then cut a glance to where Grace had turned her attention back to Goblin. Alphabet leaned forward, arms folded on the table and it looked like he was talking to her. Despite the distraction, she still looked like hell.

"I'm worried about her," I admitted, then pivoted to tear open the box. We needed to set it up to make her coffee. "I don't like how she seems at the moment."

"She's been this way for a while." Voodoo shook his head and there was no mistaking the element of caution in his voice. "You haven't spent as much time with her."

No shit. I spared him a look and my irritation had to have shown because he raised his hands.

"I get it, the call to take her was Bones and mine. We did it to make sure we cleared any bag and tags from her."

Aware, I just met his gaze steadily and kept my own mouth shut. I didn't need the lecture or the defensive explanations. Bones had made some questionable choices of late and we were addressing those. That said, Voodoo had been in charge of getting her here safely and she'd been hurt on his watch.

She'd been hurt on Alphabet's watch too, a nasty little voice reminded me. I slapped some duct tape over that mouth. Alphabet was already beating himself up. So yes, she'd been hurt on their watches, but they'd all gotten her out of there and kept her in one piece.

That was something, so I fisted my irritation and bottled it.

"I'll set this up," Voodoo offered. "And get the coffee going. You do the omelets?"

Equitable exchange. "Thanks." When I turned this time, I found Grace watching us. She didn't jerk her gaze away when it collided with mine, but she did lift her chin. "Hungry?" I searched her expression, then added, "I hope? I've got stuff for omelets and I can do an egg white omelet if you want."

Personally, I thought that was a waste of food cause it tasted deadly dull, but it wasn't about *me*. She needed more calories and maybe some color in her cheeks. I kept my gaze fixed on her eyes and not on her throat. The livid color of the bruising there just pissed me off all over again.

"What do you have for the omelets?" The question carried a lot of hesitation. Too much, in my opinion.

"He can make anything," Alphabet answered in a droll tone that carried far more of his humor than had been present earlier. "So make him work for it. Don't ask him what he has, just tell him what you want."

Amusement unfolded within me as Alphabet practically made it a dare. Would she do it? Rather than comment, I tilted my head and eyed Grace.

Lips compressed, she regarded me with a renewed directness that had been missing earlier. Goblin was still planted at her side, head on her lap as she kept petting him. The good boy was looking after both of them.

"Go ahead," I encouraged her. "Challenge me."

A real smile softened her expression. "Ham, spinach, tart cherries or grapes if you have them, and cheddar cheese?"

"You got it. You want the whole egg or just the egg white?" I thought I'd managed to ask the question without a grimace but her sudden laugh decried that attempt.

"The whole egg is fine. Three eggs might be a lot, so just two?"

"Well if three is too many, one of us can finish it for you." Voodoo's offer came with the sound of coffee beans being poured. "Now, what kind of latte would you like, Firecracker?"

"Flat White?" The hope in the query was a kick to the junk. She really didn't get that it was okay to ask. I turned to face the stove and the prep counter. But of course she didn't, we'd basically taken her into custody and she went where we did.

Yeah, definitely needed to address that shit.

"You wanted oat milk, right?" I asked over my shoulder.

"We don't have that," Voodoo corrected me. "Yet, I will make sure we lay in the supplies for it. In fact..." He abandoned the coffee set up for a moment and grabbed a notepad and pen out of the drawer on the far side of the kitchen. "Make me a list, Firecracker. Anything we don't have that you need or want. Just write it down."

He left it in front of her and then went back to making the coffee. The sound of the grind echoed through the kitchen coupled with the scent of fresh coffee. In no time at all, he had the coffee made and I had the omelet ready. We carried them over to the table at the same time.

"The cherry tomatoes aren't as tart as the grapes or the cherries, but they will add some acid and I added a little brie with the cheddar to give it the sweetness." I set the plate in front of her as Voodoo delivered her custom flat white with a flourish.

All three of us stared at her. It was ridiculous how important this felt.

"Thank you," she said, then set the pen down on the still blank notepad. "I'm sure it's great."

I wasn't.

"Well if you don't like it," I told her. "I'll make something else." Then a door closed farther down the hall and a silence rippled across the room. All the ease in her expression vanished at the sound of the footsteps preceding Bones' arrival.

"Good," he said as he joined us. "You're all here. Let's get this over with..."

TEN

GRACE

Boney Boy's arrival acted like a rock slide slamming into an already agitated pond. The ripples turned into waves that sent the water surging to the edges and slapping upward. It was like a storm hitting with the ionized air growing almost electric. Maybe I was imagining it, but the look Alphabet sent across the table toward Bones was downright hostile. Even Goblin picked up on it. He shifted his weight and then moved to lay so he was touching my feet with his hips and rested his chin on Alphabet's feet.

Such a precious dog.

Hands wrapped around my coffee cup, I tried to chase the sudden icy chill out of my palms. Neither Voodoo nor Lunchbox said a word to Bones as they resumed their activities. When I glanced at him again, I found Bones studying me in turn. Like Voodoo, half of Bones' face was littered in bruises and swelling. One corner of his mouth was definitely fatter than the other and his right eye was damn near closed.

I flicked a look from him to Voodoo and then back. Voodoo definitely had bruises but Bones looked a hell of a lot worse for the wear. I guess when Voodoo called it therapy, he meant more for him than for Bones. I took a deeper drink of the coffee and sighed at the bitter flavor with just the barest hint of hazelnut and chocolate underneath the rest. It was strong as hell.

Just what I needed.

"Good morning, Grace," Bones said after what felt like a protracted silence. "I hope you're feeling better today."

The words weren't quite flat, but his tone was. It wasn't the first time someone had tried to make nice with me when they were definitely not feeling it. Perfunctory peace moves were common when you wanted to reduce the level of friction on a shoot. More often than not, it was basically an olive branch offered and accepted for that moment. After, we'd go our separate ways and it didn't really matter what they thought of me or me of them.

This? This was different. I debated responding to him. I didn't really have much nice to say where he was concerned. As much as I'd like to argue I could see all of this from his side—that would be a lie. Not only would it be a lie, I didn't *want* to see things from his side of this. He'd treated me like an inconvenience since everything went wrong. As sorry as I was to be stuck with them, none of this was my fault.

None of it. Another swallow of coffee gave me a continued excuse to not answer him. Frankly, all I could think about was attacking him verbally. Or throwing something at him again. As much as none of this was my fault, it wasn't totally *their fault* either. They'd come to my rescue.

Mine and others. I'd seen them take everyone else home and they'd tried to take me home.

These were all facts that were important for me to remember. At the same time, it didn't *help* his case or mine. I said *his* instead of *their* because as frustrated as I was about our current situation, Bones seemed to have taken an intense dislike to me from the beginning. He didn't want me involved, but also didn't seem willing to just let me leave. There was simply no evading the dark look in his eyes or the hard expression on his face.

Frankly, I didn't want to focus on the coldness in his voice. Even as I ticked off the litany of various infractions from the past few days, I turned all of my attention to my coffee. Exhaustion draped me like a deadweight and it pushed my shoulders down. Even my face seemed too tired to try and manufacture a smile.

"Probably needs more caffeine," Voodoo said. The sound of the milk being steamed and the grind of the coffee had all offered varying degrees of comfort. "Let me know how that first one is for you, I went with regular milk. But we'll have oat in for you by this evening."

The ease in which he delivered the declaration made it a fact, even if it hadn't happened yet. I surrendered the coffee mug to him as I wrapped my hand around the tumbler. Oh, the flat white was so much warmer and it penetrated the icy shell of my fingers. Even better, the scent was heavenly.

A long swallow of the hot, smooth coffee was the jolt my system needed. "Thank you."

Hot on his heels was Lunchbox with the omelet and that smelled divine too. "Here you go."

I glanced up at him with a smile. It was a little easier to summon this time. "This is great, thank you." Another swallow of the coffee had my system humming. As much as

I hadn't really felt hungry when we first got down here, my stomach growled in anticipation of the food.

The pair looked pleased with themselves and I made myself put the coffee down before claiming a fork. The omelet smelled even better when I cut into it. A wave of nausea swept through me as my mouth watered and my stomach tightened. Maybe I was too hungry. It definitely happened to me previously when I skipped too many meals and even minimized water because dehydration added to my ripped look.

Not that I was ripped at the moment, but I had been avoiding food. Closing my eyes, I forced myself to breathe through my mouth rather than my nose. Deep, slow breaths to settle my stomach's objections. The last thing I wanted to do was throw up my coffee or this omelet.

After my third or fourth deep breath, I managed to take the bite without choking on it. Chewing it slowly didn't help as much as I would have hoped. The omelet tasted good but it was so rich. My second bite was a lot smaller. It was like trying to swallow a stone, but I got it down. The water glass was there, so I grabbed it instead of the coffee. As good as the coffee sounded, I needed to get my stomach to stop protesting.

Movement across the table from me pulled my gaze up. Bones had taken the seat directly opposite me. "You're fine," he said, motioning with his bruised hand toward the food. "Slower bites and Lunchbox is bringing you toast."

"I'm fine." Arguing the point was going to become automatic soon enough. I didn't want to rely on Bones for help or for him to notice anything.

"Yes, you are," he said, without an ounce of irony or scorn. "We haven't been feeding you well enough. So we're going to help you get through this."

"Bones is right," Lunchbox said as he circled the table and set a plate of dry toast down next to the omelet. He set another omelet in front of Alphabet. Unlike mine, Alphabet's looked like it had been piled high with everything—including peppers and salsa.

My stomach flip-flopped unhappily. Right, don't focus on that. "I really am okay," I said on the heels of a long exhale. "I just didn't realize how hungry I was."

"It's okay," Alphabet said and this time he brushed his fingers down my arm. "Take as much or as little time as you need. We've got plenty of stuff for an upset stomach if you need it." That was nice, and before he'd even finished Voodoo disappeared out of the kitchen. No doubt, he went to get me something for my stomach.

A chuckle worked its way through me. It shouldn't be funny. In fact, it *wasn't* funny. As far as I knew, Voodoo wasn't a doctor of any kind, but he handled most of my wound care. Or he had since we'd left that clinic. Bones still studied me from across the table. He didn't remove his attention even as Lunchbox set a plate in front of him. Nor did he when Voodoo slid into the seat next to me with a stack of little pills.

I paused with the bite on its way to my mouth as I stared at the various and sundry pills he'd retrieved. "Got a little bit of everything," he said. "Antacids, nausea, gas—pick your poison."

The earlier laugh that I'd tried to smother bubbled up through me again. "Do I want to know why you have a medicine cabinet of upset stomach meds?"

Voodoo shrugged. "Nothing nefarious. At least not right now. We know how to trigger these reactions in people too. If you're going to set someone up to be sick, it's better to make sure you don't take yourself out at the same time."

"Hangovers are ass too," Alphabet volunteered in between bites. "The last thing you want is to be puking when you need to rehydrate. So yeah, we got a little bit of everything."

"I always thought hair of the dog that bit you worked pretty well." At least when we had dawn shoots after being up dancing and drinking all night. Most of the time, I was still a little drunk when we showed up on set. "Sadly, this isn't alcohol so much." I couldn't even remember the last time I'd gotten plastered. "I didn't realize we hadn't eaten that much."

"We'll make adjustments," Bones said, another reminder that he was right there. When my gaze collided with his, he leaned back in his seat. "All of us will. No more missing meals for you. You're already scrawny and don't have enough meat on your bones to spare, much less go hungry."

I frowned. Scrawny?

Bones gave a jerk and then glared at Voodoo. If we'd been anywhere else, I would have thought that Voodoo just kicked him under the table.

"It wasn't an insult," Bones argued.

"It wasn't a compliment, either," Voodoo countered. "You should go ahead and take one of these, Firecracker."

"I was going to finish eating first." If taking something upset my stomach more...

"Probably better to split the difference," Bones suggested. "That way you can keep eating and not worry about fighting with the food after the fact."

Fighting with it—oh yeah, okay. "You have a point." One I was willing to concede. I chose a pair of pink pills. They would coat my stomach and let me eat. Easier to pick them since I had a solid idea of what they would do and how they would affect me. Once I'd downed them, I resumed my slow bites and washed the food down with coffee and water.

The guys had already decimated their meals but waited for me, without rushing or even prodding me. When I would pause to have a sip of water, they each seemed to be having some kind of private conversation with each other by exchanging looks and what I thought might be hand signals. Those ceased under my observation but since it kept resuming when I focused on the food again, clearly I wasn't imagining it.

Still, when I finished the last of my toast and pushed away the final third of the omelet, I felt a little more human. I was also debating getting up to make myself another flat white.

"Thank you for giving me the time to eat," I said, glancing at each of the guys one at a time until my gaze rested on Bones. "Are we going to actually settle all of this now? And talk? Or is this going to end with another dismissive comment that cuts me off at the knees?"

It came out far more combative than I'd intended, but I didn't regret the choice. Voodoo made it sound like he and Bones had fought and worked out some of this shit. The bruises on their faces were further evidence. Alphabet looked a little harried today, more than the day before or even after the drive and the...

The image of the vehicles catching fire and flipping as he shot out their tires and gas tanks played on repeat in my head. I hadn't seen what happened to the guy in the barn, but based on the blood that had been all over Alphabet and the knife in his prosthetic, the guy was definitely no longer with us.

Hard to find myself caring about that part too. Except...

I sighed.

"Yes," Bones said. "We are. I made some calls. We have some information. We're going to debrief—all of us."

I frowned.

"You want answers," Bones continued. "Are you up for the debriefing now or do you need more rest?"

"How is your stomach, Gracie?" Alphabet asked as though he were translating for them but I got it.

"I'll live," I said. "I would kill for another flat white though."

"Got it," Voodoo said. "Anyone else want coffee? Once we have that ready, we'll relocate to one of the offices."

Since no one else argued or even asked him why, I assumed that had to have been something they'd been discussing with hand signals and silent stares. Fine, I didn't really care where we had this conversation as long as we had it.

"Thank you," I said to the guys as they all rose and started tackling tasks from clearing the table to cleaning the kitchen. Not that they let me help. That was also fine, I took the time they were all moving to observe, particularly Bones. Something had shifted with him but I didn't know what it was or if it would be beneficial or not.

When all was said and done, we adjourned to a different room. This one had an entire wall that doubled as a screen of sorts. As soon as we were inside and the door locked, Bones faced all of us—faced me.

"Let's start with the one question you've asked repeatedly..."

CHAPTER

ELEVEN

The laser focus on Bones' deep gray eyes demanded all of my attention and that was *before* he said he was going to answer the one question I'd asked repeatedly. My stomach bottomed out. Amorette. He had to have news about Amorette. I curled the fingers of my left hand into my palm and dug my nails in even when I hugged the tumbler of coffee to my chest with my right hand.

A violent trembling vibrated outward from my core. It was like I was at the epicenter of an earthquake that increased in intensity with each passing moment. Biting down on my lower lip, I sucked it between my teeth. The sharp pinch of pain helped. Just like the ache between my shoulder blades that pulled taut with how hard I was hugging the tumbler.

Discomfort kept me in the here and the now. Still...

"As far as we've been able to tell, your sister went missing at roughly the same time as you were taken outside of her place."

I frowned. "She was there when I was?" My heart sank. Had I led them to her?

"Unknown," Alphabet said before Bones could answer and I cut a glance to him. He had his right foot up on the ottoman in front of his chair. Goblin sat next to his chair, his attention focused on Bones like he was equally ready for the briefing. I raised the coffee cup, more to give my mouth something else to do before I bit through my lip.

Finally, I managed to push out my next question even if it came out a little hoarser than I planned. "Unknown? How?"

"We don't know if she was there or already taken," Bones answered for Alphabet. "He tracked her movements right up until the Wednesday before your weekend away."

Wednesday.

I frowned.

"Do I want to know how you tracked her?" I cut my glance back and forth between them.

With a sigh, Alphabet sat forward. "First things, first. I still have a host of searches to run. I've also got some bot programs I need to repurpose and get out there too. That said..." He blew out a long breath. "I'm sorry, Gracie. As far as I can tell from backtracking her movements, she didn't go home again after she left Wednesday morning prior to the weekend you two had planned."

My heart sank farther if that was possible. The Wednesday before—I'd been busy on those shoots. I'd gone out with friends. I'd been focused on my life and looking forward to the weekend. The fact she didn't answer my messages had been *normal.* When she had a case or was really busy, she sometimes waited to answer. It was just what she did.

"She left early in the morning, stopped at her favorite coffee place—"

"Rhythms," I murmured. "She likes their breakfast sandwiches even more than their coffee—I think." It was a source of some humor. "They bake their own bread so it's awesome."

"I believe you."

It felt like the kindest thing anyone had ever said to me. Three simple words. Well, those three words and the genuine sympathy in his eyes. I took another sip of the coffee. The flat white seemed to have lost all flavor. The warmth offered some comfort so I'd take it.

"She grabbed a breakfast sandwich then?" Bones prompted, redirecting us back to the subject. I wanted to hate him and thank him in the same breath. If they had more answers, I wanted those too.

"Yes," Alphabet said before he cleared his throat. Lunchbox appeared in my periphery with one of those refillable water bottles. He pressed it into Alphabet's hand. "Thanks," he muttered before unscrewing the top and taking a long drink. He didn't spend any more time on it than that. "She got the sandwich and while she waited for her coffee, she got a call. The number was a burner—so no idea who it was, but she didn't seem upset by it."

"Probably a client," I said, tracing my finger up and down along the smooth side of the tumbler. It didn't quite feel real. None of this did. "She would sometimes get them a disposable phone so they weren't tracked by their partners. Or soon to be ex partners."

Based on everything she'd ever described to me though, those ex-partners weren't always likely to just accept a court's decision. No, Am would protect her clients with everything she had. That included protecting their communications and making sure they had access to her whenever they needed it.

"Possibly," Alphabet said, as though conceding my point. "I just can't confirm who or where."

"You could if it wasn't a burner phone?" I wasn't quite sure if that was creepy or cool. Maybe both?

"Yes," he said, no hesitation marking his answer. "Lots we can find out with a few clicks. It's just a matter of knowing where to look."

"So you looked at Am's phone log?" How else would he have figured out the burner phone? That made sense, right? If the person with the burner was there, he wouldn't necessarily know they were talking to Amorette?

"Yes." Alphabet shifted in his seat, a flicker of discomfort apparent on his face. "I know you have a thousand questions. I want to lay this out for you as far as I got—then Bones can tell us what he found."

Voodoo circled the room, his hands in his pockets and his attention not seeming to be on any of us. I doubted that. The only people sitting at the moment were me and Alphabet. The weariness in Alphabet's expression offered one answer as to why. Where Voodoo seemed to be pacing the perimeter of the room to sublimate his restlessness, Lunchbox stood with near enough the same posture as Goblin.

He was in reach for both Alphabet and me. Was I imagining the level of concern rolling off each of them? This was bad news. They weren't sugar-coating it or trying to bury the story. At least, not anymore. Course, before they just didn't answer the questions at all.

I suppressed a shudder, the sudden quiet around me was telling. Maybe the reason they hadn't said anything before was they weren't sure how I would react. That was fair. I had no idea how I would react. The fact I hadn't started screaming yet seemed like a mark in the win column.

"I can handle it," I said, focusing on Alphabet again. "I might only be a couple of steps away from throwing myself over the virtual edge, but—I can do this. Tell me what you know." My throat tightened, a warning against trying to squeeze those words out. "Please."

Alphabet continued to study me, but he didn't make me ask again. "After coffee—Rhythms," he added on the name with a little nod to me. Details mattered. "She left and walked to the courthouse. I thought she'd be going to her office, but she headed to the family court building. Camera coverage inside is a little spottier. Privacy issues." His grimace was more irritation than disappointment.

"So there's no way to know who she was meeting with there?" The obvious would be her client. It was a courthouse and there were matters of confidentiality. So that made sense.

"I didn't say that." Alphabet lifted his refillable bottle as though toasting before he unscrewed the lid. "Discovering the who is just going to be a bit challenging. Not impossible. That also means it will take us some time. I've got her appointment calendar, but all it listed was the courtroom and judge she was in front of. It didn't offer any other details on the case or the docket."

Chin dipping, I stared down at my feet. "I don't remember all of their names. Am is always careful when discussing clients. She takes confidentiality very seriously. Now that doesn't mean she hasn't told me a name here or there but... I don't remember."

Missing. She'd been missing for two days when I drove

to the beach. She'd already been gone while I was being impatient. Then…

"If she was already gone, why did someone grab me at her place?" Did that mean I was the target or she was? A dull pain throbbed behind my eye. A flash of the man who told me he'd been waiting for me danced sickeningly in front of my eyes before he vanished once more.

Alphabet motioned to Bones. "I just gave you everything I had before we had to leave for the job. I'm back on this now."

"That wasn't everything," Lunchbox corrected and when Alphabet glared at him, I glanced between all of them. "She deserves to know."

"They found her…" My voice cracked and dropped out entirely before I could frame the last two syllables. "…body?"

"No." That answer came from all four of them in varying degrees of forcefulness. Like someone had cut my strings, I sagged. She wasn't dead. She couldn't be. And she wasn't.

"Firecracker, if there was a body, we wouldn't keep it from you." Voodoo didn't make it sound like he was trying to placate me. It was just straightforward facts. That said, I still couldn't resist looking at Bones.

"We wouldn't," he confirmed. "The only reason I tabled these discussions previously was we had a job and not enough answers."

"You have enough answers now?" It landed like I'd thrown down a gauntlet. As irritating as Boney Boy was, it was a lot easier to keep together staring at him than drowning in the sympathy the others offered. The burn of tears in the back of my throat retreated.

"Also, no. We have some answers, a hell of a lot more questions, and issues we need to address." Bones was tall—all of them were really—but there was something about him standing there, a sentinel locked in place as though daring the world to try and move him. The broad muscular frame added to his intimidation factor so did the lean, hard lines of his face all weathered and rugged from hours outside. His nose had a bit of a bump that told me it had been broken more than once.

That made sense. The four men radiated military precision. Whether they were good guys or bad guys or just trained, Bones was in charge and he presented as such. He also seemed to be the one to make the final calls—or had been until now. The others weren't as willing to go along.

"What part did A-B leave out?" The nickname soothed some of the jumbled emotions still vibrating under my skin. The agitation was coming back like the tremors I'd already been dealing with had suddenly gotten worse.

"We called her office," Alphabet answered. "Lunchbox and I both did it, we called, acted like clients of *hers* and we were told she resigned."

"Bullshit." I surged to my feet. "There's no way she just quit." Am was the most dedicated person I knew. "She'd never just *leave, much* less do it without saying something to someone."

"What if she was forced out?" The question from Bones seemed reasonable except...

"Nobody makes Am do anything she really doesn't want to do. She's a fighter. She'd fight with every ounce of who she is and she's smart as hell. No, if they tried to force her out or do something illegal, it wouldn't end well for them."

I had zero doubt about that.

"That fits with the profile," Bones said. "So what we

have is a pair of sisters set up and targeted. One is an attorney and the other a model. Your sister does a lot of pro bono work, she's not corporate. You do a lot of corporate shoots and brands."

"So?"

"So, there are only a couple of places your work and hers intersect." Bones raised his eyebrows as though daring me to deny it.

"Our work doesn't intersect."

"Except you paid down her loans."

I shrugged that off. She had tons of scholarships thanks to graduating at the top of her class and being brilliant. What loans she'd needed for bridging weren't something she should have to worry about, "There are no debts between us." There never had been and there never would be. "She supports me and I support her. That's how it works." Especially with there only being the two of us now.

"Understood. Then we're back to which of the pair of you was the primary target." Bones cocked his head to the side, studying me. "We can't eliminate your sister being a target particularly after the response from her law firm."

"Arguably," Voodoo said. "They could have been misinformed by whomever took her. It could be another method of covering their tracks by eliminating who might report her missing."

That made a sick sort of sense.

"Kind of hard to do with me." I had a lot of clients and connections. Then there was Eleanor. She would take a torch and set the world on fire. It had been weeks already. She had to be...

"Hard is not impossible," Bones said.

"Okay." I didn't like the sound of that. Should I ask the question or just wait?

"There are no news reports about you being missing. Nothing local or national. Nothing on web servers or gossip sites—the closest we could identify was a possible blind item and it mentioned yachting."

Yachting. That was the last thing I wanted to talk about.

I gaped at him. "What do you mean no one reported me missing? Eleanor would be—" My stomach flip-flopped all over again. I had to put the coffee cup down when it sloshed over my fingers. "Eleanor would not buy any two bit excuse and if I scrubbed on a contract, she'd hunt me down herself."

"There is no easy way to tell you this, Grace. I am sorry to be the one to inform you that Eleanor Hightower was in a car accident. She was declared brain dead. Her family agreed a few days ago to take her off life support and donate her organs."

If there were more words, I didn't hear them. I couldn't. Not when the roaring in my ears drowned everything out. Someone swore. The table was shoved backwards. Goblin barked.

Then it all just shut off.

CHAPTER
TWELVE

"Goddammit," I swore as Lunchbox barely got the table shoved away from her with one foot as she dropped. Bloodless, she'd taken an almost haunting white pallor. The contrast with her deep blue eyes had been startling for the point two seconds before she pitched forward.

Emotional body blow after body blow had rained down on her slim form. For all that she was a looker—and holy shit was she ever—she looked like this fragile, pale imitation of herself. All the life and vibrance sucked out of her and leaving her collapsed like a broken doll.

Voodoo had popped forward and caught her head against his palm even as Lunchbox sent the table away. Bones grabbed her coffee cup as it pitched forward, launched by the force of the shove.

His sigh seemed both aggrieved and worried. The worried was the only thing that had me fisting my temper. Goblin had sounded a warning but she had already fainted.

"You could have done that with a lighter touch, Captain," Voodoo chided Bones before he picked up Grace. She seemed even smaller now than she had before. The fierce, larger-than-life personality she radiated was such a contrast to the rest of her.

"Wouldn't have mattered," Bones said, setting the coffee cup down on another table. "Hearing someone you cared about has died is never easy even if they are expecting to hear it."

"She thought we were going to tell her that she'd lost her sister." Lunchbox raked a hand through his hair as Voodoo set Grace down on the sofa.

"I saw that too," I murmured. "She didn't have any idea about her agent."

"Before you three lose your collective shit," Bones said, folding his arms. "I needed to be sure. Too many things aren't adding up. I spent the night on the phone with Fletcher and Cash." The two men were part of the committee overseeing the Network these days. Not that committee was the right word for them.

"What did they say?" I managed to pull my gaze from Grace to find Bones studying her with the same concern in his expression that rippled through my gut.

"That my gut is right," Bones said with a shrug. "I asked a lot of questions without mentioning Grace directly, they confirmed that these operations are far bigger than a model and her attorney sister. Traffickers typically avoid taking people who are connected. Granted, they were trying to get her out of the country, so that gives them more options."

"But how does an attorney get on that radar?" Voodoo may have asked the question but we were all thinking it.

"They are identical twins," I answered. It kept coming back to that, right. "That's the only angle that makes sense.

Grace is out there, there's literally gigabytes of her photographs out there—"

"You said something about yachting?" Lunchbox folded his arms where he stood like a guardian hovering over Grace and Voodoo. Not that Voodoo had surrendered his spot. He was on one knee next to her with his fingers against her pulse.

His concern hadn't shifted or turned graver, so I could hope that she would open those eyes again soon.

"Apparently, there's a lot of money in models and actors —aspiring or otherwise—being invited to their private yachts for sex, drugs, and rock and roll." I grimaced. "I've been digging down on it. Most of the information is only found through rumors and innuendo, go figure, they call it *yachting* cause it's basically dressing up escorts in jewels and furs so you can take them home to Mom without judgment."

The doubting looks on all three of them would be funny if it weren't so serious.

With a shrug, I spread my hands and then dropped one to stroke Goblin's head. He was still focused on Grace and I could practically feel the concern shimmering around him.

"So, they basically hire them out like whores?" Lunchbox frowned. "How the hell do you hire a model to be a whore?"

"Her agent?" Yes, the woman was dead now. So had she known something that could point people in the right direction? I hadn't finished pulling the background on anyone around her. I was working out from the center—I needed a wider scatter shot.

"Cash suggested that a lot of agents can be looped in to arrange introductions, even to broach possible invitations with the clients. The upside is a cut of the money and these people can afford to do whatever they want with whomever they want." Bones shook his head. "It's another form of networking."

Lunchbox scrubbed a hand over his face and glanced at Grace. "So... what? They are hired to go be pretty arm candy and entertain some wealthy fat fuck? Do they get extra if they fuck him or his friends?"

"Probably. Whether they are paid directly or not, these are wealthy men who like to be seen with beautiful women and to be appreciated by them. It can secure funding for a film or a company or an idea. So what is a few hundred thousand to invest in a project? Or get a business opportunity off the ground?"

Hate swelled through me at the idea. We were all whores after a fashion. We did what we were asked to do and took payment for it. Now? We used the skills we'd gained and put them to work for us, but we still took money. If not cash, then we worked on an exchange for influence and favors.

"The problem with all of this," I said as I tried to make the various puzzle pieces fit into the picture we'd been trying to fill in. "What would yachting have to do with the people trying to take her? That group the Vandals found her with was heading south. Toward Mexico? South America? A port so they could ship them to Asia? The Middle East? The middle of nowhere? We don't have that information. The others on that truck were not the looker she is nor were *any* of them influential or recognizable."

Because that was another key. Grace Black may not be a household name, but she had a very *well-known* face. I hadn't been able to place her, not at first. Lunchbox had though, and at some point, I needed to give him shit for being dialed in that tight to not only recognize her, but knew enough to name her.

"They weren't the first people to take her," Voodoo said into the blanket of silence that fell after my question. "It's not just one group."

That gave me food for thought. "Fact," I said, holding up one finger. "She was taken outside of her sister's place. Fact, she woke up somewhere there were multiple other prisoners—"

"Did she say if there were men and children too, or only women?" Good question from Bones.

"She didn't want to discuss it at all." A detail here or there slipped out, but she'd been guarding herself and who could blame her? Certainly not me. I raised a third finger. "Fact, the first group that took her suffered a raid. During that raid, Gracie was taken from the first group and woke up on the truck."

I wanted the names of these groups. I didn't like nebulous vague fucking details.

"Fact," Lunchbox said. "There are *no* reports that Grace Black is missing."

"Fact," Bones added. "There is none about her sister either, except that her law office is telling everyone she no longer works there. They can't believe something is wrong or there would be reports. Even a thin FBI file to indicate suspected kidnapping."

Yeah. FBI and Homeland handled a lot of human trafficking. Particularly since it went across state and national lines.

"Cash verified there are no hidden reports being buried currently?" If they had an open investigation, the last thing they'd want to do is loop in the public, even accidentally.

"As far as he can tell. Fletcher said he'd deep dive the

Feds to make sure there isn't something hidden. Right now, however, what open investigations they have don't appear related."

I snorted.

"Didn't say it wasn't bullshit," Bones gave me a look. "Just said what they told me. None of this tackles our issues with the Rojas."

Shaking my head, I pushed up from the chair. "Why isn't she awake yet?" I focused on Voodoo who still had two fingers against her pulse point.

"Because her mind might be shielding her." Voodoo's patient explanation seemed reasonable.

"I don't like it," I admitted and then began to pace. The stiffness in my right leg served as a reminder that I'd been overdoing it, combining long stretches of activity with equally long stretches of inactivity.

Thankfully, no one commented on my complaint. Goblin didn't rush after me as I walked the length of the room and back. He was as used to me as I was to him. The agitation and unsettled feeling in my gut wasn't about my leg or the damage or the phantom feelings that came and went.

"We shouldn't keep her here," I said, finally, giving voice to the voice turning circles in the back of my head. It had been growing gradually louder day after day. It finally clarified the argument when we were in Mexico. "She doesn't belong in this life."

"We can't let her go," Bones countered and while I'd expected the argument, it seemed to catch both Lunchbox and Voodoo off-guard. They whipped their gazes from me to Bones and then back. "I'm sorry..."

"You're really not," I interrupted, slicing a hand through the air. "You already have an argument for why we *can't* let her go?" Because can't was different from shouldn't and wouldn't.

"Fine, I'm not. You like her, I get it."

Did he now?

"All three of you like her and Voodoo is already fucking her. At the rate you two are going, I suspect it won't be that much longer."

"Really?" Lunchbox's tone hit a distinctly derisive note. Was he talking to Bones or Voodoo? Fuck, I didn't care.

"You want to have a problem with our sex lives or lack thereof," I said, before Lunchbox could keep going. "That's a *you* problem, Bones. I have no problem following orders in the field or on a mission, everything else? You can go fuck yourself."

A faint smile touched Bones' mouth and he shook his head. "Fine, let's put it this way. Not one of you can think clearly where she is concerned. You want to protect her. You want to keep her safe. You want to make things right for her. The problem is, all of those may be at odds with our current mission."

"We don't have a current mission," Voodoo stepped right into the fight, his deadpan delivery sucking some of the oxygen out of Bones' argument.

"Yes, we do. You made *her* the current mission."

That put a period on my argument. "Fuck." Rubbing both palms against my face, I savored the prickle of the stubble scraping my palms. "We made promises."

The harsh exhale from Lunchbox said he grasped it too. We'd made promises to Grace.

"Then we brought her here," Bones said, and before I could tackle that nugget, he raised a hand.

The gesture cast a bit of shadow over his face and high-lighted the bruises littering his face. There was a cut at the corner of his mouth that kept reopening. The petty little part of me that had enjoyed the idea of Voodoo and him going a few rounds swallowed back some regret. As fucking irritating as the captain was being, he was captain for a *reason*.

"It was my call to bring her here, no matter who suggested it." That shut off that line of argument. "I debated it. Debated finding us another safe house, especially after we proved that she was being tracked."

Lunchbox let out a low curse of his own. "I forgot about that damn thing."

"You're compromised." For the first time, Bones didn't make it sound like an insult. He just shrugged. "It happens. We've attempted to take her home and a group tried to reacquire her. They pursued her. You dealt with them. We dangled her like bait to test a theory and sure enough they came for her again. Whoever these assholes are—whether it's group one, group two, or some mysterious fucking third party—they aren't giving up."

"Bones is right," Voodoo said. "We can't let her go. With us, she stands a chance. The upside of here is no one knows where we are."

Not even Doc. Not that he had to say that. Doc was welcome at any time and he could call us. He had a number that could reach us no matter where we were in the world. But we'd built this place ourselves. Brought in the materials, did the labor, and the wiring—everything.

No one came up here that wasn't *us*.

"Exactly. Now her agent is dead and her sister is definitely missing. We have the Rojas situation. We have a lot of questions and not enough answers." One way to put it. "Fighting over her or who is in her bed is only going to get her killed."

"Don't take this the wrong way, Captain," Lunchbox damn near drawled the words, exaggerating them for emphasis. "The only one bitching about who is in her bed is you."

A snort of laughter escaped me. It popped the tension, and a soft gasp of sound filled me with relief. Grace's blue eyes were open.

"Hey there, Firecracker," Voodoo greeted her. "How we doing?"

"Eleanor is dead?" She was already pushing up on her elbows despite the harrowed look on her face. "You said she was dead. I didn't imagine that?"

The lost note in her voice made me want to assure her it was all a bad dream. Except it wasn't...

"No," Bones answered her in a firm, if even tone. "You didn't. But you also passed out so let's take it easy, shall we? Then we can go over more of what happened, compare notes—that's what a real debriefing should be."

The really weird thing about the whole argument, he wasn't wrong. Grace wanted to be involved, and she should be. It was her life. Shielding her seemed as natural as breathing. Goblin was already moving over to rest his chin on the sofa next to her and she lifted a hand to pet him, though Voodoo didn't abandon his position.

"What does she need?" Bones directed the question to Voodoo.

"Electrolytes. Water." He studied her and raised his brows. "And do you have any history of fainting or low blood pressure we need to know about?"

Fuck. Medical issues. I looked at Lunchbox but he already had a hand up like, hang on. He had it. How badly had we fucked this whole thing up?

"No, and no. Water is fine." She was already sitting up. I

really didn't like how ashen-faced she was. Based on Voodoo's nearness, neither did he.

"We can call Doc later," I said, and yes, I was calling whether they agreed or not. "If anything else comes up, we can take her to see him."

We had others we could use—like the guy at the clinic. The Network allowed us lots of resources. Doc, however, was one of us. Him we trusted.

"I'll be fine," she said to me, still petting Goblin. "I just —I can't believe Eleanor is dead."

"I'm sorry," I told her.

"Me too." The sadness in those eyes cut me. But she didn't embrace the sympathy or the sadness, she focused on Bones and raised her chin. "What do you need to know?"

"Everything." He wasn't wrong. "Every single detail and start with at least a week before you were supposed to meet your sister."

"Why a week?" It wasn't a denial from her, just curiosity. Lunchbox motioned to the door and I lifted my chin. He was going to get her fluids.

"To make sure we don't miss anything," I answered for Bones. Because taking her and her sister hadn't been an impulse. The more info she gave me, the better chance I had of teasing the data out of surveillance *somewhere*.

Yes, I liked this plan.

"Bones is right," I said. "We need to know everything and I need my tablet..."

CHAPTER

THIRTEEN

GRACE

Recounting everything that happened took way longer than I imagined. Then it became a series of explanations and questions until they knew what I did. Maybe. Who knew, since they kept discovering new questions to ask. Despite fresh coffee and all the water with electrolytes they kept pressing on me, I still had a sore throat.

Bones had a pen up on a *whiteboard* of all things, and he'd drawn an actual time line and began to link events. Any places I had gaps because I couldn't think of something and they added a question mark.

Next to the whiteboard, there was a screen with information scrolling on it—including video surveillance and images from security cameras in various areas. How Alphabet kept finding them so swiftly puzzled me, but the questions kept coming and it kept me from focusing too much.

"There," Lunchbox said, his voice slicing across mine

and I swallowed the rest of the answer. He was pointing at something on the screen—no, he was pointing at some*one*. Alphabet zoomed in. The more he blew it up the blurrier it got so he backed off a little. "Him."

"What about him?" I asked before anyone else said anything. I leaned forward to stare at the screen. Where were they? Oh, it was the Met Gala. Eleanor had gotten me a ticket cause I'd always wanted to go. She would rather put her feet up and do her crossword puzzles while binging the latest season of...

Pain spasmed around my heart. I'd just found out she was gone and instead of actually grieving, I was what? I folded my arms and tried to focus on the screen again. Thinking about Eleanor hurt.

"He's in a couple of the other surveillance images we were looking at," Lunchbox said, then slanted a look at Alphabet. "Can you run one of those—" He waved his hand in the air.

"Forensic software to compare the facial features with others in the image captures?" The desert dry tone pulled a real if reluctant smile from me. "Find me the other clips where you saw him..."

"Why are you looking at images from the Met Gala?" That wasn't recent. At least not in the window of time they'd given me.

"You were referenced in some gossip pieces," Alphabet said over his shoulder. "One of them was about this event, so I backtracked to it."

"Okay." I elongated both syllables because that didn't feel like an answer.

"We're focusing on the intelligence we have," Bones said, tugging my attention to where he stood with a marker in hand. It was funny, he looked like a teacher. "In this case, we're looking to see if anyone was watching you."

Goosebumps raced over my flesh and I folded my arms. "Watching me? Like a stalker?" I frowned. "I've had an occasional fan but nothing like that." At least none that I've known of. "Most of them are just wealthy bored men who want to have some arm candy or want to invite me to parties."

Most of them were not my type. I wasn't for sale. I didn't intend to negotiate for advances or business opportunities that way. Fortunately, it hadn't been an issue for me. There was a lot I was willing to do for myself, that just didn't happen to be one I wanted to explore further.

"Something like a stalker," Voodoo said as he returned with a tablet of his own. "But not a stalker exactly. Your sister is missing, you were taken in front of her place. One logical conclusion is to presume she was the target and they took you, possibly thinking you were her."

"Or they were double-dipping," Lunchbox said, his mouth compressing and a muscle ticking in his cheek.

"That doesn't seem unreasonable." Yet the way they were talking, they didn't seem to be on board with the idea. Except.. I frowned. "You said you tracked her until Wednesday and no sign of her after that?"

Bones touched a finger to his nose then pointed at me. "They already had her at the time they took you."

I rubbed my hands over my face and then pushed off the sofa. I was tired of sitting still. "So we're really not any closer to understanding what was going on?"

"Yes and no," Alphabet said, tossing the words over his shoulder as he kept typing on his laptop. "We have more variables to work with and I have a working theory that you were both targets. Whether it was for different reasons or the same—the jury is still out on that. But I don't think it's a coincidence that you were taken outside of her place. I also think you fucked up their plans when you went down for that weekend away."

Clearly not fucked them up enough. They'd successfully taken me. My mind flashed back to that room, the crying women. Then the man—

Nope.

Arms folded to hug myself, I paced the room. Goblin was sprawled on his back on a dog bed not far from where Alphabet sat with his laptop. The dog's tongue lolled from the side of his mouth and in that brief moment of quiet, the only thing audible was his gentle snoring.

"The trickiest part isn't identifying the *who*," Voodoo said as he rolled a coin over his knuckles back and forth. His attention on the timeline. The fact he could manipulate the coin without looking at it riveted me for a moment. "We're going to get there. The who will take a minute because there is more than one. That's the part that bothers me."

The goosebumps on my arms seemed to intensify. The soft swish of the marker on the white board squeaked periodically as Bones added more details to his timeline. Details like dates, places, and then more question marks. Weirdly, there was something relaxing about how neat his handwriting was.

Circling the room slowly, I made myself keep moving. The sense of everything closing in on me was inescapable. Didn't mean I would just stand there and let it overwhelm me. Lunchbox stood fixed as he watched a series of pictures flicker past at a high rate. The one he'd pointed out earlier from the Met stationary next to it. Could he actually process any of those images or did he not want to miss a match?

I stared at the man, the one Lunchbox said he'd seen before. Nothing about him leapt out. He was maybe five foot ten or eleven. Medium brown hair. Everyman face. Even his suit was bland considering the event. He was the picture of utterly forgettable. The cameras would skate right past him.

I wouldn't even look at him twice.

Sad comment on my part, but true. The scrolling images paused as a second image popped up. The markers were flashing. Dots on the eyes, the cheekbones, the jaw—but the two guys weren't the same.

It listed a possible match of 57%. That didn't seem like a lot.

"Save?" Alphabet asked.

"Yeah, could use prosthetics to change his look," was Lunchbox's answer.

Could use...

"Why would anyone use prosthetics to change their look to follow me? That's nuts."

Almost as one, all four men looked at me.

"It's nuts, right?" The shivers seemed to intensify. Was the room freezing or was that just me?

"Maybe," Lunchbox was the one that answered. "It's still a close match, so better for us to keep it for reassessment. We can't leave any stone unturned."

The last almost sounded like an apology. Then the images started flicking again and his attention returned to the screen while Bones went back to writing. I couldn't fathom any of this.

None of it made sense.

None of it.

The hum under my skin seemed to grow louder. The buzzing was almost too much. The noise intensified as did the agitation. It was like I'd taken a fall into some poison oak, and had to wear some scratchy burlap on top of it and then *not* react.

Abandoning the room they were working in, I headed to the hall and then toward the living room and kitchen. A glance outside showed the bluer sky had been blanketed by darker clouds. Not quite rain worthy, but definitely overcast.

I did a circuit of the living room—twice. The place was almost painfully neat. There weren't a lot of knickknacks. I paused a beat and searched the room with a sweeping glance. There were *no* knickknacks. The only thing sitting atop one of the tables was the universal remote that I'd flung at Bones.

The room looked like one that would show up in a catalog and you could order all the pieces—right down to the rug. Nothing to really focus on so I kept moving.

There were three dishes in the sink, I paused to rinse them out before opening the dishwasher. There were a few dishes in there—all ones from breakfast. So that made sense. I stacked the bowls in the top and then closed it again.

Impatience ripped through me. I checked the garbage can but it was mostly empty. Not that I would know where to take the garbage if it wasn't. With a low groan, I pivoted and found Voodoo leaning against the column that framed part of the entranceway separating the kitchen and dining room from the living room.

"You don't have to do dishes," he said and I shrugged. The pull on my back wasn't as bad as it was previously. Still not terrifically comfortable, but I'd rather feel that pinch than the sensation of a thousand ants crawling all over my skin.

"They were there and I wanted…" I spread my hands. "I don't know what I wanted."

"You're upset." The deadpan delivery seemed to make the words even more ironic.

"No shit." I stared at him. "Of course, I'm upset. Every question I answer creates new ones. You four are all fired up and on the hunt—it's impressive. But I'm still…" I gestured to the space around us then folded my arms again. "I'm doing nothing."

For the first time in a very long time, I was helpless. This was not a feeling I ever wanted to encounter. The last time had been when Maman got so sick. I pushed those memories away. I couldn't deal with that right now. Not with anxiety swirling in my gut like a violent whirlpool threatening to suck the life out of me.

It might almost make some of this easier. The moment that thought tried to take purchase, I ripped it out. No, I wasn't giving up on anything. Being lost didn't make anything easier. Neither did being dead.

It just made you dead.

"You want to talk to me about what's going on in that beautiful head of yours?" Voodoo's question reminded me that he was right there, enjoying a front row seat to my existential crisis.

"Not really." Maybe a little blunt and on the nose, but here we were. "I don't even know if I know everything going on in my head. I feel like I've been ripped out of my life and tossed into another universe where up is down and down is up and nothing makes any damn sense."

"Well, multiverse theory usually has to do with choices. Choose the red pill, you face the dark harshness of real life. Take the blue and you can continue to live in blissful ignorance."

"That's *The Matrix*." I frowned. "Not multiverses."

One corner of his mouth kicked a little higher. "The principle applies. Depending on whether we're discussing Marvel or DC, the multiverse discussion can get muddy. Particularly when they can't make up their minds if they are actual alternate timelines or alternate universes."

"Aren't those the same things? Wouldn't an alternate universe have an alternate timeline?"

"You'd think," he said and it was his turn to shrug. "Personally, I think they should have actually hired someone who understands quantum mechanics and physics to give them a plausible explanation. Spaghetti and forks are not what I call helpful."

"I really have no idea what we're talking about anymore," I admitted.

"See, that's the problem. Their convoluted explanations make it all more confusing. Butterfly effect? Totally understandable by the masses. String theory? Not so much." He pushed away from the column. "So let's talk about something else. What has you spooked?"

"Does it have to be one thing?" It didn't feel like just one thing.

"Obviously not," Voodoo said, holding out a hand to me. "And why don't we go sit down? You've had a lot of shocks and you need more rest."

I glanced down at his hand and then at him. "I don't think I can. If I sit still, I'm just gonna start screaming and I don't know if I'll be able to stop."

Admitting I was freaking out was the first step to fixing it, right?

He studied me for a long moment. "What can I do?"

I glanced at the windows. "Can I go outside? I need to

breathe. I need to walk—I just need to move where the walls aren't closing in."

Head cocked, he stared at me for another long moment, then nodded. "Yes, you can. But one of us has to go with you."

"I really don't care. I just—I just want to go."

"Give me two minutes, Firecracker and grab your boots and a jacket. Both should be in the mudroom." He was already striding up the hallway back to the room where they were tearing apart all their different angles.

By the time I had my boots on, he was back with Goblin. I welcomed the dog with head scritches as he pulled on his own boots. He was also wearing a shoulder holster with a gun in it. He covered it with his own jacket and then reached for the door.

"Ready?"

FOURTEEN

VOODOO

"I'm taking Grace for a walk. Mind if Goblin comes?" I directed the question to Alphabet and not Bones. I didn't really care what Bones had to say on the matter and I wasn't asking for his permission.

"She okay?" Lunchbox frowned.

"No," I said, keeping it as forthright as she had. "She's trying to not have a panic attack. She wants to be outside and she wants to walk. So I'm taking her."

"Take Goblin," Alphabet said as he glanced up from his laptop. "He could use the break to stretch his legs." Grace would probably appreciate his company.

"Take your phone," Bones said and I gave him a mock salute before I whistled. "Come on, Goblin."

"Go," Alphabet said, when the dog checked with him first. He really was the fifth member of our team these days. The relief on Grace's face when Goblin and I met her in the mudroom would be hard to manufacture. She took my gun in stride or if she didn't, she didn't complain.

Once I opened the door, the cooler air drifted in. The overcast clouds suggested rain, but there was no scent of it in the air. I checked my watch for time and followed Firecracker and Goblin out the door.

"Which way?" she asked as she slid her hands into her pockets. The lack of color in her face hadn't quite drained her lips of their pinkness, but it wasn't far off. It added to my worries regarding her.

"Let's head up the mountain," I said. "It's not a steep incline, but it is steady. There's some good lookouts along the way." Pretty sure there were, but what I could see when I scouted wasn't necessarily scenic.

"That means the walk back will be downhill." A hint of a smile appeared, briefly, but it still showed up. She set off in the direction I indicated and I let her set the pace. Her legs were a lot shorter than mine, so better to not make her take two or three steps for every one of mine. Goblin played forward scout and raced ahead, then circled back to check on us before dashing on again.

Yeah, he needed the exercise too.

"How long have you guys had this place?" As much as I hadn't been expecting conversation, I wasn't going to turn it down either.

"A few years," I told her. "We pooled our resources, bought the land and built what we wanted. Some of the structures were here, but the house is all us."

"You did all the work yourselves?" The faintest bit of skepticism made me smile.

"Don't think we're up to it?" It was meant to tease and another flash of her smile said it worked.

"Just seems like a lot of work."

"It was, but it was the kind of work we wanted to do. We built over the summer. Pitched tents, had campfires at night. It was almost like having summer camp without the counselors or the girls."

She rewarded that comment with a real laugh. What bugged me about it was how hollow she sounded when the laugh was done and how quickly the light in her blue eyes seem to just go back out.

Head on a swivel, I scanned the area. Goblin was in scout mode too. He would check ahead then come back and join us for a while before he took off again. It also let me keep an eye on Grace. She lost some of the stiffness to her movements the more we walked.

The wound on her back *was* healing. The bruises on her throat *would* heal. The discoloration on her cheek, the mottling of yellow and green where someone had caught her with the back of their hand was also fading. These were all positives, but it was the wounds we couldn't see that had me on edge now. The concussion *appeared* better. Looks could be deceiving.

"It's a really nice house," she said, as we reached one of the lookouts. There wasn't much here but some sheer rock faces, but the lip overlooked the valley. "Wow."

"Thanks and this is one of the reasons we like it up here. It's quiet. Few to no people. We occasionally see some bears, and a moose once. We left them alone, they left us alone."

Her eyes rounded briefly and she wrinkled her nose. "Are you teasing me?"

"Yes," I said because I definitely had been earlier. "But dead serious at the moment. There is wildlife up here. If Goblin goes on guard, it means he's scented or heard something. *Trust* his instincts."

The fact she looked directly at Goblin who was currently rolling on his back in some thick grass and wiggling as he played made me laugh. Her scowl was adorable.

"I've never seen a moose," she muttered, and turned her attention back to the valley. The breeze had picked up and while it was cool, it wasn't cold. The clouds thickened, but it still didn't feel or smell like rain. Just a weather system passing by.

It could keep right on passing.

"I don't advise trying to pet one. Or a bison for that matter."

"Are there bison up here?" Her eyes narrowed as she glanced at me.

"Not up here specifically, but we're not far from the parks and there are bison there. Tourists like to get their picture with them and don't realize that bison are not docile creatures and they really don't like it when people invade their space."

"Well, then they get what they get." She shook her head. "We're in Montana, right? You can tell me that?"

I sighed. "Yes, we're in Montana."

"Thank you," she murmured, the two words were so soft I almost didn't hear them. "You guys brought me here, to your place and I know I've been pissed at you—"

"You have a right to be." For all that we had good intentions, the choice to bring her here had been Bones' and he'd never explained exactly why. I could guess and if I was right, then I actually agreed with the choice. "Bringing you here isn't about keeping you prisoner, Firecracker."

"No?" She practically dared me, but her gaze remained fixed on the distance.

"No. Whoever is after you is extremely determined. We think there are at least two groups, but based on the timeline and what you can recall, I have to wonder if there is more involved than just these groups coming after you."

"More?" She pivoted to stare at me almost pleadingly. "More than killing my agent and manager? More than taking my sister? More than taking me? What *more* could there be?"

"Taking you permanently. Making you a part of a collection. Keeping you."

Disgust curled her lip and she shook her head. "They don't get to have me."

"No, they don't. But they *want* you, Grace." It was my turn to sigh. "At the end of the day, we can keep you safe if we keep you out of sight and away from anywhere you would normally be."

Maybe we should have had *this* conversation before.

"You are visible in your life—"

"I'm not as visible as you might think."

"Perhaps you're not a household name, but people know you. They know how to book your time." I frowned. "Why didn't they just hire you for a shoot and take you that way?"

That pulled her around. "I have no idea. Eleanor takes care of my contracts and negotiations. I'm not her only model. But she's really good at what she does and she vets every request carefully..." Her gaze went to the distance again.

Based on that description though, if the people trying to lay hands on Grace went through her manager, it might explain why they killed her. Not that we had concrete evidence on that *yet*. It didn't feel like a coincidence in any form of the word.

"I was offered a million dollars to attend a party," Grace

said. "They offered less than that but I don't do those anymore. I don't like them."

"Like—what kind of party would pay you a million dollars to show up?" Even if I was already guessing yachting, I wanted her take on it.

"A yacht party. They are very popular. Wealthy men want to buy everything. Sometimes, they like to buy the attention and company of women."

She folded her arms and I checked the color in her cheeks. I didn't want her to be cold. Goblin was still lolling in the grass. He was comfortable and she had some color again. Both positive signs.

"When I was just starting out, I would take the invitations because they were networking opportunities. A group of us would go together. Some girls liked to do a little more and if they wanted to, fine, but I wasn't for sale. Not like that." Another long sigh escaped her. "I hate this. I just want to see Amorette, to talk to her, to hug her and know she is okay. Then I want to go back to my life... Maybe it's not the life for everyone, but I liked it."

If I could stand her sister in front of her right now, I would. "We're not so bad, are we?"

"No." It came out almost grudging. The frustration reflected in expression. "I don't know what to do."

"Well, first thing's first, we're going to finish our walk." I offered her an arm. "And I'm going to let you interrogate me." That didn't come out quite how I intended it, but it fit. "You want to know something, ask. I can't promise to answer everything, but I will tell you what I can."

She eyed me then my arm. She trusted me enough that night to let me help her forget everything. Could she trust me now? Not reading into her hesitation, I waited her out. Finally, she slipped her hand onto the crook of my elbow.

"You still good for more walking?" Probably shouldn't push it.

"I thought I got to ask the questions." The tart response made me grin. "But yes, I think I'm fine to keep walking. I really don't want to go back inside yet. If I was at home, I'd go to the gym and just work out. A run on the treadmill or a stairmaster—something."

Right. I could definitely help her with that. "As much as I would like to ask what else you like to do, I would like you to take note that I am not asking you any more questions. You have the lead, Firecracker."

Goblin gave up his lolling to lope alongside us and then he darted ahead. There was another spot up the slope where she could get a good feel for the mountains themselves. It was a hell of a view.

She didn't ask me anything at first, just moved with me. Her gaze was distant and her mouth turned down. She was grieving. Maybe trying to distract her wasn't the best plan.

"What is your name?" Damn near missed the question, she asked it so quietly. "I know you go by Voodoo, but what is your—government name, I guess is the right question."

Not answering it before had been about keeping distance. It wasn't classified, but there were few who called me by that name. Bones was one, but generally only when we were alone or he needed actual help.

"My name is Bryant," I said. "Bryant Wagner."

Surprise flickered over her face. I kind of liked being able to surprise her.

"So where did Voodoo come from?"

Chuckling, I shook my head. "That's a longer story."

"I have time," she pointed out. "So do you at the moment."

At the moment...

"True, but that's definitely a story for another day."

"Hmm..." She really was cute when she was disgruntled.

"I did say, I didn't promise to answer everything."

"That's true... Bryant."

I liked how that sounded on her lips.

"Bryant Wagner." She frowned. "You really don't look like a Bryant."

"No?" I laughed.

"No," she said.

"Do I look like a Voodoo?" Yes, she was the one who got to ask the questions, but I wanted to know.

Grace glanced up at me from under her lashes. "That's definitely an answer for another day."

"Touché, Firecracker. Touché."

"I liked it." She was quite pleased with herself. "So, besides rescuing women from trafficking rings and blowing up drug labs, what else do you do?" I must have hesitated too long because she sighed. "Let me amend it to what else do you *like* to do, if you can't talk about your work."

The retort made me want to kiss her. She wasn't asking this time, so I refrained. "I like a lot of things, Firecracker, but if you want to know if I have hobbies...I do. I like to do magic tricks."

Interest flared in her eyes. "Magic tricks?"

"Sleight of hand is really useful in my line of work." I raised my hand to her ear and "pulled" a coin from her hair. It was a good, solid coin. Great for working my fingers. When I held it up, I said, "Silver dollar for your thoughts?"

Real delight lit her up and took my breath away. Right.

More magic tricks.

FIFTEEN

GRACE

One day bled into the next and rather than get bored or frustrated with the tedious task of taking each morsel of information apart, Alphabet seemed to come alive with the work. He'd zero in and stay at his desk and on his comp unless one of the guys bullied him away from it.

I'd asked if I could take Goblin for another walk just the day before and that seemed to rouse him. He'd blinked at me almost blearily. The redness of his eyes coupled with the rough dark of the stubble coating his face suggested what he needed more than a walk was a nap.

With a sigh, he glanced at Goblin then at the screen. Before I could backpedal my request, he keyed in several things then checked his phone before he stood. The cracks of his joints had me wincing, but they didn't seem to faze him in the slightest.

Goblin bounded to his feet and turned in a circle next to me without getting in Alphabet's way. "It's supposed to be colder out there," he warned me. "Storms coming through. Grab a jacket?"

Even his voice was hoarse and rough. "Maybe you should take it easier," I said. "You sound bad."

He shrugged then shoved his hand through the disarray of his hair. Three things happened in that moment, his raised arm sent a waft of distinctly *unwashed* and *musky* man in my direction. The smell of sweat wouldn't usually bother me, but sweat laced with onions and something I couldn't identify was *really* bad.

My nose wrinkled and I backed up a step before I even registered I was moving. He shot me a brief frown, then made a face himself before tested his own smell by raising his arm again. Oh, yeah. That was like old sweaty gym socks left in the bottom of the hamper bad.

"I can just go get that—"

"Fuck," Alphabet said with a scowl. "I reek."

"I mean," I began, fumbling for something that might be a polite response before I gave it up. "I don't think you're quite corpse-like yet, but it's definitely nasty. Can't be healthy."

With a snort, he glanced down at Goblin. "And he definitely needs a walk. Ten minutes?"

What was I going to say? *No?* "Of course."

"Thanks, Gracie." Then he moved at a steady, if faintly limping pace out of the room. I frowned at the hitch to his gait. Maybe I should have just said no so he could get some rest.

Lunchbox stuck his head in the door not even a full minute after Alphabet and Goblin disappeared. "Good job, Gracie. A walk and some air will be good for him."

"I hope so," I murmured, then followed Lunchbox out to the kitchen to wait for Goblin and Alphabet. After his shower, and a shave apparently, he seemed in much better spirits. Even if his eyes were still red. He was also armed, a gun in a holster on the back of his belt.

The guys didn't wear them in the house, but *none* of them seemed to leave without having it on them. After Mexico? Well, they wouldn't get an argument from me. We walked for over an hour, lingering until the first spits of rain hit us and then a little longer.

By the time we got back to the house, dinner was ready and dark swept in soon after. I didn't think the sun had gone down but the pitch dark nature of the storm clouds made the night come early. Rumbles of thunder rolled over the house while we ate. It wasn't long before I excused myself to sleep.

Even after the walk, I wasn't that hungry. The rain came down in sheets and I watched it out the windows as lightning flashed. With the lights out, I could almost pretend I was somewhere else entirely. Eventually, I curled up in the bed and listened to the storm. Sleep eventually swallowed me.

Following the debrief, the guys had fallen into a routine. Alphabet seemed permanently attached to his computer. But I might try to get him out for another walk today. Lunchbox started every day with a fresh loaf of bread. He smoked a brisket one day. On another he cooked up a batch of savory chili.

Voodoo spent more nights in my room than he spent away. Even if he wasn't there when I went to sleep, I'd snap awake between one and two in the morning and there he'd be. More than once, he'd just been murmuring to me and wiping away tears I hadn't even been aware of shedding.

Then there was Boney Boy.

I had no fucking clue what he was doing or where he

was, but he didn't bug me and I didn't go looking for him. The problem with the passage of time was, I seemed to be losing track. I had no idea how many days it had been since I'd been rescued from the truck or we'd gone to my apartment or after we got back from Mexico.

Worse, I had no idea how long it had been since the last time I saw Amorette. My gaze tracked to the photo on the dresser. I looked at it every morning and every night. Still, she felt a million miles away. Blowing out a breath, I made myself turn away. Voodoo wasn't in my room, but I could see from where he'd moved one of the chairs and the blanket there that he'd likely slept there with his feet up.

It surprised me that he hadn't asked about sleeping in the bed. Despite me mentioning it during one of the times he was soothing me, he'd merely pressed a kiss to my forehead and told me to sleep. He would be right there. His staying wasn't about sex either, cause we weren't having any.

A part of me regretted that. The night we'd had at the hotel had been both desperate and... No there was no "and" about it. I'd been desperate to feel anything beyond what I'd been experiencing then. Voodoo had made it all go away.

As grateful as I was for that respite, I wasn't sure what it meant going forward. Should I pursue another night? Would it help me forget? Or at least push it all away? And yeah, sex as stress relief or as a coping mechanism didn't seem the best idea. Not after everything else.

Restless with the circumstances, but even more impatient with my own thoughts, I shoved out of the bed and headed for the bathroom. A lot of my bruises had faded. The soreness between my shoulder blades also seemed to have faded.

Twisting to look at myself in the mirror, I eyed the pinkish and ruddy line. It was thin but there. I didn't need any more bandages, so that was good. After brushing my teeth and washing my face, I dragged my hair back and into a ponytail.

I went through the dresser to find clothes I could run in. Even though I'd never been a fan of running, or exercise of any type, I needed to do *something*. The spandex shorts hit me mid-thigh. The racerback tank top with the built-in sports bra was perfect. Socks took a hot minute then I had to find shoes.

There were boots and shoes in the mudroom, but I needed something for the gym. If I had to run in my socks, I'd do it. I delved into the closet and found a stack of shoeboxes in the back. I could have sworn these weren't here before. Frankly, half the stuff in here still had the tags on it, but I hadn't paid that much attention when we got here beyond seeing if there was anything I could use to get out.

"Score." Second shoebox had running shoes in it.

The gym was in the basement, so that was where I headed. The house was quiet and the sun wasn't quite up outside, though there was some light. Weird. The scent of coffee tickled my nostrils and damn near convinced me to detour to the kitchen.

"After," I ordered even after I caught the faint whiff of maple syrup. Too much sugar. If I didn't do something, I really was going to just start screaming and not stop. The walks helped, but agitation churned in my gut like I'd become some kind of plasma ball. Everything zapped me from the inside.

I followed the stairs around and then down the set to the basement. There were a lot of rooms down here, but thankfully, I didn't have to prowl and sneak peeks behind every door.

The gym door stood wide open. It smelled like a gym too—a combination of sweat, cleaning products, and an old air freshener, maybe. Pungent and musky. I studied the layout, the equipment, and what supplies were here. There was a huge matted area, benches, basic weights, and multiple cardio machines including a Stairmaster, two treadmills, two bikes, and an elliptical.

There were four of them. They obviously needed to work out. Probably did it at the same time. Shelves in the corner had towels, a spray bottle with some kind of cleaning solution, and roll of paper towels.

Cool.

I'd kill for music, but I didn't see anything that looked like a remote or a stereo and I was still sans a phone. The earlier irritation swarmed through me, and my heart hammered as I clenched my fists.

Yep. Time to run.

I chose the closest treadmill and studied the buttons. Most of these had programs that would alter everything from incline to speed, but I just wanted to move. Basic start. Excellent.

Got it going and kept upping the pace over the next few minutes until I was at three and half miles per hour. My legs protested right from the outset. I'd been too still for too long. The more I thought about it, the more irritated I became and the faster I ran.

Could I actually outrun my frustration? Or would I collapse from the effort? The answers were maybe and most definitely, and in that order. The hum of the machine and the slap of my shoes against the treadmill's belt. At thirty minutes, I had the beginnings of a stitch in my side so I dropped back to three for a bit even though I'd finally found that place where all the noise in my head quieted.

Running *sucked*. It was good for keeping me trim and for endurance. I needed endurance on long photo shoots. It actually demanded a lot of energy, whether I had to scowl or wait for the light to be in the right position, or summon some sultry smile.

Part of it was playacting, inhabiting a role that the camera could catch. In the beginning, it had been me. I was the person in the photo, and I struggled to find something to care about—especially when the demand for sensual shots grew.

Then one day, I just pretended.

Pretending was easier.

I loved my job. I loved the places it took me. Most of the time, I even loved who it demanded me to be. The stitch subsided and I hit the speed back up, passing three-point-five for three-point-eight.

At forty-five minutes, I pushed past the four to four-point-five. Not only had the noise in my head quieted, but the tension which stretched out inside me and threatened to snap and break at any moment seemed to ease. Sweat slicked my face and trickled down my back.

I slowed it all the way down to a walk at the one-hour mark. My legs burned and so did my lungs, but fuck it felt good. Real good. The scuff of a shoe against the hard floor had me cutting a look over my shoulder.

Lunchbox crossed the room with a large bottle of water in hand. "Hey..."

My brain stuttered a moment as I processed his greeting. For just a few blissful moments, I'd forgotten everything. Where I was. Why I was here. The fact my sister was missing. It all rushed back in, bringing the tension with it, a milder form of it, but still back all the same.

"Hey," I said, finally. At least my breath was already coming back under control. "Thanks." I accepted the water and tilted the bottle up for a long drink. I damn near gulped down half of it.

"You doing okay?" The guarded way he asked the question had me cutting off the treadmill entirely so I could face him.

"Not really," I answered and tried to summon a smile. "But my back doesn't hurt really anymore and the bruises are fading. I can't keep sitting around all day. It's driving me crazy."

"Hence, the running." Arms folded, he studied me as though he were trying to peer right into my brain. Hated to break it to him, it was messier in my head than in my apartment. Probably better that he couldn't see.

"Yep." I stepped off the treadmill and moved in little circles. Probably kind of dumb to run for that long after not running for even longer. I'd probably end up stiff as hell.

Worth it.

Head cocked, Lunchbox pursed his lips. "Talk to me, Gracie."

"About what?" I drained the last of the water before heading for one of the towels in the corner.

"About you." He didn't follow me but he also didn't look away from where I stood wiping my face.

"Not much to say. I'm still here. You guys are still searching. None of us have answers." I was back to being ready to scream again. That had me grabbing the spray bottle and a couple of paper towels.

"You're frustrated."

The urge to say *"no shit"* bubbled away inside. Thankfully, only some mildly ironic laughter escaped as I wiped down the treadmill. "You could say that. Going for the walks was helping, a little."

His frown deepened. "I thought the debriefing helped."

I shrugged. "It did until it didn't. Not much is helping. I need to be doing—" I spread my arms and motioned to the room as if the answer should be lurking around somewhere. "Something. Anything. So—I ran. Now I'm going to shower and find clean clothes."

That would keep me occupied for thirty or forty minutes. Then I'd be back to nothing. Maybe I could take Goblin out for a walk and head downhill this time. The main road had to be down there somewhere, right?

The moment the thought hit, I discarded it and the used paper towels in the trash before putting the bottle of spray cleaner back. I couldn't take A-B's dog. They were such partners. I also had no idea how far I'd have to go and I was really not built for survival or had I ever taken survival training.

"Do that, then come down to the kitchen. I'll have your coffee waiting and..." He studied me for another long moment. "I think you need cinnamon rolls. Big fat ones. Light on the frosting, because you think it's needless sugar."

Was that so? "I didn't say needless, I said too much."

"Same thing," he said with the faintest of smiles. "Cinnamon rolls need the sweet. Especially hot and fresh from the oven."

My mouth watered and my stomach gurgled away. I could practically taste them and it sounded fantastic. "You're really going to make them?"

"Yes," he returned with a glance at his watch. "Get

going, Gracie. I'll have everything ready for when you come back down."

I must have hesitated too long because he frowned.

"Don't tell me there are too many calories in the rolls. You just did an hour on the treadmill and you've been hiking. Carbs are good."

Snorting, I shook my head. "I wasn't going to say no, I'm still back at—the offer. Thank you." Cinnamon rolls were my favorite and I wished they were ready right now.

"You're welcome," he said, ushering me out of the gym and up the stairs ahead of him. "Now, hurry up and shower. You're finally excited about something I'm making you, I don't want the moment to pass."

I was almost to my room when the guilt stabbed me. Had I really not expressed my appreciation for all his cooking? The man was a machine and he made something different for every meal. Very few items seemed to be repeated.

Giving myself a look in the mirror, I shook my head. I needed to be better about how I responded to them. They were trying to help and they had saved my life. It wasn't perfect. Not yet, I needed more answers than we'd found. They were busy men, that much I'd gleaned, and they did *mercenary* work that included blowing things up.

I needed to keep their interest on finding Am and getting us home. Then we could all go our separate ways. But if another job came up and I was being a bitch...

Yeah, I couldn't afford that. We—Am and me—couldn't afford it.

CHAPTER

SIXTEEN

The sheer tenacity and stubbornness housed in Grace's petite frame blew my damn mind. Each time I thought I had a bead on her, she changed the game. She was as fragile as a grenade with the temperament to match. Little seemed to intimidate her. If anything, Bones' attempts to glare her into compliance only served to make her more defiant.

It was fucking hot.

I was almost humming as I collected the supplies together. I made bread enough that the guys enjoyed it, but no one had a sweet tooth. Not really. So cinnamon rolls, which I loved, were something I rarely indulged in. I'd make them daily if necessary to keep feeding the sudden light that had appeared in her eyes at the mention of them.

"What are we doing?" Voodoo asked as he made his way through the kitchen. Hair still damp from the shower, he was already armed and had my list for the supply run he was about to do.

"Making cinnamon rolls," I told him. "I have a few more items to add to the list. I'll text you once I get these ready to go."

Eyebrows lifted, Voodoo studied me for a moment. "She gave you a favorite?"

"Not directly." Because she really hadn't. "But when I mentioned them..." I spread my hands and he nodded. "How is she sleeping?"

"Still badly." Voodoo sighed. "I thought last night was the best one she's had in a while. The nightmares worry me."

"We can't help her until she talks about it or is willing to." That advice still sounded as shitty now as it had when the doctors informed us of that for both Doc *and* Alphabet.

Fucking bullshit. There had to be a way to help someone even when they weren't there yet. Watching her suffer sucked.

"I'm not a fan of that advice any more than you are." Voodoo ducked into the mudroom and returned with a suede duster. "Unfortunately, we can't make her trust us."

No, but I thought she trusted us more than she was willing to admit. Unsurprisingly, Bones appeared, also ready to go. We had some leads on the group that hired us and sold us out. They were trying to hide.

It wasn't going to last long.

"We'll be back later this afternoon," he informed me. "Keep an eye on Alphabet."

"Always have one eye on him." I was working the dough slowly. I needed to get it folded together before I rolled it out. Not that Bones waited for the answer so much as just strode out.

"Today is going to be fun." The dry as a desert deadpan comment from Voodoo made me grin.

"Happy hunting."

He answered with a middle finger before following Bones out. Snorting, I made swift work of the dough and getting it rolled out. My hum returned as I spread the butter over the flattened dough then the brown sugar and cinnamon.

With care, I rolled it up before slicing each section. I set the first rounds into a glass baking dish then set it aside to rise before starting on the next one. Better to make a couple dozen, maybe more. I'd make sure Gracie got hers. I doubted the guys would have a problem with letting her have hers, but better to be safer than sorry.

The only bad plan was not having one. I kept one eye on the stairs while I rolled out the next. I had three glass baking dishes set up to rise by the time Grace descended the stairs. She'd showered. Her thick, dark hair fell in a straight line. The damp strands seemed even darker than usual but there was already the hint of waves appearing at the ends.

She slowed on the last step and gave the area a slow glance. Checking for the others? The hesitation put her right between a shadow from the hallway and a faint trail of light beaming down from one of the skylights above. The gritty, raw woman dripping with sweat and panting from the gym was gone, leaving behind a far more ethereal one.

When she turned those brilliant blue eyes in my direction they seemed to shimmer. The contrast seemed to frame her, trapped in a moment between vulnerability and strength.

Just like that, it was over. Her eyes shuttered and her expression smoothed to something more neutral. The imaginary snap of shutters closing echoed through me. Right.

She was protecting herself. How could I possibly fault her? No matter how much it pissed me off that she saw us as something she needed protection from. No matter how far down we managed to get the walls, she'd shore them up and they'd be high again.

I summoned up a smile. "Feel better?" It was a weak ass fucking question but we had to start somewhere. Voodoo had been working on her. Goblin too. I was pretty sure somewhere in there, she and Alphabet were fighting to form some kind of friendship.

That meant I could damn well do my part.

"Oddly," she said, folding her arms to cross the living room toward the kitchen. "I kind of do. I mean, I'm tired but I'm also... energized? Not sure that's the right word."

She'd dressed in an oversized sweatshirt, leggings that made her seem even younger and smaller somehow, and a pair of huge fluffy socks that climbed almost to her knees.

"Sounds good," I told her and then glanced at the glass dishes before checking the time on my watch. At this altitude, the yeast rose faster, which meant these fast-rising rolls would be ready for the oven in half the time they would elsewhere.

Useful.

"Are the others off on some mission?" The quiet question pulled my attention as I shifted to the espresso machine. She liked flat whites. I could do that.

"Sort of," I told her. "Voodoo and Bones went on a supply run. Alphabet's sleeping in."

He'd been up most of the night digging down into the accounts of every single attorney at her sister's firm. He had been, at least, when he wasn't working on tracking Rojas operations, locations, and other resources.

Gracie wanted answers.

We wanted to give them to her.

"Should we let Goblin out?" She stood near the table, arms folded still, a worried frown tightening her brow.

"He's probably fine. Alphabet was up until early this morning. But..." I considered for a moment as I steamed the milk and held the answer until I was done. Then I glanced at her. "If he isn't up in the next two hours, I'll get Goblin."

That startlingly blue gaze tracked to mine and some of the concern bled away from her expression. Real relief reflected in the faint smile flirting with her lips. "Good. He's been really nice about letting me take him for walks."

"Goblin is a big fan too," I told her as I passed the coffee cup to her. The cinnamon rolls were almost ready to come out. "Alphabet doesn't mind at all. Probably wishes he could go to walk with you both. I bet he jumps right into it when we're all caught up."

Another flicker of a smile but she didn't say anything, just nodded. Fair. At least she took the coffee and wrapped both hands around the cup before taking a sip. She let out a slow, but intensely satisfied little sigh.

With a nod, I gestured to the table. "Grab a seat. First round of cinnamon rolls will be ready. Now, do you prefer bacon or sausage?"

She tilted her head. "With the cinnamon rolls?"

"Protein," I said. "The rolls will be excellent carbs after that workout, but you still need protein."

Taking another sip of the coffee, she watched me over the rim for a moment. "Egg white omelet? Or even scrambled egg whites with mushrooms and spinach?"

A part of me wanted to argue. That wasn't a lot of calories. But I hadn't brought up calories, I brought up protein. Egg whites or not, it was still an excellent source of protein.

"Let me check for the spinach. I definitely have mushrooms."

"Just mushrooms is fine." No disappointment marred the words. My jaw clenched, caging my automatic response. The last thing she needed was me scolding her. Still, fighting to hold those words hostage had me damn near grinding my teeth.

No fresh spinach in the crisper. I snagged my phone and fired off some texts to Voodoo. "I'm adding spinach to our list," I told her. "Any other fresh veggies or fruits you like?"

"It's not that important."

Lips pursed, I pivoted to face her. "They are already out. They are already planning to pick up food. Give me a list. Giving them something to do will help keep them out of trouble."

Humor sparked in her eyes. "I like carrots, especially baby carrots. Broccoli. Raw. Lettuce. Tomatoes."

I typed the requested items into the text field. At her pause, I shot her a look. "Apples? Bananas? Oranges?"

"Melon," she added, scraping her teeth over her bottom lip. "Cantaloupe. Honeydew is fine, but I prefer cantaloupe."

"Got it. What else? You have a snack you like? Nuts? Chocolate? Trail mix?"

Another flash of amusement but she shook her head. "I try to avoid too much in the way of excess sugar. One because I like it too much and two, it's a lot of empty calories."

"Dark chocolate then?" I offered. "Very healthy in moderation, low in sugar, and it can boost your mood."

"My mood?" Another sip of coffee hid that luscious mouth and how her lips moved to frame each word. "Is something wrong with my mood?"

"I'm not going to insult you by pretending that everything is fine. It's not." Maybe I shouldn't have to say it, but facts were facts. "I get grief. I get trauma. Maybe it doesn't show, but we've all been through it."

I hadn't hit send yet.

When she didn't respond, I pressed the advantage. The scent of cinnamon and sugar wreathed the kitchen as the rolls cooked.

"You don't want to talk about what's happened to you outside of some basic facts. That's—that's a survival technique. You're controlling what you can control and you're not focusing on what you can't." Fuck, I felt like an asshole. This needed to be said, however. "It's okay to not be okay. As much as I'd like to wish it wasn't true, everyone copes differently. Unfortunately, pretending it didn't happen doesn't mean it didn't."

The light in her eyes had gone out. How darkness could swim inside such beautifully jeweled eyes baffled me. Yet there it was. The oven beeped and pulled my attention away. Pivoting away from her, I took the reprieve to pull the cinnamon rolls out.

The icing would take a minute to whip together. That was pure sugar though, so better to check with her. I set the fresh ones on the rack and put another dish in to bake. Then I hit send on the list before going for the confectioner's sugar.

"Icing okay?" I mean, they were edible without it. They were more than edible. Still, the cream cheese and confectioner's sugar icing just added some pizzazz.

"Maybe half and half?" Another scrape of her teeth over her lower lip.

"Done. I can add some vanilla to it or even a little coffee

if you want to add some coffee to the flavor?" Lots of ways to dress it up. "Then I'll get your omelet going."

"A little coffee? Maybe?" she asked after a minute.

Good girl. "You got it, Gracie. Coming right up." We didn't speak while I put it together. I set two of the fresh cinnamon rolls on a plate. I put icing on half of each. Then spread it over the rest of the ones in the dish. When I was done, I carried the first two over to the table.

She licked her lips. "That looks good."

"Enjoy. Gonna get your omelet going."

With a glance up at me, she pulled a chair out. "Thank you."

"Anytime." I held her gaze for a heartbeat before retreating out of her space again.

I'd just finished whipping the egg whites together when she said, "Lunchbox?"

"Yeah?"

"I know pretending doesn't work. I've been trying to pretend you guys aren't keeping me captive." That had me looking at her and she held a cinnamon roll in hand. The other one was gone and there was a smear of icing on her lower lip. "Yet, here I am, and apparently it comes with dessert."

The droll comment lightened her gaze again and she toasted me with her cinnamon roll. I grinned and went back to work on food. Yeah, we needed to just keep including her. Earn *her* trust...

This was step one—no, the debrief had been step one. But I wasn't sure how much ground that got us. This was step two.

I snagged my phone and fired off another message to the guys.

Time to plan for step three.

CHAPTER

SEVENTEEN

Three days after eating the fresh-baked cinnamon rolls in the kitchen with Lunchbox and drinking coffee, I jerked awake, heart pounding, and breath coming in short, desperate pants. They were coming.

The man with his big hands was dragging me down the hall to escape, but more hands tangled with my legs and I sank into the floor. I could barely move. It was worse than trying to wade through heavy mud. The sucking sensation threatened to pull me even deeper.

Trapped, I couldn't turn around. But they were coming. The pound of their feet, the pop of the weapons, and the screams—it was all happening behind me and I couldn't see. I couldn't do anything.

Then...

I snapped awake and I couldn't suck in enough air to keep from being dizzy. Sweat had my tank top clinging to me and feeling gross. Even worse, the air was almost too damn cold against my skin so I could add chills to the shivering going up and down my spine.

Voodoo wasn't in here again. I hadn't seen much of Bones or Alphabet at all the past few days, but Voodoo and Lunchbox had been there. Most of the time, Voodoo woke me up before the dreams got too bad or he'd be right here to talk to me if I snapped awake.

Tonight was the second or maybe third time he'd been absent. Maybe Lunchbox was right, maybe I needed to talk about this shit so the dreams would stop. But I didn't want to talk about the dreams any more than I wanted to talk about the events populating them.

I was a big girl. I didn't need someone holding my hand. But rather than go back to sleep and risking more shadows, pain, and fear, I headed for the bathroom and a shower. Showers couldn't fix everything, but they could help you feel better.

Even a smidgeon better was *better*.

The bathroom was filled with steam by the time I finished. While I couldn't wash away all the shadows, I could at least warm up from the chill they left behind. It also helped clear up the fog and left me far more awake than tired. I had no idea what time it was, but I didn't want to stay up here by myself.

Maybe downstairs by myself wouldn't be much better, but I needed to do *something*. Guilt raked against my belly cause in and around wishing that Voodoo was in here, I was also annoyed that he wasn't. It made absolutely no sense to be alternately grateful and irritated.

It wasn't his job to look after me. It wasn't any of their jobs. Despite that, here we were. The conflicting reactions competed for dominance over my mood and left me even more restless than when I'd tumbled out of the nightmare.

Dressed in an oversized sweatshirt, again, and a clean set of sleep shorts, and thick socks, I finger combed my wet hair so I could go downstairs. One second before I reached for the door handle, I hesitated. Most nights when I woke up and Voodoo was in here, I didn't leave the room.

What if they'd locked the door again?

Would they do that? They hadn't since those first days, but would they when I was asleep and didn't know? Wrestling with the *what ifs* was just giving me a headache. Now as annoyed with myself as I was with them, I turned the handle and the door opened.

See.

The mental castigation didn't do me any good. The house was dark save for a couple of night lights that led to the landing the stairs. Dark and quiet. The other doors along the hall were quiet. Weirdly, I didn't know where anyone else's bedrooms were. I'd not bothered to look.

Note to self, time to stop soaking in my self-pity stew and figure that out. I was supposed to be convincing them to help, to keep looking, to do more, and was I doing any of those things?

Eleanor would slap me, if she could see me right now.

The thought stopped me dead at the top of the stairs and pain bloomed around my heart. Eleanor was dead. She wasn't going to be doing anything anymore. She was dead and I had to ask myself if that was *also* my fault. Was it really an accident? Even when the guys described it, they didn't make it *sound* like an accident.

Grief twisted up my insides. Tears clogged my throat, and I had to swallow hard to try and choke that emotion back down. I'd never see her again.

Never hear her salty tone when she wanted me to get my shit together. Never savor the laughter in her voice when she chortled over coming out on top with a competitive deal. Never share a toast when we cross another item off the bucket list of my career and hers.

Closing my eyes, I dipped my chin and fought the tsunami of emotion threatening to drown me. The silence closed in on all sides, leaving me alone with the painful thump of my wounded heart. Flexing my hand against the newel post, I wasn't sure how to breathe anymore.

Then a masculine sound drifted upward, piercing the quiet. A hum of a voice. I could hear them speaking, but I couldn't quite make out the words. Someone was awake. Blowing out a breath, I made myself head down. Once on the first floor, I recognized the voice

It was Alphabet.

Following the sound, I found the door to Alphabet's office open. Light spilled out into the hallway, and his voice grew clearer and clearer with each step I took.

"Standby, I've got the codes. I want to be fully into their system before you make entry." Music rolled out of the room, but it wasn't cranked up.

It was also *disco*.

I blinked at the clear notes from Donna Summer singing about *MacArthur Park*. Cool song, but also... weird.

"Okay, I'm in," Alphabet said and I moved closer to the doorway. Goblin sprawled on his bed, completely flipped onto his back and snoring. He shifted a little when I appeared and his eyes slitted open. He thumped his tail twice, but when I didn't come any closer, he seemed to go back to sleep again.

"Keep your pants on, Bones. This isn't just picking a lock. I am rewriting their logs to erase any trace of us being here." Alphabet sat at his computer, his screens all lit up with a dozen different images including what looked like security camera footage.

Arms folded, I frowned. Bones was clearly off on some mission somewhere. If he was gone and Alphabet was here, I'd bet that Voodoo or Lunchbox or both were with Bones wherever *there* was.

"Cycling the power now. Fence is shutting down, you're clear to go through it or over it. Dealer's choice." He rolled his fingers against a track pad and the camera angles changed.

There the guys were. All three were visible briefly. The images were kind of green and they were moving at speed. Something landed on the top of the fence. Then they were over it. One. Two. Three.

It was almost blink and you would miss it. They were off the cameras again.

"Hold, ten seconds," Alphabet ordered and his fingers flew as he counted it down. When he got one, he merely said, "Go." Then the screens rotated again. I couldn't see where anyone was or even where they were. It was all dark, even with the green tint.

"You are clear in three, two... go."

His fingers flew in a little symphony of their own over his keyboard.

"Doors open, boys. Come on in." Then the screens changed to interior shots. The sudden brightness had me squinting even across the room from the monitors. Alphabet had a headset on, so he could hear the guys and I couldn't...

Wait, there they were. They were dressed in dark clothes and masks or balaclavas or whatever those things were called. The guys were moving steadily through wherever the hell they were. I glanced over at Goblin again as his snores climbed in volume once more.

Whatever they were doing, it wasn't upsetting. At least it wasn't upsetting for Alphabet at the moment. I had a dozen questions, but I didn't want to interrupt. An entirely different tension wound through me.

Hot cocoa.

I was going to get hot cocoa for me and for Alphabet. At least that was something useful I could do. I needed the damn cocoa if nothing else. I could make it on the stove, but we had an espresso machine so I could also steam the milk. I went through the cupboards first to check for chocolate.

It really depended on what kind of chocolate they had. Once I found that, I could decide how to make the cocoa. They had to have chocolate. My side ached and so did my gut. It rolled, cramping a little. Maybe I was hungry, but I didn't want food.

The chocolate was in the pantry. There were containers of powder, also a couple of boxes of standard hot cocoa mix, there was also some Hershey's chocolate syrup. Plenty of options. I grabbed the second and the third before retreating back into the kitchen proper.

Steaming the milk was the way to go. Yes, it was noisy, but I doubted that it would bother him if he even heard it through the headphones. It didn't take me long at all to fix the two huge cups of hot chocolate. I sipped mine once it was ready.

It tasted a little like heaven. Chocolate might not fix problems, but it went a long way towards making them easier to deal with. Even better than a shower, really.

Fisting both mugs, I headed back to Alphabet's office and made it just in time to hear him say, "Behind you..."

Flashes on the screen showed one of the guys with a

gun raised as he fired it. There were bodies down. It was—surreal. Like a movie or something.

Only it definitely wasn't a film.

It was real.

It was people I knew.

A cold band tightened around my core. I dragged my gaze off the screen and then glanced down at the hot cocoa in my hands. What was I doing?

The soft woof pulled my attention down to Goblin. He'd abandoned his dog bed and leaned against my leg. The soulful look in his eyes reminded me why I'd come in here. A glance at the screen showed the guys moving through some facility, but they weren't shooting at anyone anymore.

Alphabet had also turned away from the screen and his deep blue eyes fixed on mine.

No backing out now. I was here and he knew it.

So I held up the hot cocoa mugs as an explanation.

CHAPTER

EIGHTEEN

"Hold," I ordered, not bothering to check if they listened. After all this time, we'd long since mastered the art of working together. We didn't have to be getting along to communicate in a shorthand as familiar as our own heartbeats. I tracked the motion of a security patrol.

As late as it was, and with as little sleep as I'd had over the past few days, I was still restless. I was also more than a little annoyed. My irritation wasn't aimed at the guys—not even Bones with his attitude. Grace wasn't the cause either. Stubborn, fierce, and defiant to the point of obstinate, she fascinated and amused me in equal measures. I only wished she'd trust us.

Really trust us.

No, I was pissed that the clients who hired and then sold us out on the Rojas job in the first place. They'd made a call, determined they were better off writing us off as a loss and chose sacrifice.

Fuckers.

One of the reasons we vetted clients so damn thoroughly was to avoid situations like this. Since vetting was *my* job, I blamed myself. I'd missed something.

Wouldn't happen again.

The only faint light in the clusterfuck was the identity of the man in the barn proved him to be just a drifter. He had no ties to the Rojas. Bastard still hurt Grace, but he was not a loose thread and he'd already been cut off.

"Status?" Bones asked in a tone that was both commanding and patient. The request wasn't an attack or a demand. I didn't tell them to hold for shits and giggles.

"Standby, Captain." I stared at the screen, the patrol continued up the farthest hallway on an external perimeter on the far side of the building. The laboratory facility was "closed" for the night. Night staff consisted of a pair of janitors—already done for their shifts—and a light security force.

Everything on paper said it was a standard laboratory processing medical specimens. All the licenses were current and inspections up to date. It was clean and neat, formal, nothing to look at twice. Which was exactly why we were looking twice.

The Rojas were a syndicate, smaller than most other Mexican and South American cartels. They produced high end product, and definitely illegal. The difference was they didn't distribute directly over the border. They stayed on their side of the line. That meant they had to have a distributor *here*.

"Security cleared. Continue. You should be good for the next five minutes. No lab staff on surveillance. Start timers now." I've been monitoring security at this building for the past three nights, they never varied. But it didn't mean I was going to just trust three days of data.

I hit a button on the screen to start a timer going for me as well as the guys split up. Lunchbox headed straight for the primary lab. He would get in, get samples, and a solid look at what they were doing. He was also the best suited for that task. He would know what he was doing.

Bones headed to the computer room, long-term data storage and the terabytes of data kept there. Voodoo diverted to the upper levels and corporate offices maintained here. Bureaucracy took on all forms. Pharmaic's Neurosin lab was all about research. That would totally explain the security. It might even offer some insight into the military-grade encryption.

Legitimate businesses didn't generally hire mercenaries to eliminate drug labs in a different country to shore up the stock price. Their executives had been busy little boys. As soon as Bones made it inside the data room, he'd get my thumb drive into place. My worm would go to work and I'd have control of *all* of their systems.

A whisper of motion behind me had me flicking a glance to the window in the upper left of my screen. We didn't monitor everything in the house, but we had cameras installed for a "rainy day." Currently, it seemed to be pouring, particularly with only me and Gracie in residence.

No one knew our location. We'd buried the deeds and bought up the surrounding land via separate LLCs. It was as secure as we could manage and as distant from who we were as possible. Base needed to be a place we *could* relax.

Freshly showered, Grace studied me with quiet, intense eyes. The crisp freshness of her shampoo and soap touched my nostrils. Three smothered pops tugged my attention from her to the screen.

Ambush? I narrowed my eyes, but the captain studied the interior of a room not on the plans I acquired nor on the surveillance. "Secure, Cap?"

"Secure," he answered. "Blind spot?"

"Looks like, I'll dig deeper." I didn't like blind spots. "Sweeping ahead. Watch your sixes." I also didn't like leaving bodies behind but since we weren't planning on leaving the *building* behind, I guess that would deal with that.

A grunt of acknowledgement came from Lunchbox and a snort of laughter from Voodoo. Yes, watching our own asses was also second nature.

Bones was already on the move. A glance back to the door showed Grace had gone. I spared a moment to twist and study Goblin. He snored away. Gracie hadn't *looked* upset but if she had been, he'd have reacted.

Trusting him, I refocused on the screen. Once they were clear, I'd go find her. We should've told her the guys were taking this mission. Guilt raked across my belly as if threatening to eviscerate me. Getting used to having Gracie there also meant we were taking her for granted.

We needed to do less of that and more of looking after her. We already had one discussion about revisiting our protocols. He wasn't wrong. That said, I didn't actually have the time to do it right this moment. "I will," I murmured as much as promising Goblin as myself.

Bones finally made it to their data room. "Going dark," he said as he swiped a card and accessed the room. The signal cut once he was inside. I started another clock. If necessary, I could divert Lunchbox or Voodoo toward him.

For now, we were on schedule. We'd been hired by a

small conglomerate of wealthy business owners based in and out of the States. They'd tried to root their businesses in Central America or make it look like that was where the contract came from.

Digging deeper had taken me through a series of shell companies that eventually led back to business interests State side. They'd deliberately set out to mislead us to eliminate an "illegal" enterprise choking out their "legal" one. While that might be partially true, the companies entangled in this little cabal were not clean.

If anything, they had their hands in a lot of shady shit. I didn't like to be used.

With three seconds to spare, Bones was out of the data room and on surveillance again. "Locked and loaded."

The programs were already waiting for the signal and I started the download. Over the next few minutes, I'd have every drop of data they had stored there. The backups were also on site. Normally, when a client attempted to fuck us over, it was about money.

I could go and get the money and take care of paying out what was owed. This was different. These so-called captains of industry were playing war games on a global level. That was no bueno.

The soft drag of a foot pulled my attention again and there she was, holding two large mugs of—

I sniffed. Hot chocolate?

Fuck me, that sounded amazing. I cut a look from her to the screen then back. Right, she was here. I tugged a second chair over and patted it once then pressed a finger to my lips. She passed me one of the huge mugs and it smelled even better being this close.

She curled up into the chair, pulling her legs up. The

back of my free hand brushed against her legs. Despite the sleepy eyes and flushed cheeks, her skin was freezing.

"Secondary lab coming up," Lunchbox said. "It looks like there's an ancillary data room here too. I take it you are going to want what's in here?"

"Yes, please," I answered. "The first round of data mining is still going." But that was a *lot* of data to pull out. We needed to streamline it. I pushed my chair to roll to the side where I could snag a blanket and then rolled back. "Let me work on this."

"Got it."

I draped the blanket over her legs and she blinked at me with those spectacular blue eyes. They were so much more intense than a bright sky over the bay. I had to make myself look away or risk missing more.

"Voodoo, back it up five paces. What was that?" On the screen Voodoo did exactly what I asked and he faced a wall of thick glass looking right into an empty lab. Or at least it looked like an empty lab *space*, but the secure locks blazed red. There was also a warning.

"Not something I really want to open unless it's necessary." They had some PPE gear with them, but not enough to risk any kind of failure. Couldn't really blame Voodoo for that. I wrote down the number on the door.

"You're good, keep going." I even managed to sound gracious about it.

"Thanks, dick," Voodoo said with a chuckle. I grinned wider. Bones was almost to the corporate offices. They were on the far side away from the labs. Lunchbox was inside a lab, his white suit covered him from head to toe.

I took a sip of the hot cocoa and about fucking died. It was creamy, a hint of sweet with a little kick that added a burn and the chocolate was out of this world. I licked the flavor off my lips to glance at Gracie and toasted her with the chocolate.

A small smile softened her lips and Goblin bumped against my chair as he moved to rest his head against her blanket-covered lap. Yeah, she was more upset than she let on. But of course she was.

"Locked and loaded," Lunchbox said as he left the cleanroom and began to strip off the hazmat suit.

The secondary set of downloads had already begun. This was going to take a lot more time than I wanted. "Set the timers to plus five when you're on exodus."

"We still need to finish evac," Bones reminded me.

"I got it, Cap, don't worry." Speaking of onsite staff. I tracked down the security. They were crossing over at the farthest point on the perimeter and beginning to circle back around. "Also, time to pack it up, boys."

I wanted them well and truly gone. I double-checked the file tree being built. The names were mostly letters and numbers. Nothing actionable.

Yet.

Like any other puzzle, I just needed the pieces so I could begin sorting them out and putting them together. It was like the dossier I was building on our Gracie. The surface image was very different from the woman underneath.

A part of me attributed that to gut instinct. I trusted that instinct, but I needed the evidence to back it up.

"Heading out," Bones said. "Meeting at exfil."

"Copy." Lunchbox's response was a beat before Voodoo's. With care, I started setting off some of the smoke alarms elsewhere. We wanted everyone out before we blew it. Collateral damage was to be expected. We already had some, but I'd rather avoid more.

"Tripping alarms. Standby." My fingers flew over the

keys as I set up more alarms, including evacuation measures. The lab's lockdown features would come in handy for this bit of misdirection. "Jamming cell signal in fifteen. You're a go for exfil."

They moved. I tracked them as they took different exits, but linked up outside. The security staff left on site were also evacuating. Their vehicles raced for the guardhouse at the gate while the guys headed west and into the open land that bordered the facility.

It would take them a little longer but they weren't going to run into anyone and that was how I liked it. The first data room's downloads completed at the three second mark. The second data room finished just a second later.

"Two—one," I said, counting it down for the guys as much as for me. "Boom." The explosion was impressive. At least what I could see of it on the screens before the cameras went down.

External cams would also go offline without the internal network. I gave it another few seconds. Then there was a crackle over the line.

"We did not use that much C-4," Voodoo complained.

"No shit," Lunchbox answered, but there was a note of faintly hysterical laughter under it. They'd survived, and that was always the sign of a mission well done.

"We said they were cooking something up there. Any ideas, Alphabet?" Trust Bones to stay on target.

"Not yet. I'll start parsing soon. Get clear and then get back here."

"Might be a little late," Voodoo commented. "I'm starving."

The ribbing continued, as much for their own distraction as they committed to the hike as it was to begin decompressing. This hadn't been as much of a challenge as it could be and I was undecided on whether that was a good thing or not.

Blowing out a breath, I hit mute on my side and glanced back at Gracie. She was sound asleep and Goblin had gone to sleep on the floor between us. I reclaimed what was left of my cocoa and sipped it. Much cooler, but still rich and creamy, I soaked in the sight of her.

Sighing, I returned my attention to the computer. I wasn't crashing until they were completely out of the zone and on their way back. So, I might as well start decrypting the data. Do this, wait for the all-clear, then I'd get her back to bed.

That was the plan.

CHAPTER

NINETEEN

The next time I opened my eyes, it was dark save for a single light burning in the corner. Or maybe in the bathroom? Squinting, I turned my head. I hadn't gone back to bed, had I? Awareness trickled back in and the thump of a tail pulled my attention to the floor where Goblin wiggled across the carpet toward me, toward the bed.

"Hey," I whispered a greeting. Wherever I'd woken up, it wasn't my room. Goblin's wiggling seemed to intensify and he went from sliding on the carpet to standing up. "How you doing boy?"

Then he had his paws on the side of the bed and I ran a hand over his head.

"Want to come up here with me?" He hadn't slept in my room once since I'd been here, but that didn't mean I didn't get to play with him and hang out. I loved dogs. Always wanted to have one, but my job took me everywhere and that wasn't fair to a puppy.

Goblin swiped his tongue over my face repeatedly, giving me kisses even as he did a full body wiggle of happiness. A soft laugh escaped me because he was determined to give me lots of *kisses*.

"Come on," I invited him, patting the bed as I scooted backward to give him room. I froze when I pressed against a warm back. I wasn't in the bed alone. Before I could even process that information, Goblin was on the bed and wiggling against me in between slurpy kisses and me petting him.

It was wild, how swiftly he would slide onto his side, but kept drowning me in kisses and I couldn't go anywhere. Even when I tried to pet him, it barely slowed him down. Goblin was just so damn happy. Laughter spilled out of me as I tried to avoid getting his tongue in my eye or my mouth. Though I swore he was gonna go up my nose with his enthusiasm.

Masculine grumbles rising in volume behind just added to my amusement as I half-wrestled, half-just played with Goblin. We were definitely *not* in my room. I guess I fell asleep in his office while he worked. That meant he'd have to have been the one put me in his bed? Not that I could focus on that very much. Not when I had a wiggling pile of canine joy just demanding everything from me.

Laughter bubbled out of me as I alternated between petting Goblin and defending myself from them. When the bed shifted behind me, Goblin's whole body just seemed to vibrate at a higher frequency. Then he was climbing on me to wiggle and slurp at Alphabet.

This time, I didn't try to smother the sound as I cracked up under Goblin's full frontal assault. He was acting more like a puppy than he had at any other time since I'd met him and it was just...

Wonderful.

"Goddamn, Goblin," Alphabet said, the faint raspiness from sleep adding a deeper dimension to his voice and a subtle sensuality to the way he enunciated the syllables. "You're soaking Gracie down and I didn't sign up for a bath."

Despite the denial, he didn't sound all that upset. Though he threaded an arm between me and Goblin to help create some room. The drape of him against my back sent a wave of warmth over me that would probably suggest I was blushing if I hadn't been laughing so damn hard.

The wet kisses really were drenching me, but I wasn't remotely upset about it. "He's in a good mood," I managed to say from behind the shield of my hand to keep Goblin's tongue at bay.

"Clearly, he likes waking up with you, Gracie-girl." The relaxed confidence resonated in his sleep-husky voice. I could listen to him all day. Probably why I'd drifted off when he was talking to the guys.

"Maybe," I said, still smiling so hard it made my cheeks hurt. "Or maybe he's just happy that I'm not blocking him from you."

His snort was deliciously derisive. "He wouldn't even be on the bed without you, Gracie-girl. He makes me get my ass up when he wants me up."

"Oh." I frowned. "Should I have not..."

"Shh," Alphabet shushed me, and shifted to push himself up on one arm. "You're fine, Gracie. Goblin and I have a deal, he makes sure I don't hang out in bed when I'm down and I get up when he asks me for it."

I turned that revelation over. It was kind of sweet that he and Goblin worked together, but it also made sense. Goblin kept depression at bay? Or maybe his trauma? I didn't know enough about it, but I loved that Alphabet had him. Goblin's happy squirming settled as he rolled onto his back, legs spread wide, with a look of ecstasy on his face as we both rubbed his belly.

"This is kind of nice," I said, aware that while he was present, he wasn't grinding on me or anything else. It was just "comfortable." Probably not a word I should share with him. Most guys I'd ever met didn't like being told they were comfy or even friendly. A sigh escaped me.

"If it's so nice, what's making you sad, Gracie-girl?" The soft question hinted at intimacy and asked me to trust him. The damn thing about it was I wanted to trust him. I wanted...

"It's—" Before I could just sort of shrug off the concern, he shifted his hand from Goblin to press a finger to my lips.

"Don't lie. If you don't want to tell me, that's fine. But let's just make it a rule to not lie to each other."

That had me blinking and I twisted, laying against the pillow to look up at him. He met my studying gaze with a kind of quiet patience.

"Yes, I know what I'm saying. You don't have to tell me everything. Do I want to know? Yes. I wouldn't ask otherwise. But..." He shifted his attention to Goblin for a moment and blew out a breath before glancing to me again. "But," he repeated. "I want to trust what you say to me. I want you to trust what I say to you. I want there to be *no* questions about that. So, if you don't want to answer something, just say you don't want to and I'll do the same."

"So if I ask you what the guys were doing last night?"

"I'd tell you I don't want to answer it until they are back and we debrief." He scratched at the scruff on his jaw. The tousled hair, blue eyes, and rough stubble gave him this kind of rugged charm that had me curling my toes. "Not everything I don't tell you has to do with you or your sister, directly. We've involved you in a lot, it's better that we all have consensus before we involved you in more."

I ran my tongue over my lower lip as I considered that answer. No deception echoed beneath the words. Goblin sat up and looked at me. Well, looked at us, since neither of us were petting him now.

"I don't know entirely what is making me sad," I admitted. "It could be a lot of things, most obvious being my sister and everything that's happened." That was the truth. "But that feels almost too simple an answer and I don't know how to answer it for myself much less for you."

"Fair enough," he said. "So... we have a deal?"

"Yes." No hesitation. I wanted to be able to trust them. Hadn't I been beating myself up on this for days now? "Deal." Then I gave it a little more thought. "Caveat?"

"Name it."

"This is between you and me for right now. I'm not sure the other guys apply *yet*."

"Acceptable. We'll add it to the discussion."

That—seemed reasonable. I held out my right hand to him. "Then we have a deal, AB."

Goblin slurped my fingers a beat before Alphabet shook my hand. We both laughed.

"Yeah, I think he wants out..."

"I can do it... unless there's some code I need to enter to open a door."

"There is," he confirmed as he rolled onto his own back and reached for his phone. "But I can key it in here. Just let him out the back door and he'll take care of business. Then we'll get him breakfast. Goblin, down."

The sweet boy hopped right off the bed and sat waiting like a gentleman, tail wagging.

"I'd kill for coffee."

"I got it," he said, sitting up even as I slid out of the bed. I was still in the shirt and sleep shorts. The room was a lot chillier out from under the covers and all the warmth. "That hot cocoa, by the way, was the best I've ever had. I need to work on points to get you to make it again."

He shoved the blankets back as I raked a hand through my hair. My first realization was he'd slept in sweatpants and no shirt. There were scars and tats on his back. None of which were any of my business. The second realization came when he reached for something instead of getting straight up. His prosthesis. I'd forgotten about it and he needed to put it on.

And I was staring.

Yanking my gaze off him, I looked at Goblin who sped up the thump of his tail. "C'mon, sweetheart. I'll let you out."

I was at the door and Alphabet had just stood when I glanced back to where Goblin waited.

"*Gaan.*" The word seemed to galvanize Goblin and he trotted right after me. "I'll be out in a minute," Alphabet said to me.

"Sounds good." I followed Goblin along the hallway—Alphabet's bedroom was downstairs, not that far from his office, actually. That made me feel a bit better. He hadn't had to carry me up the stairs or something.

At the door, I trusted what Alphabet had said about putting in the code and unlocked the door. The moment it was open, Goblin took off like a shot. He made it a dozen feet before he peed a river.

Poor baby, we made him wait a long time.

Folding my arms, I stepped down onto the stone patio they had set up. It wasn't much more than a slab of stone and some edging, but it had potential. I walked to the edge to watch Goblin as he dashed around after he relieved himself and went in search of somewhere else to do some business.

The sun was already up. We'd slept late, it was high and the day was really lovely. The breeze carried something that smelled like sweetgrass on it. It wasn't cold, exactly, but definitely cooler and I'd want pants if I planned to stay out here.

There was a chattering of birds, but all I really heard was the quiet. It was so deep it was almost frightening how empty it was. It had taken me a long time to get used to the city, the undertone of regular traffic, sirens, and a kind of just—hum of humanity.

None of that was here.

It was just—silent.

Then the sound of the coffee grinder echoed from the kitchen and I had to laugh. That wasn't so quiet, but it sounded good. Smelled better cause there was already a round of espresso going by the time Goblin dashed back to me and we headed inside.

Alphabet was in the kitchen, gray sweatpants low on his hips, and his foot tapping as he pulled another shot. He hadn't bothered with a shirt, but then I didn't have on pants and we'd just shared a bed so this was—cozy.

Comfortable.

There was that word again. Alphabet glanced over his shoulder. "So, tell me, do you have any other hidden talents like magical cocoa making?"

I raised my eyebrows. "Such as?"

"Cooking."

I shrugged. "I can, it won't be fancy. I survived on

takeout and the basics. A lot of my diet ran to steamed chicken and salad."

His grimace was downright comical. "That's not a diet."

"It is if you need to maintain low body fat. The camera adds plenty." It was just another part of the job.

"Well, I hope you like cereal." He motioned to the pantry. "We have a few different kinds. I know we have fruit."

"You don't cook either?" But I had to admit I was curious about the cereal too so I headed for the pantry.

"Well, Lunchbox and I have agreed to disagree on that one."

I poked my head back out as he started the milk steaming. "How is that an answer?"

"Well, I say I can cook. Lunchbox says I can't—especially not with his utensils or pans."

I bit the inside of my lip. "What happened to his pans?"

"Could be that I like to blacken sausage and steak... and burgers sometimes. You know—make it extra crispy."

"Burned?" I mean, it was a way I supposed.

"You say poh-tay-to." He shrugged, but there was a grin and his eyes were dancing. "I say blackened. Blackened fish is excellent."

"Uh huh. This is why you and Lunchbox agree to disagree."

Alphabet winked. "Exactly. So, cereal it is or fruit or we can figure something out."

I suddenly had a dozen questions. I had no idea what order to even ask them in or if I should ask them at all. Filing those away, I settled for, "What's your favorite cereal?"

CHAPTER
TWENTY

"Put her on for me," Voodoo said from where he stood in the corner. We had maybe thirty minutes before the rendezvous, and should already be moving. Lunchbox was going over the vehicle Voodoo secured for this leg and he'd called Alphabet to check-in.

I checked my watch. The check-in was a good call. The change in plans couldn't be helped. As long as they were still secure, we wanted to finish this.

"Hey, Firecracker," Voodoo's voice dipped. His gaze collided with mine briefly before he turned to pace away. The landing strip at the small Nevada airport didn't offer much in the way of shade, but he just slid his sunglasses on as he stepped out of the hangar.

I sighed.

"You heard Alphabet," Lunchbox said, as he closed the trunk. "She's been up for the past two nights—late. Real late. That means she's having nightmares."

"I'm aware." Just like I was aware that Voodoo had been spending more and more time in her room.

"We should have briefed her." Not an unfair conclusion or one I wanted to argue with him over.

"While she has a right to information about her and her sister," I said, willing to concede that much. "This operation has nothing to do with her."

Once we finished this, it would be done and we could reorient our focus to her.

"I get that," Lunchbox said, folding his arms before leaning back against the side of the vehicle. "But it's also bullshit, Cap. Do you get that?"

Voodoo returned, cutting off any response I would have made and tossed the cellphone back at me. "I got shotgun, Cap. You haven't slept in the last two days. This is at least a two hour drive, get some sleep."

Tucking the phone into my pocket, I pulled open the back door and slid in. It was an oversized SUV and that left me with room to stretch—some. Like the boys, I was dressed in dark fatigues, a dark shirt, and dark combat boots. It was common enough wear and we didn't stand out.

I pulled on a dark cap and my own sunglasses even as Lunchbox pulled out of the hangar.

"Two hours there," Voodoo said. "How long do you think we'll need for questioning?"

"As long as it takes," I answered in tandem with Lunchbox, then folded my arms, tilted my chin down, and went to sleep.

～

"Cap." One word and I lifted my head. It barely felt like I'd gone to sleep. The lack of grit in my eyes said it had definitely been at least an hour, though not quite two. "We're ten minutes out."

Voodoo passed back a takeout cup that smelled of strong black coffee.

"Thanks," I said, voice a little rough but I took a swallow of the bitter brew. It was strong enough to sheer paint from the walls. Good thing. "Any word?"

"Just a text," Lunchbox said. "They are there and waiting for us. Didn't beat us by much."

I nodded, then took another swallow of the coffee. It was hot, but not really scalding. I definitely wanted to burn off all the cobwebs.

Our destination was a nondescript, dead little town in the middle of nowhere. The roads out here weren't much to comment on, old state highways that were just two lanes for a hundred miles or more.

The dusty little town boasted a sign that was old, and hanging crookedly by a single chain while the other swung brokenly against it.

Settle Down.

Founded 1889.

Someone had a sense of humor. The town beyond it wasn't much to speak of. If there was more to it than the main street, I didn't see it. While it was back from the state highway, the only visible road was a rough gravel and dirt scattered path.

The storefronts were right out of some old Western show, the tired and faded colors a mere echo of what they might have been. There was debris on the porches—or what passed for their porches. Maybe a boardwalk that joined the old storefronts together, and gave people a place to walk that wasn't the dirt streets.

Since more than one step looked busted in half, I'd go with the idea that they weren't secure. There were actual fucking tumbleweeds rolling along in what would presumably be a hot breeze.

"What a shithole," Voodoo said, studying the town a lot like I was. "Probably do ghost tours and shit out here."

"Probably," Lunchbox said. "Though I don't trust the sturdiness of the buildings. The one on the end is starting to lean."

He wasn't wrong. Still, he pulled down the main street then around the back to park behind a squat adobe building right next to another SUV. I didn't wait for Lunchbox to put it in park before I set the empty cup down and slid out. The stifling air that greeted me was every bit as roasting as opening an oven door.

Sweat dotted my face even in the achingly dry air under the relentless sun. Yeah, it was a shithole in the middle of a desert. But it would serve its purpose.

A backdoor on the squat adobe building opened and a former FBI agent stepped out to scan us. He was armed, but the gun was secured and clearly visible in his shoulder holster. Since we were similarly attired, I didn't worry about it.

I crossed the short distance and held out my hand. "Cash," I said by way of greeting. "Thanks for taking the time." Though to be fair, I actually hadn't expected one of the heads of the Network to be our delivery agents.

"Don't mention it," the tall man with the light hair, hard eyes, and square jaw stated. "Seriously, don't. Come on in. It's fucking miserable out here."

Though I doubted it was much better in there. A feminine laugh, low and husky, drifted out as I stepped in behind Cash with Voodoo and Lunchbox a few steps behind me.

"You didn't have to come," Vienna Drew stated from where she was seated at what was probably once upon a time a desk for the sheriff of the town. Unlike the wood outside, it seemed to still be in good shape.

The lean, athletic blonde woman reclined with her feet on the desk. For all that she had to be over a decade younger than any of us, I would never mistake that for inexperience, much less weakness and vulnerability.

Cash just snorted and turned briefly to greet Voodoo and Lunchbox with handshakes. It definitely wasn't that much cooler inside the adobe, but the shade afforded some relief.

Swinging her feet down, Vienna rose and held out a hand to me. We'd met on a handful of occasions—four that I could count. More often than not, we spoke to her on the phone or via a message. Since they reorganized things, she seemed to be taking a more active role.

That might make the next few hours trickier.

"It's good to see you," she said, shaking my hand once before sliding her hands into the back pockets of her jeans. "Hello boys."

"Ma'am," Lunchbox practically drawled the word and she grinned.

"Vienna." Voodoo just nodded then leaned against the wall closest to the door. The room was a little small for all of us, but as long as we were friends it would be fine.

"Before you try to find a diplomatic way to ask why she's here," Cash said, easing a hip onto the desk with a little more confidence than I thought the furniture deserved. "The names you tagged and the info you pulled led right back to one of ours."

Vienna's easy expression darkened and her eyes narrowed. "By ours, he means a broker within the Network. We backtracked and confirmed that he was double-dealing." Oh, she was not happy. "More than that, he's been actively seeking out jobs where he can bill twice. Not acceptable."

"Great, so there's more backstabbing motherfuckers in the Network. Just what we want to hear." Lunchbox didn't sound even a little irritated, more just bemused.

"Exactly," Cash said, spreading his hands. "We've been cleaning house the past several months but cockroaches always scatter. Sometimes, you have to kick shit over to get them to come out."

"Unfortunately," Vienna said with a slow shake of her head. "I wanted to ask him some questions myself, but I also know you are owed a debt."

"This wasn't your fault," I told her.

"Perhaps not entirely," she agreed. "But we've been making an attempt to clean up the Network. You should be able to trust the people and the information you obtain within it. Just as those of us in it should be able to trust you and yours when you take a job. If either side falls down... It leads to more problems. I've had enough of those."

Ferocity echoed beneath those last five words. "Well, then we appreciate you taking the time to do this."

"You're welcome," she said with a long exhale, then glanced at Cash. A groan rose from somewhere behind her. "Oh, look at that. I win." She held out a hand to Cash.

He smirked, then pulled out his wallet then retrieved a twenty before he gave it to her. "You win. Fair and square."

She grinned, then looked at me. "I said he would be

awake by the time you got here and that I did *not* give him too much sedative. Cash didn't agree, so we made a little wager."

"What I said was between the concussion and the drugs, it would make getting him lucid a little more challenging." Still, Cash just tucked his wallet away. "Anyway, we'd like to stay for the questioning. If you don't mind. Then we can handle body disposal."

"A body in the desert doesn't need that much disposal," Vienna said, strolling down a short hallway to—

"Is that an actual cell?" I asked as I followed her.

"Yep." She looked pleased as she motioned to the cell and the man inside it. He sprawled on what was left of a rotted-out cot. The frame had long since given up and I doubted there was anything of a mattress left.

Almost as unexpected as Vienna and Cash's presence, was the appearance of the man in question. Roger Edwards was a balding, middle-aged man with a bit of a paunch belly and a sallow complexion. He looked more like an office manager than a broker for mercenaries.

Then again, middle management was middle management.

"You know," Lunchbox said almost conversationally as the man in question started to sit up, still groaning. He hadn't even registered our presence yet. "I almost feel bad for the guy."

"I don't," Voodoo said. "He wanted to play with fire, he gets burned."

"But he's—dinky-looking." Lunchbox grimaced. "And he just pissed himself."

The strong scent of urine hit me at the same moment. The guy stared at us, his mouth moving without sound before he shot a look at Vienna.

"Small doesn't mean docile or safe," I reminded them. If nothing else, Grace should have been a powerful example of that. "Do you need anything from him?" I asked Vienna.

"Nope," she said, leaning back against the wall, arms folded like she was settling in to watch. Cash joined her and held out a bottle of water to her. She made a face but took it anyway.

"This won't take long," I said then turned the old iron key that was protruding from the lock. The creak of the hinges was like a shriek of a banshee. That seemed appropriate.

"Look," the man said, scrambling to his feet and tripping over the debris of wood. "I can pay you..."

"We don't want your money." I cracked my knuckles. The man blanched so hard, I was surprised he didn't just pass out. He did piss again.

I didn't sigh. This wouldn't take long and I somehow doubted I'd even have to hit him.

"What do you want? I can totally give it to you. Anything. Name it." His babble came out on a wave of spittle as he backed all the way up against the wall.

"Roger," I said. "I want a list of who else you sold our schedule to and whether you hired us because someone wanted to kill us or you arranged for us to take the job then sold the information to someone else."

"That's it?" The man stammered.

Yeah. This wasn't going to even be that interesting. Fuck.

"That's a start..."

"Then I can go?" He looked from me to Vienna then back again. I didn't turn around to see their expressions, I just kept mine dead neutral. Beating this guy wouldn't offer much in the way of satisfaction.

I also didn't answer his question. "I'm waiting."

"Look, Bones—you're the one they call Bones right?" His wobbling voice seemed to find some balance. "Of course, you're Bones. That's who agrees or doesn't agree to a job."

"Still not an answer."

The man scrubbed at his face, then seemed to swing his gaze around like some answer was going to just magically dance out of the air for him. Or maybe he thought he had backup that would save him.

"I—" He licked his lips then glanced down. Yeah, no answers down there. "I'm so dead."

"Probably," I said. "How you die is still up for grabs though."

"I didn't mean to sell you out." He didn't look at me. He didn't look at any of us. "I'm a broker. I connect clients and contractors. Once I have my fee, I'm out."

He cut a glance up. Fuck me, was he *crying*?

"I was good at it. Then one day, I had a job come across that was like the exact opposite of a job I'd just contracted and so... I didn't think about it, I just gave them the information. Made twice the fee. I told myself, one-time thing, Roger. Just one time."

"But it wasn't just one time..." I prompted when he fell silent.

His long, almost mournful sigh did make me want to punch him in his pudgy fucking gut.

"No. There were more... It worked out, only one party ever came out the other side so no one knew."

"I can see how that worked out for you." I shook my head.

"It did and... you guys are good, you know. I didn't think it would hurt you. I got paid. You got paid. The other guys?

They'd be dead. So no harm?" Pathetic was written all over him.

"No, Roger," I told him. "Not no harm."

He deflated once again. "You were hired to take out the Rojas first. Then another client reached out because they wanted the operation and heard that their competitor had hired someone..."

Through a series of fits and starts, Roger spilled his guts. Not literally, I wasn't going to bother getting my knife dirty for that. It was all a financial transaction for him. We'd been hired to eliminate the Rojas by one organization. Another organization wanted information to take it over themselves.

It was inelegant, stupidly basic and simple and he'd made a hefty profit over the last several years. He also put my men in danger.

That, I wouldn't forgive.

When he was done, swearing up and down he didn't know anything else, I broke his neck. Pathetic or not, he'd put a knife in our backs.

No way did he get to live to do it again.

TWENTY-ONE

GRACE

The sun had gone down already when Alphabet and I went outside with Goblin. I'd prepared two large mugs of cocoa and the cloudy skies had finally cleared out. When Alphabet invited me to go out to see the stars, excitement threaded through me.

While the milk heated, I dragged on the sweatshirt he grabbed for me. It was huge, but it was also warm. The faded green with the Army logo on the front was kind of like being wrapped up in a hug.

Putting a pin in that fanciful thought, I passed one of the oversized mugs to Alphabet.

"Thank you," he said, then held up a remote in his free hand. "Once we get to where we want to look, I'll shut off the external lights."

"Okay." I wrapped both of my hands around the mug. The warmth made a wonderful contrast to the chillier air. "Where are we going to look?"

Alphabet flashed a smile at me. "Right over there." He

pointed to somewhere in the darkness beyond the perimeter cast by the light. "Go slow, we're going to let our eyes adjust."

I'd done walks in front of dazzling lights and camera flashes, I knew how to focus *away* from the light to keep from squinting or reacting. But the plunge into darkness was going to be a bit more challenging.

When he offered me an arm, I adjusted my grip on the coffee mug so I could put a free hand on his forearm. What hesitations remained in me toward Alphabet had been falling away steadily. He wasn't grabbing my arm or ordering me. It was an offer, pure and simple. I could refuse and he wouldn't object.

That made it all a lot easier. *He* made it easier.

"It's dimming." Surprise filtered through me.

"Yep," he said, sounding quite pleased. "Easier on the eyes." He whistled once and Goblin came trotting out of the darkness even as the light seemed to melt back.

Bit by bit, the brighter light faded into the darkness. But what seemed inky dark wasn't quite so intense. If anything, it seemed to have a texture.

"Here." Alphabet slowed. My eyes had to have adjusted because I could make out shapes on the ground. There were patio chairs out here and a small table. "I brought a blanket out if you got cold, but it's not so bad right now."

No, it really wasn't. He and Goblin stuck close until I got myself comfortable on a chair then Alphabet settled on his. Another swallow of the hot chocolate and I shifted to put the mug down. Settling back, I glanced upward and forgot how to breathe.

It was the Milky Way. My mouth fell open. It was just like in the books. The stars spread across the sky like blue diamonds scattered against navy silk and velvet. It was so intensely beautiful.

"Told you she would like it," Alphabet said in a low voice, probably to Goblin, but I couldn't look away. I didn't have the words and I didn't want the moment to end.

We sat out there until the hot cocoa was gone and beyond. We didn't say anything at all. Until his phone let out an alert and shattered the peace. It was like slowly coming out of a dream, and I wasn't altogether sure what was reality and what wasn't.

"They've landed," he said. I didn't have to ask who *they* were. Voodoo had apologized to me on the phone, when I spoke to him. Their *trip* had been delayed. Instead of coming straight back they had to make another. I hadn't been given an ETA.

To be fair, I hadn't asked either. We'd avoided some of these topics, save for when Voodoo had wanted to talk to me, and Alphabet said they should be heading back soon. That was it. The past two nights we'd slept on the sofas in the living room, watching movies. Tonight...

Tonight, I'd go back to sleeping in my room. The sofa wasn't good for Alphabet. He'd been turning himself into knots to look after me, and it was my turn to look after him. "How long until they get here?"

"Probably a couple of hours yet."

A couple of hours. "Was their trip about Amorette?" It was asking the one question I'd been avoiding.

"No," he answered on a sigh as he swung around to sit sideways on his lounger. It prompted me to do the same. "It was something that needed to be handled, but it's not about your sister. If we had anything... anything at all, I would tell you."

I studied him in the starlight. He'd promised to not lie

to me. Maybe he couldn't tell me everything but he said no more lies. Did I believe him?

Despite feeling like eternity elongated while I weighed my answer, it couldn't have been more than a few seconds. I believed him. "Okay," I said. "Thank you for answering."

"You're welcome, Gracie."

Goblin bumped his head against my knee and I rubbed a hand over his head. "I think I'm going to go up to bed." I didn't want to wait up for the guys. It was already late, and if I withdrew now, they could come in and get some rest from their trip.

We could tackle everything else tomorrow.

"You sure? I don't mind setting us up in the living room. I'll even build a fire." He held out a hand to me as he stood and I took it. "You're freezing."

"No, not that bad and yes, I'm sure. You've slept on the sofa for two nights and you've been great. It's time for me to be a big girl again." I went for self-deprecating, but there was something in his soft huff that said he didn't believe me. "Thank you for showing me this."

"My pleasure. We'll do it again. One of the best parts of having our base here... the sky goes on forever." The wistfulness in his voice tugged at me and I spared another look up. He was right, the sky definitely did that.

GUILT NIBBLED at me after I bid Alphabet and Goblin goodnight and went up to my room. I felt like a bit of a coward and a hypocrite. I'd kind of—no kind of, I *had* enjoyed the last couple of nights. Alphabet was good company. Our agreement had done a lot toward making it easier to just talk and enjoy him.

He promised when the guys came back, we really were going to drill down on the issues. Well, he hadn't promised *exactly*, but I read between the lines and it was what he *wanted* to do. I believed him. That was enough for me.

What I didn't want to do was have a fight with the others tonight. They'd been gone for three days and I'd only seen part of the operation. It was safe to assume they would be exhausted. If not—well, they deserved to return to base and rest up.

We could always fight tomorrow.

I went through the motions of getting ready for bed then went to the photograph of me and Amorette on the dresser.

"You'd probably have ripped their heads off by now." I traced the lines of her face. "You'd have a dozen different arguments ready and turn them inside out. Or you'd have already persuaded them to do everything." Another long sigh escaped me before I set the framed photograph down. "I miss you."

I had to make myself turn away after that. Turn away and get ready for bed. Once I was under the blankets, though, and the light off save for a low one in the bathroom, I just stared at the ceiling.

My mind raced. Watching movies had helped distract me and let me sleep, but I didn't have a television in here or even a phone to listen to something on. No, it was just me and my thoughts and they started going faster, and faster. Around and around in circles alternately drenching me in ice cold fear, unsteady nerves, or just pure, existential dread.

"Enough, Grace," I told myself. "Enough. We have to sleep. We have to sleep if we're going to do this." I tried to focus on good things, positive memories, even just fun things I wanted to do…

My mind flitted from event to event, thing to thing, and just wouldn't settle. It was so damn irritating. Blowing out a breath, I sat up and stared around the room. I'd go for a run on the treadmill in the morning. Exercise could help, maybe. The restlessness invading my whole system aggravated the shit out of me.

I considered and rejected getting up. Dealing with everything else in the morning would be better. Especially with my heart pounding, my hands clenching, and a headache threatening. I'd just be spoiling for a fight to relieve the tension.

Just not a good plan.

I flopped back against the pillows and resisted the urge to thump my hands and feet against the bed and scream. A little huff of laughter escaped me at the mental image of my tantrum. Still staring at the ceiling, I thought about all the things I would have done if I were home in my place.

Watch a movie or catch up on some show that I was behind on.

Listen to music.

Play on my phone.

Read a book.

None of those were an option in here. Especially if I didn't want to leave the room.

I ran a hand over my face. Well, an orgasm would definitely help with the tension. A shudder of anticipation vibrated right through the taut feeling in my body. Yeah, an orgasm would do nicely.

The lack of toys or a partner were not deterrents. Not in the slightest. In fact…

I cupped my breasts and teased the nipples through the

cotton of the sleep shirt. One thing about knowing my own body, I knew exactly how much pressure to apply to elicit a response. Even better, I could savor the feelings because I had no intentions of edging myself.

Still teasing a nipple with one hand, I slid the other to dip into my panties. Teasing my clit, I stroked back and forth slowly. A memory of Voodoo in the hotel room stealthed out of my memory, a tempting wraith that had my cunt clenching around emptiness.

Fuck.

Having felt the bunch of his muscles and the way he moved against me... The heat of his mouth against mine... The swipe of his tongue... Gentleness and demand... I arched my back, the memory leaving me slick and needy.

Circling my clit with two fingers, I applied the pressure I wanted even as I pinched and twisted a nipple. The competing sensations made me arch and shift as I spread my legs.

A toy could increase the speed and force. But my fingers were just fine. My pulse increased as the band of tension that had bound me up so tight earlier, stretched out. The only thing that would make this better was if he were right there...

Squeezing my eyes shut, I let my imagination wrap around the memory of Voodoo as he slid into me. Oh, there was a feeling I wanted to savor and the pleasure crested, and burst through me with a kind of swift surprise that made me gasp.

Laying there, I tried to catch my breath and let a smile widen on my mouth. That... oh that was exactly what I needed. The profound relief swept through me from head to toe. Yes, just what I needed and wanted.

Pulling my hand from my panties I went to wipe them

on the bedsheets when a hand locked around my wrist and I jerked, a half-scream clawing up my throat.

As if conjured by my actions, Voodoo braced one knee on the bed as he pulled my fingers to his mouth and sucked them against his lips then cleaned them off with slow, deliberate swipes of his tongue.

The tension rebounded, binding me up in knots as I stared into his eyes. There was no mistaking the intensity in them or how his dark hair fell rakishly against his forehead. He was a dark angel, come to life...

"If this is a dream," I whispered. "I don't want to wake up."

His low chuckle had me curling my toes. "It's not a dream, Firecracker. It's just my turn." Then his mouth was on mine and I had my arms around his neck. My hand was in his hair, fisting it as he dragged me out from under the covers.

The cooler air had my nipples tightening further. Voodoo had on too many damn clothes..

I tugged at his shirt and he broke from the kiss long enough to rip his shirt up and over. All that skin, taut muscle, and the light dusting of hair that had me eager to explore every inch.

He bit my lower lip, a swift kiss, before he grabbed the hem of my shirt and tugged it upwards. I wiggled out of it then reached for his belt.

"Fuck," he muttered. "Stay right there."

Then he stood, his belt came free and then he shoved his jeans down. Thankfully, he was already without his shoes or socks. Maybe that was why I hadn't heard him come in.

Drinking in the sight of him, I licked my lips. Then I flopped back to peel my panties down. I didn't make it far before he grabbed them and ripped them right down my legs. Then he lifted them to his nose and took a deep breath.

"I thought slipping in to check on you and finding you pleasuring yourself was the best thing I'd seen all day."

"Yeah?" I answered in a rush. So not a dream. Okay. That worked for me too. Now that he was here, the longing I'd been burying burst free. I just wanted to touch him.

"Yeah, but I was wrong."

He all but fell over me, bracing one hand against the bed near my head.

"You, spread out like this, with want on your face? That's fucking gorgeous, Firecracker."

The heat and weight of his cock was against my thigh and I slid my legs apart, bracketing his hips with my knees as he settled himself against me. The length of him pressed along my cunt and I arched to stroke him and myself.

"This... this is the best damn thing I've ever seen or felt." Then his mouth fused with mine. The kiss, long, slow, and deep. It was like he savored the taste of my soul and dragged me into the pleasure of it all.

I skated my nails over his shoulders and then his back. The bunch and flex of his muscles offered delicious terrain to explore. The tangle of our tongues had me groaning as he began to rock his hips. The tease of his rigid length against my clit sent little sparks through my system.

"Voodoo," I whispered against his mouth in between drugging kisses. "I need you inside me."

"Oh?" There was just the barest hint of teasing in that syllable. "You seemed to be doing just fine with those fingers..."

It was my turn to bite his lip, then I traced a line of biting kisses along his jaw to his ear as I fisted his hair.

"That's because I was imagining you in the hotel... when you fucked me the first time."

A full body shudder went through him and then he lifted his head, his gaze fixed on mine. "Yeah?"

"Oh, yeah," I said, abandoning the whisper. "I want to feel you inside me again..." I wanted it so goddamn much. I don't know which of us reached for his cock first, but he wrapped his hand over mine.

He was so hot and hard, and his skin so silken. We teased his tip against my entrance. I was so soaking and ready, but he took his time, never looking away from me. Then he pressed forward and I arched up to meet him.

What patience we seemed to possess snapped in that instant. He slammed home to the hilt and swallowed my cry with his kiss that was all tongue, teeth, and gasping breath.

"Fuck!" The word exploded out of me as he pounded into me, every thrust as wickedly sinful and welcome as the ones I'd imagined. The stretch was a burn that just fed into my pleasure. I dug my fingers against the bunching muscles of his ass as he increased the tempo.

Maybe it was the first orgasm, or the tension, or the fact that he was here and satisfying the very real desire to see him. Or maybe it was just the way all of his focus and strength powered into me, but the orgasm that caught me up had me writhing against him as he kissed my throat.

"I'm going to come so deep inside you, I'm going to leave a mark," he promised and I locked my legs around him, digging my fingers in to hold on. Then our mouth fused again as he drove all the air out of me over and over until I was dizzy from it.

Only then did he shudder and let go. The heat of his release seemed to bloom inside of me like liquid fire. We lay there, locked together with his face buried against my throat. The softness of his beard tickled my skin as much as the little hairs on his chest teased my nipples.

We floated there together, all the tension and frustration had drained out of me. This was… right.

"Give me a few minutes, Firecracker," he murmured.

"For what?" It was a challenge to push those two syllables out.

"To get my second wind."

I blinked and then focused on him. "Really?"

"Oh yeah, you definitely feel like *more*." Was that a challenge?

I clenched around him and he hissed. "You're starting to feel like more too…" Mine definitely was.

His grin was feral, then he kissed me again and there were no more words.

CHAPTER
TWENTY-TWO

VOODOO

Finding Grace curled up against me when I opened my eyes was a damn good way to greet the day. Waking her with slow kisses before eating her out until she was screaming was an even better way. Finishing it off by sliding into her was the crowning glory.

Her brilliant blue eyes were drowsy, but pleased. I really liked that look on her face along with the flush in her cheeks. Nuzzling kisses to her cheek, I slid a hand through her hair. "I need a shower and some coffee," I murmured. "Want to grab your own shower and meet me downstairs for the second?"

"Are you trying to tell me I stink?" Playfulness wound through her voice and I snorted.

"Definitely not getting me with that one." I winked. "But I do want coffee." Trailing a finger down her nose, I savored the way her lips widened into a smile. "If I take a shower with you, that's where we're going to stay and then right back to this bed."

As plans went, I could get behind it. Frankly, I hadn't planned on the extended absence. I wanted to make it up to her.

She caught my hand and pressed a kiss to it. "That's my job," I told her, before I lifted her hand, returning the favor. "And if I don't start moving, I won't."

"I'm finding it challenging to encourage you... even though I know we need to talk today."

Yes we did. Right. Hammering all of this out was important for her and for us. Still reluctant, I forced myself to get out of bed. After dragging on my jeans, I scooped up my abandoned shirt before I leaned back down to kiss her again.

"Come find me downstairs in fifteen," I told her, stroking a hand through her hair. "I'll make your coffee."

"Might take me a little longer than fifteen minutes."

"That's okay," I said with a grin as I headed for the door. "I *will* wait."

Once in the hall, I ran a hand over my jaw. Leaving her and her room took a heroic effort. Blowing out a breath, I headed straight for my room. It took me ten minutes to shower, dress in clean clothes, and head downstairs.

Lunchbox and Alphabet were already in the kitchen. The combined scents of fried potatoes, bacon, and coffee proved incredibly alluring. I didn't even make it all the way into the kitchen before a fist slammed into my face.

The move staggered me. "What the fuck?" I blocked the next punch and glared at Lunchbox. He was usually the steadiest of us so this was some unexpected shit.

"We get back and the first thing you do is head straight to her room and fuck her?" He delivered the accusation in a low, ice cold tone. I stared at him.

"And?" I rubbed my jaw. The blow definitely hurt. "Since when do you care?"

"Don't be a dick," Lunchbox said with a cutting look.

"I didn't think I was being one," I muttered as he stalked back into the kitchen. I followed with a little more caution. Lunchbox didn't usually *snap*. Alphabet sat at the table, coffee in hand and a faint smirk on his face. "You planning on hitting me?"

"If I decide to do that, you'll be the first to know." He toasted me with the coffee cup.

Snorting, I headed for the espresso machine. I'd barely reached for the portafilter when Lunchbox said, "She's been through enough. She doesn't need to just be used for sex."

Facing him, I raised my brows. "Excuse me?"

"You heard me. She's been through hell. She's not here to service us."

The comment flicked a switch on my temper. "I love you like a brother, but I will take you the fuck apart if you ever say that again. I am *not* using her."

"Then why the hell did you just go dive into her bed?" The snap in his tone crackled like fire licking over wood.

"I don't owe you any explanations. The only person with right to that information is Grace. She's the one that matters." I wasn't going to bring up what I saw her doing or how fucking hot it had been to watch. I'd gone up there to be there for her dreams and instead, she was pleasuring herself. "So maybe take the stick out of your ass before I yank it out and beat the shit out of you with it."

"You want to go a few rounds?" Lunchbox took two steps forward. This shit was new. I expected crap like this from Bones. I talked him down or we went a few rounds. Whatever was eating at Lunchbox needed dealing with, because this was an escalation that went from zero to a hundred.

It was also not him.

"Lunchbox is jealous," Alphabet said in a tone that was at least partially amused and undeterred when Lunchbox switched his glare to him. "He doesn't like that you and Gracie have hit it off so well."

"Too fucking bad," was my only comment on it. "If this is going to continue to be a problem then we solve it right now. We're not doing this to her and she doesn't deserve the vitriol or the bullshit."

"Oh, that's what she doesn't deserve." Right, all that anger came lasering back to me. "But after she was kidnapped by some trafficking ring, abused, and we know it was sexual, and there's no way she wasn't raped, you just drag her into bed and what...?"

"First," I said, keeping my tone level and my own temper in check. "I didn't drag her anywhere. Nothing was done with Grace that wasn't done with her consent. Maybe you missed the memo, but she's an adult. We might be keeping her here and restricting her movements, but we don't *own* her."

That last seemed to rock him back on his heels. Good, maybe I could slap some sense into him without violence. Particularly because I hadn't had a cup of fucking coffee yet and she could be down here any second. This morning was the first time I'd seen her truly relaxed since we'd met her.

I wasn't going to let *anyone* fuck that up for her.

"Second," I continued, holding my ground. "Since when do you lump me into a category with rapists and abusers? Because if you are and do, then we have a much bigger issue."

None of them had been in that hotel room with her that

night. None of them had seen how broken and desperate she'd been.

Lunchbox held my gaze for a long moment, then bowed his head. "Fuck. I don't lump you into that category. I know you're not." He raked a hand through his hair then stalked over to the stove.

"Like I said," Alphabet commented. "He's jealous."

"Fuck off," Lunchbox snarled at him over his shoulder, but some of the heat in his tone had definitely bled away.

"Nope," Alphabet answered with a grin, but he sobered as he looked at me. "You know he has a thing for her too."

"So do you," I said, completely aware.

"Not denying it. But also not pushing anything."

I nodded. "Fair enough. Now, if we're done with this…"

A door closed, but it wasn't Grace striding toward us. It was Bones. He had definitely showered and shaved. His eyes were cool as he surveyed the room upon entering the kitchen. "Problems?"

Letting Lunchbox take that one, I returned my attention to the espresso machine. I'd promised her coffee. I was going to make it.

"Nope," Alphabet said behind me. "We're just great. How are you?"

Silence greeted his comment and the grinder sounded almost abnormally loud in the room.

"Really?" Bones did not believe him. Well, never let it be said he couldn't read a room.

"Yes, really. We're fine," Lunchbox said into the silence before cracking some eggs to get them going. "Just tired and want to get this debrief on so we can get shit sorted out."

The silence thickened as I pulled the shots and it grew

even harsher when I retrieved the milk from the fridge. I caught Bones' speculative look.

"Maybe we should ask you," I said, easily enough. "Problems?"

He shook his head. "You three are fighting over Grace."

"Hey," Alphabet said, pointing bacon at him. "Point of order, I am not fighting anyone. Neither are they."

"That's why Voodoo has a bruise and Lunchbox's knuckles are red." The blunt assessment was on the nose. "If you're not fighting over her, what are you fighting about?"

The hiss of the steamer rose filled the quiet. Then Lunchbox flipped the eggs. "We were having a disagreement over eggs."

"Eggs." The level of doubt Bones managed to infuse into that single syllable almost made me laugh. Cause, seriously, eggs?

"Yep," Lunchbox said. "It's settled. So don't worry about it."

"You want coffee?" I asked Bones as I finished prepping Grace's. It was a damn miracle she hadn't walked into this stupid conversation yet.

"Sure, as long as I don't have to debate *eggs* with you."

Not missing a beat, I nodded. "I'll let you off—this time. No guarantees for tomorrow."

There was a snort of laughter from Alphabet and a huff from Lunchbox. With Grace's coffee ready, I made Bones' before I started on mine. Lunchbox bumped my shoulder and I glanced at him.

The apology was there and I just lifted my chin. We were good. He nodded, then there was the sound of a door closing again. This time, the light steps that followed told me Grace was on her way down. The shift in the room was palpable.

When I turned, she paused in the entryway to the kitchen and she swept her gaze over all of us before coming to me. "Problems?"

The distinct echo of Bones' earlier question was almost funny.

"Not precisely," Bones said. "However, I would like to have a discussion with these three before we debrief with you fully."

"She can have breakfast first," I said, carrying her coffee over to her.

"It's okay," Grace said, taking the coffee and smiling up at me. "I'll just take Goblin outside for a few minutes, then come back in." She rose up on her tip toes and I dipped my head so she could brush a kiss to my jaw. "Thank you."

"Grace," Alphabet said. "Voodoo's right, you don't have to go anywhere. Whatever Bones needs can wait."

"Maybe," she said, though her smile was undiminished. "But I actually don't mind giving you the time. And I like going out with Goblin." Something passed between the two and I wasn't the only one who noticed.

After a moment, Alphabet nodded then murmured something to Goblin. The dog rose and bounded over to Grace. Good boy.

"I can start your breakfast while we're talking," Lunchbox said. "What do you want?"

"Right now, I just want coffee. Then maybe some yogurt and fruit. But coffee first." Her lips twitched at Lunchbox's fierce frown.

"What about some fried potatoes or bacon? I have some ham I could slice and fry too..."

She squeezed my arm lightly then brushed her hand

against Alphabet's shoulder on her way to Lunchbox. His whole posture shifted at her approach.

"Let me have the coffee, then maybe the yogurt and fruit. If I'm still hungry afterward, we can talk then, okay?"

Everything about his posture said he wanted to argue, but he only blew out a breath and nodded. "Fine. You need more than just yogurt and fruit."

"So you've said," she told him with a grin. "Also, if I haven't said it. Welcome home. Alphabet and Goblin took very good care of me and I tried to take care of them while you were gone."

"She did a great job," Alphabet volunteered. "Notice, we didn't burn down the kitchen or anything."

Her laughter just made me smile. Yeah, she was definitely feeling a little better.

"Now if you'll excuse me, I'll let you boys work out whatever it is Boney Boy wants to work out."

I *almost* laughed out loud. The Boney Boy moniker wasn't going anywhere. With that she turned and headed for the backdoor with Goblin trotting alongside.

"Not going to say anything nice to me?" Bones asked as she passed him. "Give me some assurances? Or comfort?"

The snark filled his tone with challenge and he tossed it down like a gauntlet.

She paused, lifting her chin and focusing on him. I couldn't see her face. None of us except for Bones could. His eyes narrowed.

"I don't care if you have a pulse, much less a nice anything, Boney Boy." The comment was delivered in the same light tone she'd used when she spoke to the rest of us. "In fact, I don't have much to say at all. Enjoy the fact I'm leaving you to chat since you didn't want me in here for that."

With that, she sailed outside into the cooler morning with Goblin racing alongside, leaving Bones to stare after her with a scowl.

I chuckled as both Alphabet and Lunchbox cracked up. Goddamn, I really like feisty Grace. She was every bit the firecracker I knew she could be. Her serving notice to *Boney Boy* would be good for him.

And entertaining for me. I passed him his coffee. "Spill, because she has waited on all of us long enough."

Bones' sigh carried a wealth of meaning, but he didn't deny the observation. "I spoke to Vienna and Fletcher late last night... We have another problem and it involves Grace."

Son of a bitch.

CHAPTER

TWENTY-THREE

It was a scant fifteen minutes, if that, before Voodoo stepped out to call me. Goblin and I hadn't gone that far. The morning was cool, but sunny. Fat, poofy white clouds decorated the vivid blue of the sky. I'd been soaking up the sun and drinking my coffee.

Some of the tension Voodoo had melted away the night before and this morning corded around me. He waited for me at the door and his expression gentled. "It's not that bad."

His soft words actually made me smile.

"I hope it's not." Goblin darted up the two steps and passed Voodoo to get inside. "Not even sure what *bad* is at this point."

"That's fair," he told me, stepping back to let me in. The combination of rich scents of coffee, bacon, potatoes, and, oh, biscuits surrounded me like a welcoming hug. Bones was at the table with Alphabet. They had plates piled high with food. Lunchbox set out another plate, most likely for Voodoo, before he set up his own.

A rich glass bowl of yogurt with side dishes of granola and fresh fruit waited in front of the empty seat next to Alphabet. My smile grew. "Thank you," I said to Lunchbox.

He nodded once. "I have extras of everything else if you're still hungry."

I appreciated it. Sliding into my seat, I reached for the spoon and set my coffee down. The first bite was welcome. I added the granola and fruit to the mix.

Voodoo settled in front of the plate of food in front of the chair to Bones' right. Alphabet sat to Bones' left where he occupied the seat at the head of the table. That left the chair directly opposite me for Lunchbox.

Conversation waited for Lunchbox to sit. Once we were all there, Alphabet leaned back in his seat and turned his attention to Bones. Lunchbox and Voodoo both flicked their attention to him as well.

After a swallow of coffee, Bones leaned forward. "Alphabet. Report."

"Currently, digital searches haven't turned up anything on Amorette Black." Alphabet slid a look to me, the apology in his blue eyes. "Expanded sweeps haven't found her at any legitimate border crossings or via any CCTV at airports."

My stomach sank, but I made myself keep eating. That wasn't unexpected. Alphabet had already told me he hadn't turned up anything new.

"The law firm is still being cagey. We've had no luck in getting any answers out of them. Even when we've played clients..." He sighed. "I dug into some of their servers, just surface skimming. But they've taken her name off everything in the firm. Sorry, Gracie. We've reached out to another hacker—one we trust—to do his own deeper dive to see what he can find."

I nodded with a sigh. "Thank you... I mean that. Thank you. She represented women primarily. So I don't think they'll buy that a man is one of her clients." The fact they'd stripped her name off everything. "If we could get her client list, I could try talking to them directly. But I am guessing we can't get that if they removed her name."

Alphabet shot her a sorrowful look. "No information is really ever gone. You'd need to delete and overwrite at least seven to ten times. Even then, data can be reconstructed. I don't know if they've taken that kind of time."

They'd clearly taken *some* time. "Even if they remove her from the firm, she had court cases. Based on what I remember from Amorette, you have to file with the court to withdraw as counsel. You don't get to just ditch and say hey, I don't feel like repping these people anymore."

"But if her firm is still representing those people?" Lunchbox said.

"She'd still be an attorney of record. To change that, she'd have to file or the attorneys in her firm would. It wouldn't matter how much overwriting they are doing at the firm itself. The courts are entirely different and if the judge or judges don't sign off on it, then she could be facing fines or censure or something."

"So, we hack the courts—" Alphabet muttered. "See what cases she's tied to and what papers were filed. I can do that. I'll get started on that as soon as the debrief is done."

"If you find the names of her clients, I can call them..." It may or may not help. I disliked intensely that her firm seemed to erase her. "Did you find her so-called resignation letter?"

"No," Alphabet said. "Any file detailing hers had been archived. I could see the names, but not content, and I couldn't open them without getting into their archive."

I really hated that. I scraped the last bite of yogurt out of the bowl.

"On that note," Bones said and it forced me to focus on him. His expression was steel, though he didn't seem angry. "The operation you were rescued from was an independent contractor with links to everything from South American cartels to Eastern European syndicates and a few operations right here in the States."

That... was unsettling. "Independent?"

"Independent," he confirmed. "We didn't have anyone to question. Our allies, including Doc, are funneling any information they can turn up on these people to us but it doesn't look like they were the ones who took you in the first place."

I didn't scream. I wanted to scream. But I didn't.

"One of the reasons we want to get into your sister's cases is to see if the reason she was marked had anything to do with those."

My stomach sank.

"That said, we can't discount that you two weren't targeted because of who *you* are." Voodoo met my gaze and I could almost feel the edge of regret. "You already told me about the yachting parties—the bidding. The guys who wanted to pay you for your time."

The icy heat shifted as it seemed to glide over my skin. "You think because I said no, they decided to force my hand?" Did that fit with the man I'd woken up to? The one who'd said he'd waited for me?

He hadn't been remotely familiar.

"It's a possibility we can't ignore," Lunchbox said.

"Human trafficking is a multi-tiered, multi-national, multi-sourced enterprise that basically deals in human slavery whether it's commercial, sexual, or worse."

I frowned. "What's worse than commercial or sexual?"

"Big game hunting," Bones answered and I pushed the bowl away from me. The yogurt and fruit sat like a lead weight in my stomach. "Research. There are others... none good."

No, I supposed not. "Are there any reports of me being missing?"

"No," Alphabet said. "Another cause for concern, because someone has gone to a great deal of trouble to erase both of you."

Erase.

I clasped my hands together to try and keep them from shaking.

"The number of attempts to reacquire you also leads us to believe that you were the primary target, at least for one of these groups of traffickers." Little emotion seemed to touch Bones' voice. "The death of your manager, agent—that also suggests that whoever wants you doesn't want anyone looking for you."

Eleanor wouldn't have stopped. Neither would Amorette. It seemed almost wild that of all the people I had contact with and knew, that those two had been specifically targeted...

Coincidence didn't come with such a stretchy waist. Her going missing right around when I was taken and her firm acting like she quit? No police reports? Nothing? She was just *gone*.

"There's more," Voodoo said, pushing his own plate away and focusing on me. "Bones confirmed this morning that there is a bounty out for you. It's being floated through some areas that we have access to. The accounts where the money is being floated will be back traced and drained. We'll use their own tools against them."

"Already working on it," Alphabet said and he bumped my clasped hands with his gentle fist. "No one is going to take you, Gracie."

"No one," Lunchbox confirmed and Voodoo nodded.

"We won't let anyone touch you. But we can and will tear this apart to find out *who* and *why*." Voodoo's promise wasn't as reassuring as it could be, but I believed him. I believed them. *That* helped.

"How? You want to dig into court cases, check out these accounts, and keep looking, but what about Amorette? Is there a chance we can still find her? Is she still here in the States? Or in one of those other places?" Because that was the real fear. What if she disappeared into the ether? What if I never saw her again?

I raised my clasped hands and bowed my head, pressing my lips to the knuckles of my index fingers. These were not outcomes I even wanted to consider.

"What about law enforcement? What if we report this? I don't know how much of what you do is illegal... I can report it without involving you..." No sooner did I make the suggestion than I sighed. "But how would I explain any of it without involving you."

"If it were just a matter of using our names to get you into the right hands, Grace," Bones said in a rock-steady voice, "we'd have already done it. Talking to law enforcement might help here in the States, but you'd have to get into it with Interpol, or other agencies for the global search and we don't have enough to direct anyone to a possible where."

Squeezing my eyes shut, I battled back the tears. I did not want them to fall. Period.

"As for the rest, we're not taking you back because we don't think Homeland or the FBI or one of the others wouldn't look... we're not releasing you because we don't know that they could protect you." A harsh, if blunt reality and Bones didn't soften it.

"What he's saying," Lunchbox said, picking up, "is we don't know if they don't have people on their payrolls. These types of operations are incredibly sophisticated. Whether they are moving one person or a dozen. You shut down one conduit, another opens. It's just as likely that you would go into their custody, nothing happens for a few days, maybe a few weeks, they send you back to your life and the ones who were waiting just scoop you up then."

That was horrifying.

"Or worse, you get someone on a protection detail with a gambling debt or underwater financially and they take a bribe or a payment to look the other way. Corruption isn't always about evil," Alphabet said. "We like to think of the world as a balance of good versus bad, but... it's not that simple. Some things? Yeah, some are absolutely heinous. So the demarcation is clear. But not everything."

"This is why you've kept me all this time and didn't want to answer my questions?" I focused on Alphabet.

"Yes. And no. I know that's not as clear-cut as you would like it. My instincts said you needed to stay with us *especially* after the attack at your apartment."

"Agreed," Lunchbox said. "My instincts said the same."

"Mine too," Voodoo admitted. "It's why we brought you *here* where we could see anyone coming and we know the lay of the land. No one is getting near you."

"At the same time, we also had other jobs that could not

wait. They had to be completed and as frustrating as that is for you, Grace," Bones said, his cool tones helping to tamp down some of the wilder bits of frustration. "We've done what we can for those at the moment."

"So, you don't have any other jobs?"

"We have the job to find your sister, and find out who is targeting you." Voodoo offered me a small smile. "We know you are still a target because we received another call this morning."

Honestly, I wasn't sure my heart could sink any further.

"It *could* be connected." Alphabet put a hand over my clenched ones as I lowered them back to the table. "At the moment, we *don't* have confirmation."

"What?"

I searched their faces. It had to be something. Or they wouldn't be this intense. Right?

"There was a plane crash late last week, a private flight headed for Europe, crashed somewhere in Nova Scotia not that long after takeoff. Mechanical failure is being investigated." Bones' expression was utterly unreadable. "It may not be connected, but the coincidence would be a little far-fetched."

"Who was on the flight?"

"Jock Giardan and Lloyd White as well as two assistants, a hair stylist, and..."

He kept talking but the roar in my ears drowned out his words. Jock and Lloyd. I'd known them forever. They were fantastic photographers and genuinely gifted. I knew their stylists and their assistants.

"...at the time, there were no survivors." The words fell like heavy stones.

"It may have nothing to do with you, Gracie," Alphabet said.

"But you don't believe that." They were dead.

"I don't know what to believe yet," he qualified. "But Bones is right about coincidence being unlikely. Your agent and manager being eliminated makes a certain amount of twisted sense. This could be exactly what it looks like. An accident."

Could be. Maybe. But we didn't know.

"So, people who know me are dying… might not want to hang onto me, guys." It sounded as hollow to my ears as it did to my heart.

"I fucking dare them to come at you or us," Lunchbox said, reaching across the table to lay his hand over mine. Alphabet added his to it and Voodoo stretched to place his there as well.

"No one is taking you, Firecracker. No one."

For some reason, I looked at Boney Boy. The hardass. He'd been the harshest so far. "Not making you promises," he said and that seemed fair. "Save one. They're right. No one is taking you or touching you. Period."

CHAPTER

TWENTY-FOUR

GRACE

As hard as that first conversation had been, the next one proved even more challenging. We moved back into Alphabet's office. Bones was back at the whiteboard and adding data that had been gathered.

Lunchbox dragged a chair in and set me up next to Alphabet so I could look at any images as they were ready. Voodoo disappeared for a few to "take care of a couple of items" and Lunchbox said he was putting lunch in the oven.

My lips twitched at the comment and he gave me an amused look. "You can laugh."

"I'm trying to not be rude, but... Lunchbox making lunch sounds funny."

He gave me a one-shoulder shrug. "As long as it makes you smile."

There was a strange kind of comfort in his ease. It also made it easier for me to snap back, although in this case it was more just a retort, not a slap. "And eat?"

"One can only hope you'll let me feed you." Then he winked and headed up the hall.

A sigh escaped me as Goblin bumped my knee and I stroked a hand over his head. He always seemed to know when I needed a distraction or a reminder. When I glanced up, I found Alphabet grinning. More, I caught the understanding.

"He's a good boy," I said, then focused on Goblin for a moment to lavish him with love.

"Yes, he is." His fingers tangled with mine briefly as he added his own pets. After giving my hand a gentle squeeze, he nodded to the computer. "You ready to dive into this?"

Some distant part of me was reluctant but I gagged that part. They were invested and we needed to know who was doing these things. Who killed Eleanor. Who killed Jock and Lloyd. Took Amorette. Took me.

So ready or not, I was doing this. "Yes."

"What was the name of the man who wanted you to yacht with him?" Bones asked and pulled my attention to him. Definitely not a comfortable topic of conversation.

"Maurizio," I answered with a new sigh. The older man was a bit much but I'd never seen him as a *threat.* "Maurizio Gallo. He's an Italian businessman. I think he actually runs hedge funds. I didn't really pay attention to that part. I know he's ridiculously wealthy and he's invited me to events before in Milan, Rome, Paris, and Nice. I met him during Paris Fashion Week a few years ago."

"Him?" Alphabet asked and I cut my gaze to the screen. In his sixties, Maurizio cut a fit and trim figure with steel gray highlights overtaking his darker hair. His dark eyes were canny and sharp, and his smile wide and generous. The heavy mustache he favored made him look more like a benevolent grandfather than a rake. Then again, he joked only boys were clean-shaven.

It was an opinion.

"That's him."

"Gallo, age sixty-seven. Married three times, twice divorced, widowed once. Currently maintains four residences in Rome, New York, Singapore, and Paris. He tends to travel via his yacht, but he owns four different private aircraft. His net wealth is in the billions." Alphabet read off the details as more information populated his screen.

A printer spit out several sheets. Bones turned to take the top one and studied it before he put it up on the white board with a magnet.

"He is tied to several figures in both the entertainment and financial worlds. He likes to gamble. Also dabbles in politics. Travels extensively and has ties to three syndicates in Eastern Europe, including one I know for damn certain has Bratva ties."

"Money laundering?" Bones asked as Voodoo returned to join us.

"Probably." Alphabet shrugged. "I'll dig down. I doubt he's more than an expensive client or investor. Nothing in his profile indicates he'd be engaged in the trafficking directly."

"You think he's one of the traffickers?" I leaned forward as Goblin settled on the floor between me and Alphabet.

"Maybe," Bones said over his shoulder as he added more details to the wall. "You said he offered you a million dollars to join him before you went to see your sister?"

"Yeah, he did things like that. The yachting—well it's not something I really enjoy but I can't imagine any of them kidnapping women, locking them up, or raping them the way they were." A shudder went through me and Voodoo settled a hand on my shoulder. I leaned into the contact. "I've met Maurizio several times—I know that he can make things happen for people. Models and actors, he can introduce you to people who can make things happen."

I swallowed around a sudden lump in my throat. Even if I hadn't wanted to go yachting then and I didn't care how much he offered, that was a long leap to get to him being tied up with the traffickers.

"Why would anyone who keeps upping their offer and goes as high as a million dollars just take 'no' for an answer?" Bones raised his brows and there was a blunt challenge in his words.

"Eleanor—" Pain spasmed at the mention of her. I forced myself to push past it. "She got him to agree to stipulations in the contract—no sex, no demands for nudity. That was when he was offering a quarter of a million."

Doubt reflected in Alphabet's expression when he looked over his shoulder. Voodoo's downturned lips didn't offer a much better assessment.

"I guess that does sound shaky." I hated admitting that. "Eleanor would never have made any kind of agreement if it involved that kind of danger."

"Perhaps." Bones didn't sound like he believed that. Not really. "How would she enforce such an agreement once you were there? What recourses would you have after boarding his yacht? What about him? Does he have staff? Security?"

"I hate this." I folded my arms. "I've gone to parties before, parties hosted by clients and other wealthy men. Some women too. I've been hit on more than once, and while I'm never going to judge someone who traded sex to get a leg up in the industry, that's *not* me. If it came down to fucking someone to get a modeling gig, I'd pass."

"Unless you weren't given a choice," Lunchbox said as he returned to the room. "I put a lasagna in the oven. Garlic bread will be ready later."

"Good, hopefully we all have an appetite after this. Can you give us some more names?" Voodoo asked and I tilted my head back to meet his gaze. "Other offers you may have had? Someone who was pushier? Have you ever met with a client or a company that wanted to hire you during contract negotiations?"

"Do models audition?" Alphabet frowned.

"Yes, we do. I still do now, though nowhere near as often. But when I was starting out, I had to do a lot of auditions. They need to know if you can walk a runway or how you stand. How comfortable are you in front of the camera. That means sometimes you have a portfolio, it would include a number of different shots. Art directors and casting agents need to know."

"But you haven't had to since you established yourself?" Bones asked. "Or was it only *rare* that you would have to."

"A little of column A and a little of column B. Eleanor made them pay me for auditions, particularly if I had to fly somewhere to meet them." She could be every bit the hardass as Bones. They probably would have hated each other. For some reason that thought made me smile. "I have an extensive portfolio and number of returning clients that I've worked with over the years. Most contract negotiations just went through Eleanor. When she liked the deal, she would come to me about it."

"So you always signed off on every deal?" Lunchbox dropped onto one of the other chairs near the whiteboard.

"Eleanor always knows..." I sighed, closing my eyes for a moment as Voodoo gave my shoulder another gentle squeeze. "She knew what kind of jobs I would take and what kinds I wouldn't. When I was just getting started, I rarely said no unless she advised me against it. You need work to build a reputation and to command a fee. So, I had a list of hard lines I wouldn't cross. I didn't mind posing nude, but I wouldn't do the overly sexual. It had to be more artistic. That kind of thing. There were some photographers I didn't like after I worked with them and others who had shady reputations. She avoided those. Eventually, we had a great rhythm between us and I trusted her judgment. The longer I've been at this, the more I liked to control my schedule—especially if I had already let her know I wouldn't be available."

"So, we leave Gallo on here and dig down." Bones nodded once. "Give us the other names."

It took me time to remember them all. They had questions about all of them. Not always the same questions. About music maven Lucinda Cross, they wanted to know, "Did she ever hit on you? Or was she only using you as entertainment for her guests?"

"I was there to pretty up the place." Not an answer any of them seemed to care for. She stayed on the list.

"John Aldridge," Alphabet said as he pulled him up. The man was seventy years old, married happily for fifty of those years and his wife was wonderful. "What about him? What did he want you to do?"

"Marry his youngest son, I think." I made a face cause that jerked all of their attention around. "He was really shy and very much not interested in his dad's business. He liked gaming. So when he had to do these formal events, he never took dates. I think they were worried he might be gay. I know that Teddy—Mrs. Aldridge, asked me about a few male models that I would recommend inviting so they could find out."

Bones stared at me. "They wanted their youngest son to date and get married so they put out hundreds of thousands to invite you to parties?"

Considering all our conversation so far, I could see why he thought that. "It wasn't hundreds of thousands. But, yes. Their oldest son and daughter were both in happy relationships and popping out grandkids. Robbie is my age and he's sweet. But he couldn't care less about having kids or getting hitched. I think he wanted to design games or be a tester or something. Not anything to do with his father's luxury goods business."

"The old man never hit on you?" Voodoo verified.

"No." I made a face. "I will say that Robbie taught me to play Mass Effect and I got pretty good at it. We had 'dates' when I was in town just to get his parents to leave him alone, and before you ask, no he isn't gay and no we didn't actually go out. We just played online. He might be a little socially awkward and his family is a little over the top, but they aren't shady."

I just couldn't see it.

"Put them on the maybe list." Bones shook his head. "Next name?"

It was like pulling teeth and by the time Lunchbox returned with lasagna, I was actually ready to eat some pasta just for the comfort.

Morgan Whittingham. Oil, Gas, and Mineral Rights Company, CEO. He was a little handsy and I only ever went to one party as a favor to a friend. He stayed on the list.

Marcus Gentry. Studio Executive and Investor. His parties often involved illicit drugs and orgies. Once was enough, and I ditched out as soon as I saw where it was going. Stayed on the list.

Cameron Kapnek. Tech boy, the founder of three different social media apps. Big into crypto. His parties were always on land and he just liked to surround himself with beautiful people. They dropped him to the maybe list.

On and on it went, until I couldn't think of anyone else. I finished all of my lasagna, appreciating the fact that Lunchbox only gave me a small portion. Eventually, Voodoo called it and Alphabet seconded the motion.

"She needs a break," Alphabet said over his shoulder. "And I need some time to pull out everything I can find then we can rank the targets."

I opened the bottle of water and took a long drink as the guys split a look between them.

"Four hours," Bones said. "Then we reconvene. Split the list, Alphabet. I'll take two. Lunchbox two. And Voodoo will take two as well." Then he eyed me. "Do you need a nap or want to rest somewhere else?"

Well, it was better than just being kicked out of the conversation. "Actually, I think I want to go for a run or a walk or something. Just get out of my head for a while. Do you mind if I use the gym?"

"Of course not," Voodoo answered, and then held out a phone to me. "You can use this too."

I stared at the device and then up at Voodoo. "Really?"

"I told you I would get you one. We haven't sat still long enough to make that a reality. I already put you on the wifi here. Our numbers have been added and before you ask, yes, there is a tracker in the phone. It's just in case we get separated and need to find you. You can also find us." He flipped it open to show the location sharing.

Cradling the device, I almost ruined the whole thing by bursting into tears. I could call people.

"We'd advise that you stay off your social media for now, and maybe don't reach out to anyone just yet." Voodoo made it sound like a suggestion and not an order. "Until we know who is safe and who isn't. If there's some other app you want on there or anything, just tell us and we'll make it happen."

I bit my lip as I hugged the phone to myself. "Music?"

"Anything you want," Alphabet said. "We've got a big library. I can log you into our movie account too."

Blowing out a breath, I stood up and I wasn't feeling all that steady. I kept hugging the phone then I dropped a kiss on Alphabet's cheek before I turned and gave Voodoo a hug.

He set me back on my feet. "If you want to run, do you want earbuds for it?"

"Yes," I said. "Please."

"C'mon then," he said, taking my hand. "Let's get you set up."

"Four hours," Bones called and I glanced back.

"I'll set an alarm." I had a phone and I could do it. "Thank you." Then I looked at Lunchbox. "Thank you for lunch too. I might even be hungry at dinner after I run."

"Good deal," he said and gave me a thumbs up. Still a little dizzy, I tried to get my breathing back under control.

"You okay?" Voodoo asked when he paused next to another door I hadn't opened, but it turned out to be a closet with more storage.

"I think so," I said, glancing down at the phone again. "Thank you for trusting me with this."

"You're trusting us." It was a reminder and he was right. I was. "Seemed about time we did the same." Then he handed me the earbuds.

When I took them from his hand, he clasped mine and reeled me in for a kiss that stole every bit of breath. A low groan tickled the back of my throat even as he devoured my mouth.

Lifting his head, he grinned down at me. "You need any help for your run?"

"Somehow, I don't think I'd be running if you came with me." I meant it as a bit of a joke, but he just raised his eyebrows.

"You're probably right. We can save that for later." Then he winked. "We're here if you need us."

"I know." This time, I really did know. I backed up the hallway, still hugging the phone. The feeling carried me all the way up to get changed and trailed me into the gym when I went downstairs.

Trusting them wasn't so bad. I just hoped we were all on the right track.

CHAPTER

TWENTY-FIVE

Maurizio Gallo was in France. He'd been vacationing near Nice and according to the reports Alphabet dug up, he was even now enjoying some time in a villa on the French Riviera.

"Taking her to Europe is going to be challenging." I studied the map Bones had been building based on the data we'd collected. At the moment, Gracie had gone up to shower after her run.

As irritating--and hot—as it had been to listen to her cries of pleasure the night before, I couldn't fault the shine in her eyes earlier in the day. That same glow seemed back after her run.

We'd locked her down and it was smothering her. From the way Bones and Alphabet watched her, I wasn't the only one who'd noticed.

"We'll make it work," Bones said in the same tone he'd used when he said we'd finish a mission or get Alphabet through recovery. It was a foregone conclusion, we *would* do it. Which meant we would also figure out the *how* of it.

"On our side," Alphabet said as he pushed his chair back and stretched. There was a hesitation in movement present when he stood. He needed a break. "No one has reported her or her sister missing. It pisses me off that someone is going to all the trouble of erasing her, even if it also means we may not have as many challenges to get her from point A to point B."

"Maybe," Voodoo said, arms folded. He was also staring at the map on the wall. The details on Gallo, his holdings, and the number of "dismissed" legal actions against him. The only reason we even knew there had been lawsuits at all was the gossip reporting. Once they were "settled" or paid off, they were erased entirely.

Another red flag.

"Issues?" Bones said, pivoting to face Voodoo.

"Depends," he said, rubbing his jaw. "She's a pretty well-known face. You recognized her, Lunchbox."

I shrugged. "True, but you guys didn't." A point in our favor. "Considering how many models are in the world, how many can you name off the top of your head?"

"But we still take precautions. Better to avoid any possible incidents." Bones braced his hands on the back of a chair. "We've whittled down her list to four names. No guarantee that one of them is involved in this."

"Then we'll start peeling back another layer." We'd do it until we found the problem. Blowing out a long breath, I studied the map. "We need to settle one more point before she comes back down." I checked my watch. I didn't miss Voodoo's measured look.

Slugging him earlier had sanded some of the edge off

my temper. It was hardly the first time for any of us to solve a disagreement with fists. More than likely we would do it again. With this much on the line and building an op on the go, we couldn't afford to keep dancing around the gorgeous woman in the room.

"Cards on the table," I continued when all three just stared at me. Maybe they didn't want to discuss this right now, but I wasn't going to let it go. Assumptions could get us killed. "We've been basically running by unspoken agreement. Alphabet and I got Grace out of New York because someone was after her. You came to back us up, then you," I said with a nod to Bones, "sent Voodoo to take her and lure out any possible pursuits. Eventually, we got her here."

"I don't have a problem with her being here," Alphabet said as he leaned a hip against the side of his desk.

"I didn't say you did. I also do not have a problem with her being here," I told him. "But we've never discussed the fact that we brought her *here* to *our* place. While Doc has a room here, even *he* hasn't been here."

"What's done is done," Bones said and I could almost hear him dismissing the topic. "But perhaps you three will take a little more care when it comes to our missions. The more she knows, the more she can compromise us."

"No one objected to her coming here," Voodoo said. "None of us. We could have, before we got on that plane. We didn't."

"No," Alphabet said with a sigh. "We didn't. It's not just about not having a problem with it. I like having her here."

"That," I said with a nod to him, "is the point. I like having her here too. I know you do." I lifted my chin to Voodoo. "That was very clear last night."

"And this morning," Alphabet said with a wry grin. Bones just scrubbed a hand over his face. "But Lunchbox is right. If we want Gracie to stay here, we have to know where all of us stand so we can be clear on where *she* stands."

"Involving her is a good first step," I said. "I want to help her. I want to nail whoever these bastards are that have turned her life upside down."

"The fucker who had her from the first scoop is still out there." Voodoo's voice held a quiet threat in it. The guy was out there and that was something we definitely needed to take care of. "Then there's the bastards who tagged her. The ones who put her on that truck..."

"And the ones who have her sister," I added. "If she's still alive."

"Killing her would be impractical," Bones said and it was such a cold assessment I frowned at him. "They've invested considerable resources into acquiring both sisters, into erasing them, and eliminating those around them like her manager, the photographers... You don't profit if you kill the product."

Hating that description, I tilted my head back. She wasn't a *product*. But wasn't that what all of these people were treating her as? A face. A body. A smile. It was all about how she looked.

"Until we have verifiable proof otherwise, we work with the assumption the sister is alive and we *will* find her for Grace."

"That's mighty damn optimistic of you, Bones," Alphabet said and the cap just gave him a bland look. Not that it had any effect on him. "You haven't said whether you want her here or like having her here yet."

With a snort, Bones looked at the board. "She doesn't really care what I think, remember?"

"She isn't the one asking," I countered.

"If I said no?" He raised his brows as he turned back to face us. "What would you all say then?"

I opened my mouth, then popped it closed. What could we say? Alphabet frowned, but it was Voodoo who said, "I'd call bullshit. But you're not asking me."

"I am committed to helping her. We'll find the problem, then eliminate the problem so she stays safe. That'll have to be enough for you, Lunchbox." Then he left the room.

"Well, that went well," Alphabet said. "I need to walk and stretch. Goblin could use a break too."

"You want company?" Voodoo asked and Alphabet shook his head.

"Nah, I'm good. Keep an eye on Gracie. She seems better today and I want her to keep feeling better."

"Already on that," Voodoo nodded, then Alphabet and Goblin left and it was just me and Voodoo. He eyed me. "Spit it out, before you choke on it."

"I like her." Not even going to mince my words. "I like her a lot. So does Alphabet."

"Same," Voodoo said, shrugging. "Not complaining about your interest or his. Not apologizing for mine."

"Don't recall asking you for an apology." I rubbed the back of my neck.

"Just saying," Voodoo said with a shrug. "One piece of advice, though."

I raised my brows.

"Leave Bones alone on this subject." The other man nodded to the board. "Let him focus on that. He doesn't want to split where his attention is and she is very much a distraction. His problem with you and Alphabet has everything to do with your interest in her in the first place."

"I'm sure you bedding her five minutes after he passed her off to you really went over well."

He shrugged again. "I don't care what he thinks either. It works out well. I have some work to do. I want to get some feelers out there, pin down supplies and transport, especially if we're going to France."

Yeah. Once he was gone, I turned to face the board again. I had the information, the names, and the faces memorized. If any of them were behind the hell she had gone through, we'd disassemble them piece by piece.

Wasn't sure it would be that easy though.

Putting a pin in that, I headed for the kitchen as Grace descended the stairs. Her damp hair fell around her shining face. She moved a little gingerly and I frowned. "Overdo it, running?"

"Maybe," she admitted. "I haven't been that active and I may have pushed it." Then she held up the phone. "The music helped."

"Good."

"C'mon and hang in the kitchen. I'll find you something to help with that." I waited a beat to see if she would follow, then made myself move. Giving her a choice also meant getting out of her way so she could make it for herself.

It took her a moment, but she did follow me. "Where is everyone else?"

"Alphabet went for a walk with Goblin," I told her as I went to get the meat out for dinner. I studied the contents of the fridge. We needed to go through whatever was defrosted before we left. No sense in letting food go to waste. "Voodoo is working."

"And Boney Boy?"

I slanted a look at her over my shoulder. "Do you really care?"

Her grimace was adorable. "I suppose I deserved that."

"Maybe." I pulled out all five steaks. They were large, but I could section hers down if she didn't want as much. Probably should have defrosted some fish for her. Right, I could work with it. "But he also went to get some work done."

"Oh." She moved to stand at the counter. "Can I help?"

"Not right this sec, but keeping me company is nice." I headed for the dry storage. We had plenty of potatoes in there. I carried a sack out. Could bake them or roast them.

Bake.

Stopping at the first aid kit, I flipped it open and grabbed the acetaminophen. I put the bottle in front of her.

"That will help with the aching. Don't sit still too long so you don't get stiff."

"Good advice." She turned the bottle around.

"We worked out a rough plan," I informed her as I washed off the potatoes. "We've got to tweak it a little, but we'll be moving soon."

"Toward one of the people I gave you?" Was she worried?

Of course, she was worried.

"Yes, the first one. Gallo. He's in France, so we'll have to go to him. We just have to work out some kinks in the plan so we can fly over. I don't think it will take more than a day or two to get that sorted. So take it easy on the overdoing it. International flights are not fun when you're stiff."

She released a long breath.

"I told you, we were going to help you. We just had to carve away the distractions. Now you have our whole focus." I got the oven heating and paused to look at her before I broke out the steaks. "We will help you. What we said about keeping you safe? We meant it."

"Why?" The soft question probably shouldn't surprise me but there was just a bit of a bewildered look on her face. "Sorry, that's probably rude."

"Direct, not rude." Wiping my hands off, I crossed to her. Better to keep her gaze on mine while we discussed this. "In the beginning? We wanted to help you because you needed help. You were caught in a really shitty situation. We wanted to get you home. Then those assholes came for you there."

Still fucking pissed me off.

"After that, it was a matter of honor to keep you safe. That, and we don't like bullies who go after defenseless women and children. Traffickers? They are the worst kind of bullies."

Then I traced a finger down the gentle slope of her nose and tapped it gently.

"Now? We want to help you because we like you. We're going to include you in the decisions. There may still be times when we have to do stuff on the fly and we won't have time to explain it. You're going to have to just trust us. The rest? The rest you'll have a say in."

She shuddered, then scraped her teeth over her lower lip. "It seems like a lot. You guys just kind of met me and now all my problems are in your lap."

"Lucky for you, we're pretty big guys. We can handle it." Then I dropped my head slowly, telegraphing my intention to give her a kiss and letting her have the time to back up. Thank fuck she didn't, and I kept it light and simple. A brush of my lips to hers.

Surprise flickered in her eyes but she didn't shove me away or slap me. Seemed a positive note.

"We like you Grace," I repeated. "Keep that in mind."

"Okay..."

"Now, I'm going to get started on dinner." I backed off and turned back to the steaks. "How do you like your steak?"

We were definitely going to keep her safe. Then we could work out the rest.

TWENTY-SIX

GRACE

Building out their plan included disguises, photographs, costume changes, more pictures, and testing facial recognition against their changes. Maybe I'd never had to build a brand new ID before, but I'd certainly had to build new looks, new attitudes, and inhabit them.

"What about dying her hair?" Bones asked after I'd pulled my hair back into a chignon to give myself a more severe look that I could enhance with cosmetics.

"No," I said, slicing a hand through the air. "For one, dying my hair would require bleaching the color out of it in the first place and you're talking a time consuming process that would not only need to be repeated a few times, it's damn hard to replicate and it could seriously damage my hair. Add to how fast my hair grows and the dark growth would be at the roots in a matter of days. No. We're not dying my hair."

"You have distinctive hair." He didn't add any qualifiers to it, but he also didn't push on that train of thought. "Maybe a wig would work."

"Possibly," Voodoo said, though he had leaned away from the handful of hair pieces he'd brought back with him from his supply run. "The trick is securing them. Most security agents aren't going to challenge you on the wig, but they may want to search under it. We are trying to draw *no* attention to you."

My stomach sank before I even made the next suggestion. "What if I cut it? Take it super short." I suppressed my own shivers. It was hair. It would grow back. "If I close crop it, then it can look like I'm just getting my hair back after some hair loss or something."

I really didn't like that idea.

"No," Alphabet said from the laptop he was working on. We weren't in his office or my room, but an entirely different kind of room filled with all sorts of costumes, cosmetics, prosthesis, including the kind to adjust the shape of a chin or a nose. I hadn't seen this much gear outside of a movie studio's special effects and makeup departments before. "One, even if it would alter the shape of your face enough, the longer hair gives you more options in styling. Second, you don't want to cut it."

I frowned. "It was my idea."

"Maybe it was your idea, Firecracker," Voodoo said from where he was checking different cases. "But you don't *want* to do it and if it were life and death—specifically yours— we could revisit it then. We have ways to do this that can distract facial recognition *and* help minimize people noticing you."

I didn't think of myself as having notoriety. "I don't

really know how many people in general would recognize me. People in the business? People I've done ads for? Maybe. But the average person?" I shrugged. "Then again, Lunchbox did, but nothing about any of you is that average."

"Thank you," Voodoo said with a grin and a wink. He pulled out a case and carried it over. "I think this color palette is the closest to your own. We can do some minor adjustments with your nose, add a little sharper point to your chin. Maybe a little more fullness to your face."

He flipped it open to reveal the contents.

"Colored contacts will disguise the eyes. Maybe a birthmark..." He tilted his head as he studied me, his assessing eyes probably didn't miss much. "You know, a little mole right there at the corner of your upper lip."

"Reshape her face, add some contours," Bones said, circling around to glance inside the case with Voodoo before studying me. "Maybe a little pallor and some shadows under her eyes—"

"Won't make her any less pretty," Alphabet stated with a shake of his head. "I mean she's standing here bare-faced of any cosmetics, hair in a pony tail and wearing an oversized sweatshirt and she's drop dead gorgeous. What the hell do you think some dark shadows are gonna do?"

I bit my lip. "Thank you."

"You're welcome," he said, pivoting to look at us. "We can go glasses. Different shapes can alter the look of the face."

"You can't put on eyewear for passport photos," I reminded him.

"Don't need to worry about that." Alphabet's confidence didn't waver. "Passport photos are generally shitty quality, it just has to *look* like you and then you need to look mostly like it."

They went around another circle. The amount of work they wanted to do might help with the identification, then getting through the security both at the airports and on entering France—where I'd need a visa. Fortunately, it would just be a tourist visa, still...

"What if we went the military ID route?" Lunchbox suggested and it was my turn to give him a bland look.

"No one is ever going to believe I was in the military." They were mountains, and I was definitely a molehill.

"Shortstop, don't think like that. Military is full of all types and tiny doesn't mean weak or powerless." He gave my nose a gentle tap.

"Thought about that," Voodoo said. "Problem is we don't want anyone side eyeing the ID, and military comes with its own preconceptions."

When Lunchbox handed me a tall, frothy and very green drink with a straw in it I raised my eyebrows.

"Smoothie, fruit—and the spinach and ginger you mentioned. High in antioxidants, got some proteins, plant protein not the heavier kind. Also some boosters. No extra added sugar." He managed to deliver the description without sounding too pained about it.

He wanted me to eat more and I just could not eat the sheer amount of food he prepared. Especially when I was so sedentary. The protein shakes were a compromise. One sip and I tested it. Not bad. The second sip was better. The third made me smile. "I like it."

His little fist pump was sweet.

"Thank you," I said, brushing a kiss to his jaw before I resumed happily sipping my drink.

"Anytime." He eyed the others. "So where are we?"

"Still trying to put a plan together." Irritation stroked through Voodoo's tone.

"Maybe we're making it too hard," I offered and that got all of their attention.

"How so?" The sharp firing the pair of syllables from Bones demanded a response.

"You want to make me *not* standout. That's a good idea, but...what if instead of changing my hair, we add some colorful extensions. Maybe purple or blue or both. Feather them through the hair. It's a bit of a pain in the ass, but doable. Then add some brighter cosmetics—like glitter and sparkle stuff."

Four pairs of eyes riveted on me and all of them skeptical.

"We want you to blend in so people don't look at you twice," Alphabet almost sounded like he was apologizing to me and I felt bad for laughing.

"I get that, I really do. But the thing is...standing out a lot makes you almost as invisible as if you don't stand out at all."

A sweep of their expressions didn't reveal any faith in that idea. Bones, however, folded his arms and focused on me. "Explain."

"All right," I said, before taking another long drink of the smoothie. It really was quite good. Licking the taste off my lips, I put the drink down and then spread my hands. "Everyone notices something different about other people, but most of us—at least here—are conditioned to look away, don't stare, don't comment, even when you video some altercation or whatever. People tend to avoid eye contact because horrors..." I clutched at my heart. "If you make eye contact, you might actually have to smile at that person or talk to them."

They were still frowning.

"Look, guys do eye contact with a woman either by accident, because they want her to notice them, or they have noticed her. Then if she doesn't respond, they get a couple of other reactions—most usual? 'You should smile more,' or 'What's wrong sweetheart? Where's the smile?'" I rolled my eyes. "Lots of people make jokes about it, but until you've been told fifteen times in one day that you should smile more or worse, snarled and pursued and told to smile more, you won't get it."

"Someone has actually snarled that at you?" Voodoo's tone dipped low and quiet.

"More than a few. Not the whole point right now," I said, waving that off. We didn't need to get bogged down in the weeds. "Bright hair colors, over the top cosmetics, even fun and fanciful clothes and jewelry are really popular. Do they get attention? Yes. But what do you think people see or say? Oh, did you see so and so at the airport? Or did you see that blue-haired chick? What about the lady with all the streaks?"

I spread my hands, eyebrows up as I glanced from one man to the other.

"They are looking at the plumage," Lunchbox said slowly. "Like most people can't describe what a peacock looks like, but they never miss the fan of feathers on a male. Most don't even realize the females *don't* have the fan tail."

"Exactly." I snapped my fingers and pointed at him. "If you want me to disappear, then we just need to make them look at some part of me that isn't associated with me at all. Adding the streaks, the glitter, and the fun clothes. Make me the peacock..."

"Then the rest of you fades." Bones finished the thought. While he didn't dismiss it all the way, he didn't seem fully convinced. "What if someone locks eyes with you and sees your face? What then?"

"Not an unfair question."

"Thank you." His voice was dry as the desert, but I shrugged that off.

"Have you ever met a celebrity before? Or better, run into someone you knew from work, but you're seeing someone else entirely and utterly out of context?"

"Context defines expectations." Alphabet leaned back in his chair. "Guys from base, guys we used to work with—we were always in uniform or fatigues, drop them into civvies..."

"They don't quite *fit* the context." Voodoo nodded. "That's almost uncomfortable in its simplicity."

I shrugged. "Too much noise. There's so much media, whether it's on our phones or on the wall screens around us or whatever. Then you throw in huge crowds of people all trying to get from point a to point b. You don't go sight-seeing in an airport. You're going to drop your luggage, get through security and get to the damn plane in time. You don't notice other people unless they are in your way, and even then, you're more likely to walk around them than focus on their looks."

"Accepted," Bones said after a protracted moment. "That doesn't account for cameras and surveillance. What about the one person who *does* notice you?"

"You already wanted to shift my features a little. Add a little weight to my face, maybe a beauty mark. If we do the contouring just right, it can help with the facial recognition, in theory it shouldn't matter as long as *I* match whatever identification I'm carrying."

They weren't dismissing it out of hand, but they were frowning. None of them liked it.

"It's not perfect." How could it be? I reclaimed my smoothie. "I don't think anything can be perfect. You want to go to France, you don't want me traveling as me—which is good cause I don't actually *have* my passport or my driver's license." Or credit cards or anything else.

At some point, I would need to deal with that. My credit was probably already well on its way to being fucked and my apartment gone. For now? I could fix those things if I were alive to fix them.

"What do you need to do this?" Voodoo asked and I dug out my phone.

"Let me find some examples. I have no idea where you can get it all here, but maybe we can get most of it." I settled down, taking sips of my smoothie while I searched. There was something about having a phone in my hand and actively looking for something that would help all of us.

It took just under an hour to put together a list of everything I could think of. When I passed the phone over to Voodoo, he studied the supplies.

"I'll have to head into town, probably a couple of them. We might have to make do..."

"If you can only find like blond or white extensions, grab some crazy hair colors. I can dye them if they are real hair. Fake hair won't hold the color, but it's still doable."

He nodded. It took him a minute to send my list to himself before he handed me the phone.

"I'd offer to go with you to look but probably not safe for that yet."

"Probably not," he said, with a small smile. "But we're working on getting you out of here, Firecracker. Right..." He looked to the guys. "I'm going to get these, text me with any additions."

Then he was gone, and it was just the four of us left. The weight of Bones' regard settled heavily on me.

"Are you sure this is how you want to do it?" It almost sounded like there was just a hint of concern in his chilly tone.

I shrug and says, "Have a better idea?"

"Not at the moment. Unless it involves leaving you here." That had come up already. Lunchbox and Alphabet both glared at him, but I shrugged.

"That puts you a man down. You guys already decided that. None of you have been to these parties or dealt with Maurizio before. I have. I also speak the language. Fluently."

"So you've said." He rubbed his jaw. "The rules still stand. You do what you're told, stay where you're told and if we say go or run, you do it, no questions or arguments."

"Acceptable," I said, mimicking his tone. "For now."

Lunchbox turned but not before I caught his smile or Alphabet's soft huff of laughter. I met Bones' bland stare with one of my own.

"Well, I guess we're going to find out then. Ping me when Voodoo is back."

Relief had me sagging. Up until this moment, I hadn't been one hundred percent sure we would find a way. But we had and they were willing to do this.

I looked at the remaining pair. "So, what do we do while we wait?"

"Biometrics," Alphabet said and tapped the sofa next to him. "Come here..."

I'd finished the smoothie and Lunchbox claimed the empty cup from me. "You guys work on that. I'm going to work on food. Then we'll look at packing everyone for the trip."

"This is going to work," I told Alphabet as I sat next to him and he shot me an amused look.

"You know this, because?"

"Because it has to."

It *had* to.

CHAPTER
TWENTY-SEVEN

GRACE

"Merci," I told the attendant as she brought us fresh coffees and a light breakfast. We would be landing soon and they were giving us time to freshen up. I suppose it shouldn't have surprised me that we were traveling business. I would have thought coach or even premium coach would have been less conspicuous.

Voodoo, however, eyed me when I'd asked after we checked in at the Toronto airport for our flight. "We could make do if we had to, but I'd rather be able to stretch out."

Well, I couldn't fault him there. They were all tall men with damn near a foot or more on me. So, yes, the desire to stretch their legs made sense. Also, I would never mind being able to lay my seat down and nap.

For all that I thought I would have trouble sleeping, I'd drifted right off. Voodoo woke me with a brush of his knuckles to my cheek. That gave me a few minutes to use the facilities, check my appearance, and brush my teeth.

Cosmetics held up and so did the extensions with their

streaks. It was funny, I'd never thought about putting blue, purple, and fuchsia streaks in my hair, but I kind of liked it.

I added a faux nose ring. It had taken a little time to get used to, but it was also fun. Beyond the hair, the jewelry, and the cosmetics, I'd gone for a little more of a brash look.

The black sleeveless tank coupled with a padded bra gave me a bigger boob profile. The black lace leggings looked painted on with the purple plaid skirt just this side of being too short. The knee high Doc Martens with their platforms also gave me an extra couple of inches of height.

It was all about the packaging.

Bones had given me a long hard look when I walked out wearing it before we all split up and I shrugged. "No one is looking at my face."

I swore his lips twitched. The stone face of his might have cracked if he'd given in to the desire. He definitely looked like he almost smiled. "You have a point."

Splitting up would draw less attention to us. Initially, I thought that meant we'd just be flying separately on the same flight, but the guys had their own flights and travel plans.

The coffee was strong, dark, and tasted a bit like nirvana. A bubble of excitement shivered through me the closer we got to Paris. With my new ID listing me as Canadian, I was traveling as Monet Morel. Monet for Amorette and Morel because Noir would have been too on the nose.

Voodoo had me calling him Harry for the flight and when I'd teased him about it being Houdini, he'd just grinned. Before too long, they cleared away the dishes and we were getting ready for landing. The excitement threading through me seemed *inappropriate* and, yet, we were on the move.

We were doing *something*. That *something* was important. It was another step on the path to finding Amorette.

My stomach bounced a little as the plane wheels touched down. The taxiing didn't take all that long and then we were deplaning. Voodoo grabbed my carryon bag from the overhead and gave me a gentle nudge. I had a purse strung crosswise over my torso and a hoodie that I'd tied around my waist.

"Mare See Bow Coop." The *horrendous* French from Voodoo had my eyes bugging a little and I gaped at him. He nodded cheerfully to the attendants who were welcoming us to Paris and thanking us for flying with them.

Fortunately, amusement filled their faces as I offered up a swift apology for his "joke." "*Merci pour le vol et ignorez son accent, ce n'était pas en mal.*"

They waved us on our way and then Voodoo's hand clasped mine once we were through the jet bridge.

"They appreciated my humor just fine, Firecracker," he teased and I snorted even as we linked fingers. He also shortened his stride. Even with extra height afforded by the Doc Martens, my legs were still nowhere near as long as his.

"Maybe," I said, shaking my head. "But it just sounded so *bad*."

"Well, not all of us have your very talented tongue." The playful wiggle of his brows had me snapping my mouth closed with a click, even as a snort of laughter escaped me.

"You're terrible."

"Yes, I am," he said with a grin before raising my hand to kiss the knuckles. "And you're laughing. So it's all good."

Passport control was ahead and they had e-gates which was always nice. We followed the others in the queue but had to split up because Voodoo traveled on a U.S. passport and I had Canadian.

"See you on the other side," he said, then winked. His confidence helped. He held onto my carry-on, which was fine. There were more Canadians in the line than Americans. We flew out of Toronto, so that made sense.

Still, I waited patiently for my turn and focused on *not* freaking out. Everything would be fine. I had my passport out at the gate and then set it down and looked up at the camera.

For what seemed like an eternity that couldn't have been longer than a few seconds, I stared at myself on the screen circled by the red light. The moment it flashed green, I blew out a breath and collected my passport. Voodoo waited for me not even a dozen steps away.

"Relax," he murmured as he draped an arm over my shoulders. "Told you it would be fine."

A laugh bubbled up out of me. "This shouldn't be fun."

"Who says? Hmm?"

"I—" Well, I didn't have an answer for that. Not really. "This is serious."

"Sure, but that doesn't mean we can't have some fun, Firecracker. You liked the flight right?"

"Yeah. It was comfortable."

"Slept well?" He pressed as we continued on our way to baggage claim.

"Better than I expected." I hadn't thought I would sleep at all.

"The food was good." That wasn't a question.

"I liked the portions," I retorted and that earned me a laugh from him. "But yes, it was good."

"Now we're here, in Paris. We're going to get ourselves a couple of funky t-shirts after we grab our luggage and then we'll head out."

We weren't planning to stay in Paris at all. I glanced at my watch. "Do you know when their flights land?"

"I do," he said, then ducked his head down to murmur, "don't worry. I mean it. We'll see them soon enough. Everything is fine."

Right. Everything was fine.

By the time we got to our carousel, the luggage coming out was from our flight. It didn't take long for us to collect the luggage and bypass customs because we had nothing to declare.

Once into the arrivals area, Voodoo let me pull my own suitcase as we wandered down to a couple of the gift shops. I had to laugh, he'd been serious about tacky shirts. But we grabbed them. We lingered for a bit, then he nudged us outside.

Not even ten minutes passed before a car pulled up to the curb with Lunchbox behind the wheel. He flashed a grin at us as Bones slid out from the passenger side. He grabbed the extra bags and the guys got them loaded as I climbed into the backseat.

"Hi," Lunchbox said over his shoulder. "Good flight?"

"How did you guys get here so fast?" I thought we were on the first flight.

He chuckled. "Luck of the draw. Or maybe we bumped up to an earlier flight. They had the room."

"Huh. Good flight?"

"Not so bad. You?"

Before I could answer him, Voodoo slid in next to me as Bones climbed into the passenger seat.

"Alphabet is two hours out," Bones said over his shoulder. "We rented a small apartment. We'll take you there and you can shower and change if you want. Once he's in, we'll head out again."

I blew out a breath. That fit our plans, even if we were hooking up sooner than I expected. "Are we driving down?"

"No," Voodoo said. "We'll get another car once we're there, but I need to work on sourcing some supplies." He checked his watch, then leaned forward as Lunchbox navigated us out of the airport. "If we have two hours for Alphabet and Goblin, give me another ninety minutes to get everything lined up. Then we can go."

"We can juggle," Bones said. "Grace can head south with Lunchbox and Alphabet, I'll stay with you and we'll meet them in place."

Voodoo grimaced, then nodded once. Leaning back, he glanced at me. "Lose the highlights, take your hair up into a ponytail, scrub the makeup, or take it real low key and then put on the tourist gear."

"She's gonna look like a teenager," Bones muttered.

I resisted the urge to stick my tongue out at him— barely. "I can look a little more college. Don't worry." I glanced down at Doc Martens. The lace leggings would have to go and I had some running shoes in my bags. Jeans, t-shirt, running shoes, and ponytail. I could make it work.

"Do you have a baseball hat for her?" Bones asked as he glanced over his shoulder and I felt more than saw the way he swept his gaze over me.

"I got something," Lunchbox said, handling the Paris traffic like he was a native. "Don't worry about it." He flicked a look at me in the rearview. "Still got your phone and earbuds?"

I grinned. "Yes." Now that I had them, I was *not* risking losing them. I may not have anyone to call right now, but I *loved* having the access.

"Get them ready, that way you can 'tune' us out if you need to." Then he winked. Warmth unfurled in my belly and I forced out another long breath. The flirting was... *nice*. I probably shouldn't be focusing on that.

"If we take a train instead of a car, I want to grab a couple of books." I'd kill for something new to read.

"We'll take care of it," he said, then Voodoo leaned forward to murmur with Bones. The occasional word like weapon and supplies drifted toward me. They were likely working out where to pick up the items they needed.

The place they had was an apartment on the top floor of a lovely building in the 19th Arrondissement. Bones and Voodoo slipped out to offload our luggage and Lunchbox twisted back to look at me.

"Still have a few more hours of travel to go, so pace yourself. But a shower always helps after a long flight." The advice was sweet.

"This, I actually do know." I put a hand on his shoulder. "You're coming back with Alphabet? And Goblin?"

"Can't keep me away. Don't let Voodoo talk you into bed, we won't be that long."

I snorted. "You forget, I've seen Paris traffic. But I'll be ready by the time you guys get here. Promise."

"Looking forward to it." Then my door opened and Voodoo stood there with a hand out for me. "See you when we're back!"

He brushed his fingers over my hand. My stomach clenched a little, but then I was out and I took hold of my own overnight bag from Voodoo.

"I can carry both of them if you're going to get both suitcases." Not that I thought he would go for it and his bland look said no, he wasn't.

Bones didn't say a word before he climbed back into the SUV and then they were pulling away from the curb and heading back to the airport.

"Think they have an elevator?" I asked as we went inside.

"They do," Voodoo told me. "It'll be a squeeze though."

He wasn't kidding, but then I didn't mind leaning back against him after he closed the gate and hit the button for the top floor. The ride was slow, but steady.

"Good thing we can handle cozy," I teased.

"True," he said, then slid a hand over my hip.

"Ah-ah-ah." I clasped my hand over his and pulled it back up to my waist. "Lunchbox said no hanky panky."

"Did he?" Voodoo mused. "Interesting."

Five minutes later in the apartment, Voodoo picked me up and carried me toward the shower. "Too bad for Lunchbox he isn't here to enforce that rule..."

I laughed. "We have to be ready when they get back."

"Don't worry, Firecracker. We will be."

TWENTY-EIGHT

ALPHABET

The flight had been delayed, but we made up some time once we were in the air. Goblin wasn't the biggest fan of the length. Not that I could blame him. It wasn't my favorite either. Fortunately, his service dog vest kept others from trying to pet him since he was "working." At least we both managed to relax some.

Arrival went smoothly, with the cabin crew allowing me to deplane first. Normally, I preferred to not take any advantages when it came to my prosthetic. Still, it was kinder for Goblin if we cleared the terminal and found a place for him to pee.

Also, I was more than a little stiff after the time spent on the flight. Goblin and I went through passport control swiftly enough. I had his travel papers in order and special permissions. Once we had my bag, I followed the route to the nearest pet relief area. While he emptied his bladder, I sent a message to the guys.

Their acknowledgement said they would be at arrivals

in ten. The pickup was appreciated but I needed to stretch. "Hopefully, before we get on the train…" Still, the sooner we got to the French Riviera, the sooner we could track down the jackass who wanted to "buy" Grace.

Disappointment speared me that she wasn't in the car, but Bones confirmed they had arrived safe and sound. They'd also left her and Voodoo at the apartment. It took more than an hour to get through the snarl of traffic, but then we were there and I got a good look at her.

Her smile relaxed all the tension in my spine and eased more than a few aches. Before we took the journey south, Bones and Voodoo had supplies to gather, including some we needed in case of fast extraction. Backups and weapons would be useful too. It was better for them to take the time now and since three traveled less conspicuously than five, we would go ahead. They would be a few hours or more behind us and arrive via an alternate route.

That was fine.

Three hours later, I walked with Grace and Goblin as much to let him stretch his legs as for me. Lunchbox was going ahead to take our luggage to the train. We would catch up soon enough. There was a metro we could take, and Grace knew the language and the routes.

"You okay?" The quiet question tugged at me. Grace was dressed in capri pants, an *I heart Paris* shirt, unzipped hoodie, and running shoes. She had sunglasses tucked into her shirt collar, a dark hat on to shade her eyes, her hair pulled back into a ponytail and she was absolutely stunning.

"I'm fine," I frowned. "Am I being too quiet?"

"No." A smile softened her expression. "You were just frowning and Goblin keeps checking on you."

"Oh." I shook off the malaise and paused to give Goblin

a good scratch. "Sorry—to both of you—I was just thinking plans, routes, and train schedules."

"Really exciting stuff," she said with a slow nod and just a hint of teasing.

"It can be, especially since I have the best partner in crime."

"Goblin is the MVP." She delivered the line without an ounce of irony and I had to chuckle.

"That's difficult to argue." Since she seemed to want to play, I said, "You're not so bad yourself."

"Ha." Her derisive snort dissolved into a hint of a smirk while her eyes danced with humor. "I'm practically perfect."

"Oh, yeah?" It was my turn to scoff. "Practically means *virtually*, you know."

"It also means *almost*." The retort was a good one. The breeze was a bit muggy, but the sun felt good and so did the walk. Goblin also seemed a lot happier.

"Almost perfect, then?" I tested the sound of it with a slow nod. "That works." She laughed and when I offered her an arm, she threaded hers through mine.

The train ride was a lot more entertaining than the flight. Lunchbox brought out the cards since our seats had a table. Grace turned out to be a cutthroat poker player. We were going to lose our shirts if we kept playing this way.

It would be near nightfall local time when we reached the rental, and we would be a long day away from when our planes landed. Despite her yawns, Grace skipped taking a nap even when we offered. "Better for the body clock if I just reset to whatever time zone I'm in. That means lots of hydration, exercise, eat light—too much heavy food makes me wanna nap."

"You travel a lot," Lunchbox said as he reshuffled the cards.

"You could say that. I've done several time zone hops in a few weeks. It just helps to make myself stick it out, then sleep when it's nighttime. Doesn't mean I don't get jet lag, but it works for me."

"That makes sense. I trained my body clock a long time ago to sleep on command." At her incredulous look, I shrugged. "When you might have just a limited time for sleep, you take it where you can get it. That means if I have an hour, I sleep for that hour. It's a mindset."

"What he said," Lunchbox said with a wave toward me. "So... you want to play another round?"

"I don't know," she teased, eyebrows raised. "You're both out of snacks to bet."

"Guess we need to up the stakes..."

"Or we could buy more," she said as the cart and steward came up the aisle.

"Or, you're right, we *could* buy more," Lunchbox said with a grin at me and I laughed. "M&Ms?"

"Oh yeah," she said with a nod. "Chocolate is definitely a win."

IT WAS WELL after dark before we got to the house itself. The place Voodoo lined up was a little ritzier than I would have gone for. It was also a *lot* warmer here. At the end of the drive, Lunchbox entered the code into a box and the fancy, curved pair of wrought-iron gates swung open in near silence. They looked more like they were designed for art and not security.

I just shook my head. Once up at the house, Lunchbox

did a full interior sweep before we took care of offloading our suitcases. We both nudged Grace away when she tried to help. "Take Goblin for a walk around?"

"Trying to get rid of me?" The arch comment made me snort.

"Not a chance in hell. Go on. Both of you take a walk. It'll be good for you."

A flash of her earlier smile returned and she called Goblin. When I motioned to him, he trotted off to follow her. I wasn't the only one watching her go.

Lunchbox paused then glanced at me. "You good?"

"Not according to my mother." Then I hauled another of the suitcases out. "You already find a good spot for me to work?"

"Yeah, downstairs dining room. It's central, you have good eye lines on the doors and we can secure them."

Excellent.

By the time Grace came back in, we had the suitcases lined up and open in the dining room. We removed various pieces of my computer so I could rebuild it. Yes, I had a laptop, but I wanted a more powerful machine. The hard drive was in my backpack. The motherboard had been in Grace's.

"It's a lovely place," Grace said as she moved to help us with the unpacking.

"It's definitely colorful." Lunchbox glanced at his watch and I got it. Bones and Voodoo were running late. "Why don't you get a swim?"

There was a swimming pool visible right through the glass doors. It was definitely warm enough for it.

"I didn't pack a suit," she said as she pulled out another plastic wrapped piece for the computer's fan. After she handed it to me, she studied Lunchbox. "If you guys need to talk, you can just tell me you need some time and I can go find a room."

"We're not trying to get rid of you," I told her. The ease around her eyes relaxed me some. She believed me. I'd meant what I said about telling her I couldn't answer something rather than lying about it. "But I have to build my comp. Lunchbox is going to want to check what's in the kitchen and he may have to do a supply run. The guys are late, and you've been traveling all day. A swim might be nice. You don't need a suit, or you can swim in your bra and panties. I promise to only peek a little when I'm not working."

The corners of her mouth twitched and somewhere in the villa, the air conditioning hummed to life. Good, I didn't see the need to sweat our way through anything. When she flicked a look at Lunchbox, he nodded almost solemnly.

"I don't promise not to peek or stare as long as you don't mind us seeing." It was the absolute right response to take with her, the curve at the corners of her mouth deepened.

She scraped her teeth over her lower lip, head tilting from side to side as if she were in silent debate with herself. "You're both sure I can't do anything right now?"

"For the moment," I told her. "Once I have my system set up and the guys are here, we'll go over the plan again." I straightened and stretched. At the moment, a swim actually did sound good.

"Okay." She grabbed her carry-on and headed upstairs. "I'm going to pick the best room."

Lunchbox chuckled at the declaration, then slid a look at me. "You're good with her."

"Told her no more lies." It wasn't about being good.

"It's about being honest. She's dealing with a lot. Too much. I've been there."

Between the physical and emotional damage, there was also the mental. She needed to be able to trust us and the only way to do that was to be a part of the solution.

"Yeah." He sighed then raked a hand through his hair. "They're late."

"I noticed. Then again, it's France. Voodoo had to source a few things and if they ended up driving further, then they did. Not worrying about it unless they miss check-in."

That was midnight and still—I checked my watch—another three and a half hours away.

"I might head into town and get us food..." He trailed off as the chine went off indicating a door opened. I glanced toward the back wall of windows and the now open door where a slim Grace dove right into the pool. "Fuck."

"Put it back in your pants," I advised, even if a pulse of interest had bounced right to my dick at the vision of her slim body, unbroken by anything as prosaic as underwear. "We told her she didn't need a suit."

"Yeah, there's telling then there's seeing." He blew out a breath. Goblin was sprawled on the tile near the door, keeping watch on her and me. "Right. You want anything specific to eat?"

"Nah, just whatever. I want to get the machine built. Then we need to get eyes on this jackass."

"Agreed."

∽

Voodoo and Bones arrived near eleven, gear and supplies with them. Grace looked relieved when Lunchbox said they were at the gate. After her swim, she'd showered and changed then came down to eat with us.

Instead of going to bed, despite how tired she was, she stayed up as we worked and kept watch. Her presence helped soothe me and Goblin. I wasn't that worried, but the last thing we needed was something to go wrong right now.

We could and would handle anything, but that didn't mean I wanted her in the middle of another clusterfuck. Voodoo's arrival pulled a real smile out of her, one that didn't quite dim when she glanced at Bones.

After offloading, Lunchbox brought out more food and Bones said, "It's a little late to get started tonight. We can scout tomorrow, do the pickup in the evening."

"Pickup?" Grace asked from where she sat cross legged on the floor with Goblin snoring against her lap. Lucky little shit had settled right in with her. "I thought we'd all be going."

We had discussed that. But the plan also required some refining, including getting into Gallo's security.

"If we were just planning on killing him," Lunchbox said. "Then we could all go, but it wouldn't be that much of a trip. Right now, we need answers—*you* need answers. If you're there and he's stupid, his chances of survival are nil and then we're out the answers. Better plan all around for us to scoop him up and bring him back."

Clear. Factual. Straightforward.

Grace studied all of us for a beat then nodded. "That does sound reasonable. Are we still running okay on time?"

"Yes," Bones answered. "We all need rest and Alphabet has some work to do. Tomorrow, we'll do some recon. We'll refine our plan then."

A message came through on my phone and I stared at it.

"It's Doc," I told them and pulled on my headset before I called him back.

Conversation continued with the others, but I tuned it out as I focused on Doc's request. He needed information on a place and more on a person.

Gracie let out a laugh then spritzed Lunchbox with water from her bottle. Goblin was up and while he didn't bark, he was keeping an eye on them. It took me a minute or two longer than necessary, but I got Doc what he needed.

"C'mon, Firecracker," Voodoo said, holding out a hand to her. "Show me which room you picked."

Lunchbox snorted softly and Bones just shook his head, but I got it. She had bad dreams. She trusted Voodoo with them.

"Doc good?" Bones asked after they went upstairs and I lifted my chin.

"For now." The information I gave him had satisfied him for now. "If he needs more..."

I didn't have to finish that because Lunchbox just bumped his fist to my shoulder. If he needed anything, including us, we'd go.

Now, I focused on Maurizio Gallo and his place here. I had some work to do and the guys needed sleep. Goblin settled at my feet and propped his head against my left foot. The low snores vibrated up my leg, but I just let my mind settle into the work.

CHAPTER

TWENTY-NINE

Dawn came swiftly, too swiftly. Normally, I objected to being awake so early unless I had a shoot. Even then, I wasn't a fan but I did my job. Every noise in the night had roused me. Instead of bad dreams waking me, I'd spent most of my night blinking awake as though I had not slept at all.

I would have objected today as well, but it was Voodoo sliding to the edge of the bed that woke me this time. He turned his head, glancing at me over his shoulder. "You should go back to sleep if you can."

Pushing up on my elbows, I shook my head. "I don't know that I can."

"You didn't sleep much last night." Twisting, he frowned at me.

"If you know that, then you didn't either." I meant it as a joke, but my yawn punched that out of it. "Sorry."

"Nothing to be sorry about..." He slid a hand toward me

but a light knock on the door stilled him and he sighed. "It's open," he said even as he stood.

It was Lunchbox who stuck his head inside. "Food is up." He glanced at me. "Morning, Gracie."

"Morning," I said, smothering another yawn. "Is there coffee?"

"There is, but if you want to go back to sleep…"

"She's not," Voodoo told him as he snagged a t-shirt and pulled it over his head. The muscles on his back rippled with each motion. "Mission anxiety."

"Familiar." Lunchbox shot me a look of sympathy. "Come on down then, I'll fix you something too."

The idea of food was utterly unpalatable, but I pushed the blankets back and slid out of the bed. I was already in a t-shirt, and I just needed to pull on shorts. The sun was up outside, and if it was as warm today as it had been the day before, I wouldn't need much else.

Voodoo held the door for me, but closed it as I got there and stole my breath with a quick kiss. "Hmm," he murmured against my lips. "Better than coffee."

Heat scalded my cheeks. "I haven't brushed my teeth."

"No?" He looked thoughtful, then swooped in for another kiss. This time, he licked the seam of my lips apart to plunge inside and tease my tongue with his own. I forgot all about brushing teeth or even why morning breath wasn't pleasant.

Voodoo tasted like a hint of peppermint, and then all him. The sensuous movement of his mouth against mine had me straining upward and my nipples going hard as I braced a hand against his chest.

When he dragged out my lower lip with his teeth, a shudder of pleasure danced through me. "Hmm. Tastes too good to be ignored." Then he winked at me and opened the bedroom door again. "Breakfast?"

The teasing notes in his voice excited me. His kiss had also chased away the shadows. "It did taste good." The man definitely deserved a compliment. "Though, I have to admit… not sure it quite tops coffee." I darted out under his arm as I said the last.

His little growl was absolutely delightful. Once I was downstairs though some of my good mood evaporated. Bones and Lunchbox were in the kitchen, but there was no sign of Alphabet or of Goblin. Hopefully, he was getting some sleep.

Bones gave me a long look as I padded barefoot into the kitchen, then his gaze went past me and seemed to chill even further. Whatever his problem was at the moment, though, it didn't seem to be with me. I followed my nose to the cup of straight up coffee.

No espresso.

Well, I wasn't going to complain. Lunchbox had prepared a little feast and considering how piled up the guys' plates were, I didn't protest even though I just stuck to scrambled eggs and plain toast.

The mournful look on Lunchbox's face almost made me laugh. *Almost.* Then his words from the night before wandered back through my head.

If Maurizio was stupid with me, he wouldn't survive. Lunchbox had said it so matter-of-fact and no one contradicted him. I couldn't help the little thrill that went through me at the blunt declaration.

Bloodthirsty? Maybe.

But after the past few weeks? There was also some real comfort in his words. Even more in the sentiment.

"We'll be leaving within the hour," Bones said. "It's

early, but we want to scout the location of the yacht as well as his villa. We need to get a look at his security and the number of people around him."

It took me a minute to realize he was talking to me. "Is there a strict timetable? I'm sure Alphabet already knows."

"Yes and no," Lunchbox answered. "We know where *we'll* be starting and what we need to know. Everything after that is TBD. We'll keep you both in the loop."

"However," Bones said, "regardless of schedule, we won't be back with Gallo until well after dark, unless he just decides to fall in our laps."

"It's worth mentioning that the last time I was around Maurizio, he preferred to entertain and play cards or even just drink and enjoy his pipes or cigars until well after one in the morning. Maybe it would be easier to take him in the afternoon? They are probably napping then to prepare for the evening."

"Too many eyes," Bones told me. "There are issues with acquiring a target after dark, but the risks and the chances for discovery often double if we do it in the light of day."

I nodded then took another sip of my coffee. They were almost done with their food. When they started to rinse off their dishes, I said, "I can do the dishes if you want. My contribution."

"You're contributing just fine," Voodoo told me, then dipped his head to drop a kiss on my lips. "If you can go back to sleep, do it. Tonight is going to be a long one."

My stomach clenched. "He might have answers."

"He *might*." Bones emphasized that last word as Voodoo brushed a hand against my cheek.

"I know, don't get my hopes up." Message received.

"We'll know what he knows, Grace," Bones said. "You have my word on that. Nudge Alphabet and let's go." Then he pivoted and headed out. It didn't take long for the chime of the door to signal his exit. The guys were all dressed in slacks or jeans, lightweight shirts, linen and everyone had sunglasses.

They looked like tourists. That was the point I guessed. Voodoo headed back upstairs.

"Hey," Lunchbox squatted next to my chair. "You have your phone and our contacts."

I patted the pocket of my shorts. "I do."

"Good, it'll work here too. If anything happens—*anything* and you need us back, call any of us. Even if we don't answer, we'll see the call and we'll come."

I blew out a breath and some of the tension wrapping me up tight eased. "So only call if there is a real emergency."

"That would be the plan. If we get a call from you, we're aborting the mission and coming straight back here." He lifted his hand and paused until I nodded. Then he cupped my cheek. The light stroke of his thumb against my skin had my pulse racing.

"Be careful?" It was as much a question as it was a caution.

"We'll be fine, Gracie. Look after Alphabet and Goblin."

Some of my apprehension fled. "I can do that."

"I know you can." Then he pressed a kiss to my lips and held it there. A surge of rioting emotions flooded me. The kiss was both sweet and passionate. A promise and an assurance. When he leaned back, he gave me a long look then he rose and his gaze flicked to behind me. "Ready?"

"Yep," Voodoo said. "Alphabet and Goblin will be down in a few." Fresh alarm flooded me when he paused as the front door chimed signaling Lunchbox had left the house. I glanced up at him. We were—something and he'd just seen

Lunchbox kiss me. "Don't look so worried, Firecracker. I don't mind if Lunchbox kisses you, as long as you don't mind."

"No?" Oh that came out a little warbly and feeble. I shook off the panic. "Take two, you don't?"

"Nope. He tell you to call any of us if you need us or something goes wrong?"

"He did and he said you didn't have to answer, if you saw the call, you'd drop everything and come back." The fact that two of them were emphasizing the point worried me a little. "Is Alphabet okay?"

"Yes. But we're keeping you in the loop, as promised. We don't expect anything to go wrong but only a fool assumes *nothing* will happen." The deadpan delivery only seemed to underscore the sentiment.

"Got it. Do I say good luck?"

"Good hunting." Then with a caress to my cheek, he headed out. They left through the front door and the chime signaled his exit.

My heart was a fist in my chest. Glancing down at the food I hadn't finished, I wrapped my hands around the coffee cup. They were going to find a way to kidnap Maurizio so he could answer *my* questions.

Had he done something to Amorette? I'd always thought of him as harmless. Pushy but harmless. Yet, we'd flown thousands of miles to pick him up and find the truth.

And I... I was really ready for them to do that. To find out what he knew.

But what if he didn't know anything? What if Maurizio wasn't involved? My stomach dropped and an icy heat spread over my skin. What then?

After downing the last of the coffee, I rose and carried my plate to the sink. There was a covered plate on a warmer. Food for Alphabet. I took care of the few dishes that were still there and scraped off the last of my eggs into the trash. Even the thought of eating them made me feel ill.

I took my time washing the dishes. Once they were done, I wasn't sure what I would do next. Thankfully, the sound of claws clicking against the wood told me I was about to have company.

I was drying my hands on a dish towel when they arrived in the kitchen. I'd even found my smile when I turned around. What took some effort became genuine as Goblin trotted over to me eagerly, tail wagging and I got a good look at the very rumpled, hair askew Alphabet.

"You know they make combs," I murmured and he gave me a grunt in response. "There's also coffee."

Not that I needed to tell him that, he was already making a beeline for the pot.

"Want me to let Goblin out?"

Another grunt.

And I thought *I* wasn't a morning person.

"I got it. They left you food there, too. Going to take him out back. Maybe we can walk him later."

Alphabet gave me a bleary look. I swore I could see the processing sign circling in front of him before he nodded.

"I'll be back, c'mon, Goblin. You can eat after you pee." The dog checked with Alphabet before he followed me. The yard wasn't that large. It was more of a terraced garden, but it had grass. Just meant we needed to clean up his crap.

The air was cool and the breeze came straight from the sea. The Mediterranean was visible over the roofs of the houses below. Our villa sat fairly high up. I could see the boats in the harbor. The sun had me shading my eyes, but I also tilted my face back to let the warmth hit me.

It was picture perfect and it seemed almost hollow to

enjoy it considering why we were here. Goblin took care of his business swiftly. "Good boy," I praised when he trotted back to me.

He led me back into the house and I glanced back at the ocean before following him. Alphabet was in the kitchen, right where I left him. Only now, he drank coffee and ate his food. The pot had been emptied but he'd started another.

Goblin's food was also down and he made a beeline for it. When the coffee finished brewing, I filled a fresh cup for myself and then stared at Alphabet, waiting for him to wake up the rest of the way.

Because I really needed something to do or I was going to lose my mind.

THIRTY

GRACE

"You can take a swim again if you want," Alphabet suggested from where he was downing his second cup of coffee and studying his laptop screen. They'd wired three other monitors to it so he had a full screen display, though not quite the high definition for his system at home.

Folding my arms, I leaned against the opening that separated the dining room from the living area and beyond to the patio and the pool. "Think I'll skinny dip in the sunshine where you can get a better view?"

The corner of his mouth quirked. "That's what we call a perk. But no…" He held his right hand up to shoulder height and covered the nail of his pinky finger with his thumb with the three middle fingers straight up. "Scout's Honor, not the reason I suggested it."

A laugh escaped me. "Tell me I can do something to help you."

The devilish gleam in his blue eyes twisted me up

inside. The heady combo of pleasure and apprehension had me sucking in a deeper breath of air.

"Too easy, Gracie-girl," he said on a laugh.

"I am *not*," I retorted with a sniff. Haughty wasn't my specialty but I could certainly pull off snob if I tried hard enough.

That snapped his interested gaze back to me. "Really? That sounds like a challenge to me."

The temptation to roll my eyes was right there, but I settled for a careless shrug. "You never know."

His low whistle was a reward in and of itself. "Noted." Then he huffed out a breath. "As for helping, not a lot to do right now." With a glance at his watch, he leaned back in the chair. "Really isn't a lot for us to do until they start sending me info. Scouting and collection takes time."

Right. "Then you don't need to be stuck right there, do you?"

I didn't miss how he stretched his right leg out. Now that I was more aware of the prosthesis, it proved more challenging to not see how his right foot didn't shift when he stretched.

"No," he said slowly before taking another long drink of coffee. "I want to get a few programs up and running so I'm doing my own scouting." Lips pursed, he glanced at the computer. "I figured I'd do some more deep diving on your sister's law firm while we had the downtime."

My heart did a little fist bump with my ribs. "Can you set your bot thingies to do it?"

His eyebrows rose. "My bot thingies." The corners of his lips were twitching. "Yes, I can set the bots to skim and search. They'll collect information, but I'll still need to go through it." He downed the last of his coffee and then set the mug down. "Why?"

"Cause then you can come swimming with me." Honestly, that hadn't been the offer I intended to make. I'd been thinking of getting him out of the house and going for a walk. We could take Goblin for one, it would do all of us some good.

The pool might be a lot better, though. The swim I'd indulged in the night before had helped... a lot. So, I didn't amend the offer. Surprise filtered through his eyes and he blinked, then glanced from me to the pool then back again.

"I didn't bring a suit either," he warned in a careful voice. It wasn't his voice that concerned me though, it was the shadow sliding over his expression. I wasn't sure if it was uncertainty, fear, or something else. The fact it existed at all twisted my heart.

"Look, AB, if you have to do the skinny dip, then I can too," I offered, determined to give him options. "If you want to use your boxers or briefs—really not sure what you wear but, whatever. I can grab a bra and panties. You're right, they're basically a bikini."

His continued hesitation however had my stomach bottoming out.

"No pressure, though." The last thing I wanted to do was make him uncomfortable. "If you really don't want to swim, we can take Goblin for a walk. It's going to be hotter this afternoon, but it's still beautiful."

"I don't mind swimming with you." The way he tested the words suggested he wasn't one hundred percent certain of the response. "Just..."

He dropped his glance, his attention seemingly returning to the computer screens. Somehow, I didn't think he was actually looking at them so much as through them.

The hesitation raked at me. Did I push him or did I wait? Did I try to offer to let him off the hook again? Indecisiveness twisted around me like barbed wire and it dug into my soul, gouging out wounds.

"AB," I said, finally, unable to let him hang out there alone. "You don't have to do anything you don't want to do. I was trying to offer you a break. Once they start sending data and make the move later, you're going to be glued to the computer." I licked my lips. "So, you do what you need to do and don't worry about me, okay? I'll help if I can, you just tell me what you need when you need it."

Then I pivoted to head back to the room where my stuff was. I was going to change into a sports bra and fresh panties. We didn't have sunscreen, I didn't think, so I needed to pay attention to the time out there.

Once I was upstairs, the wild cadence of my heart had my breath coming in shallow bursts. The last thing I wanted to do was hurt Alphabet.

The black with the criss cross straps in the back and support in the front looked like a swim tank. The panties were a little more lace than not, but I went with it. I grabbed a towel from the bathroom and tied it around my hips before descending the stairs.

Staying up in my room wasn't an option. If I hid away after what I'd said then I'd be lying. Our "honesty" truce had brought us a long way. Alphabet stood shirtless in the living room when I got down there. The stance caught me off guard, particularly with the top button on his jeans being undone riveted me until I forced my gaze up.

His eyes are up there, Grace. The internal stern reprimand didn't help as much as I would have liked. It was easy to forget how down right rugged and sexy Alphabet was. Or maybe I focused on not remembering it.

Voodoo and I were already lovers. Lunchbox kissed me. Alphabet? I didn't want to make any promises I couldn't keep. It was easy to promise myself I'd seduce them to my side if I needed to, but they *were* helping me. Even if I didn't understand every single choice.

"That looks damn good on you," he said, the caress in his voice raking me over. "I'm sorry for chasing you off."

"You didn't." I shook my head. At his skeptical look, I hurried to add. "You really didn't, I felt like I was making it a big deal and making you feel bad, so I backed off. But I'm here, and I'm going to swim unless you have something else for me to do."

I spread my arms, meeting his measuring look a lot more easily than I expected.

"First," he said, raising one finger. "You weren't making me feel bad. The hesitation was more about remembering I have to take off the prosthetic to swim."

I frowned.

"Second," he continued, "I don't want to pressure *you* into anything and I'm not going to lie to you Grace, I promised. You're a wildly attractive woman and I'm already interested. Getting half-naked with you in the water is incredibly appealing."

I opened my mouth and blinked. "Okay."

He cocked his head to the side. "What?"

"I said okay. You're attracted to me. I like you too." I spread my arms again. "I like all of you and yes, this is a really strange situation, how we met and stuff and this conversation is a lot more awkward than I thought it would be, but..."

It was my turn to raise a finger.

"I really like you, AB. I think that's been part of the problem from the beginning. I have to find my sister and I didn't understand entirely why you guys weren't letting me go home, and yes—I was probably being pigheaded about it."

Shut up, Grace.

"No, I was definitely being pigheaded about it. I'm having sex with Voodoo."

He knows that Grace, shut up.

"I know you know, but you don't know that Lunchbox kissed me this morning."

Seriously, Grace? Did you forget how to shut the fuck up?

"Voodoo said he didn't mind and I'm kind of unpacking that at the moment. You're my friend. I think... you're probably the first one who became a real friend here and I know Lunchbox and Voodoo are trying and I like them. Boney Boy doesn't count, so I'm not going to drag him into this conversation."

The words would just not stop coming out of my mouth.

"I guess, what I'm trying to say is that—I like the idea of getting half-naked and wet with you. I think you could use the break. The prosthetic doesn't scare me and if you have to take it off, then take it off. But if it makes *you* uncomfortable, then don't."

Was that it? I blew out a long breath.

"Done?" His quiet question asked me the same thing.

"I think so," I said. "I didn't actually realize I was going to say all that."

"Accepted." He closed the distance between us. The shadow he cast over me as he neared blocked out the sun shining through the glass doors. My feet were all but glued to the floor.

When he lifted his hands and raised his eyebrows, puzzlement trapped me. What... Oh, I shook myself out of whatever stupid stupor I was wallowing in. He was telegraphing his intention to touch me. He was giving me time to say no.

I nodded once. His earlier smile returned as he framed my face in his palms. They were rougher than I remembered, callused. Still, the contact sizzled right over my nerves.

This close, I couldn't mistake the scent of him for anything else. He was summer sunshine, salty breezes, and something a little sweeter. It made me think of the beach and coconut lotions. Or maybe that was just the blond shagginess of him.

"I really like your haircut," I said, the words bubbling right out. "I should say style, I just... yeah, I like it."

I wanted to clamp a mental hand over my mouth to shut up before I made a bigger fool out of myself.

His chuckle alleviated some of my embarrassment. "Gracie-girl, I'm going to kiss you right now, but just so we're one hundred percent on the same page. I am attracted to you and I don't care what you're doing with Voodoo and Lunchbox as long as there's room for me."

Room for—

I really didn't get a chance to process his comment at all because he dipped his head and then his mouth was on mine. It was a slow burn of a kiss, a stroke of his lips. A caress. A whisper of contact. Then he deepened it with a lick of his tongue delving deep, and I pressed my hands to his chest.

His skin was hot under my fingertips. I pushed up on my toes because he was so damn tall. They were all so tall and he surrounded me, all that strength and sturdiness. He had to truly lean down so we could kiss. Thrill raced over my nerve endings and the world slipped a little sideways.

No, it slipped more than a little. He dropped one of his

hands from my face to my hip and then he wrapped that arm around me and I was up, crushed to his chest as I slid my arms around his neck.

From slow burn to full scorcher, he turned me inside out with the kiss that demanded everything. Demanded and took, and returned so fiercely. The whole world shifted and then he was sitting down and I was straddling his lap.

He alternated between the drugging caress of his mouth with mine and the sting of his stubble scraping against my cheeks. The sweet and the bite, it was like chasing the salt and the lime with the tequila. It detonated my system with every bit the same force as doing shots did.

The shift in our positions let my knees slide onto the cushions as he massaged my back and then down to my ass. There was a tug, then the towel I'd been wearing vanished as he whisked it away.

"Gracie," he whispered against my lips. "Does that answer your question?"

I dragged my head up to stare down at him. His pupils were huge and his lips shiny. If I looked anything like him, then I was every bit as wrecked on the outside as I was on the in. "What question?"

His sudden grin was the sun coming out and then he cupped my neck and dragged me in for another kiss. This close, it was all skin on skin, except my bra was in the way. It was so much contact.

Too much. Not enough.

"You're tensing," he said against my mouth before he bit down on my lower lip and my cunt clenched around emptiness. One kiss and I was ready to climb him like a tree.

What a kiss.

"Not a bad tense," I promised him.

"No?" He fisted his hand in my hair, tugging my head back when I would have kissed him again. The heat in his eyes seared me right to my soul.

"No," I promised. "A very needy tense. But not a bad one."

I raised my left hand and covered my pinky nail with my thumb as I held up three fingers.

"Scout's Honor."

"Not the Scout sign," he chided, but the low rumbling chuckle underscoring his words turned my insides to liquid and I wanted to drown in him.

"No?" I thought that was how he did it.

"Nope," he said on a cheerful note. Then with another laugh, he devoured my mouth. Even with the bra, the rub of my chest to his had my nipples tightening. I rolled my hips against him, the bulge under his zipper a tantalizing temptation that I didn't want to resist.

A yip from Goblin had me jerking back and we both turned to look at the dog staring up at us, head canted as if he wasn't sure what we were doing.

"Not this time, buddy," Alphabet said. "Go take a break." When he lifted his chin, Goblin barked once then streaked out of the room.

I blinked after him, then Alphabet was massaging my ass. His hands were huge. It was like being surrounded and shielded on all sides. I was right where I wanted to be.

"You need a bed?" The question was so damn soft it sent flutters through my system.

I dropped my hand to his zipper and tugged it down. Then his cock was against my fingers. Someone was running commando and his nostrils flared at the contact of my hand on him.

"No," I said, answering the question as I stroked him

from base to tip and down again. The steel length of him was even hotter against my palm. "Just need this..." I arched upward and tugged my panties to the side so I could tease his cock against me.

I was already soaking, but that just ignited a whole other level of need in me. His breath came in faster pants and his hands flexed against me but he didn't change our position or urge me to go faster.

The slow rub of his tip along my labia to my clit then back again added more slickness to him or maybe it was to me. I couldn't look away for a moment.

Fair was fair though, so I grappled with some sanity long enough to ask, "Do you need a bed?"

"Absolutely the fuck not, Gracie-girl. I need to be in you though... so whenever you're ready."

We seemed to stay there, suspended in that moment when need and desire collided and I sank down. The feel of him impaling me was everything. I tilted my head back, the intimacy almost too damn much but then his hand was in my hair again and he dragged my gaze to his.

"All of me, Gracie," he ordered. "Take every single inch."

That was a command I was more than happy to follow.

THIRTY-ONE

GRACE

The moment he filled me, the need transformed into urgency and the fist of his grip keeping me focused on him only seemed to kindle a kind frantic craving. I surged up to rock against him only to have him seize my hips and drive me down again.

Our mouths collided. We both seemed to abandon the earlier gentleness. Our kiss was all teeth, tongue, and heat. Gasps of breath left him to fill my lungs even as he took the air from my mouth.

He dragged my sports bra upward but it was only to push it out of the way so he could fill his hands with my breasts. The combination of massage and teasing twists had me clenching around him.

Shifting a hand back into my hair, he demanded I arch my back as I tilted my head back. The position was a strain and it made keeping pace with riding him a challenge. Sweat slicked over my skin from both the angle he kept me at and the slam of his cock filling me.

It was difficult to maintain my rhythm then he sucked one of my nipples against his teeth and I forgot how to breathe. With one hand on my hip and the other in my hair, he guided me up and down even as he sucked, nipped, and teased one nipple before kissing a wet path to the other.

I thrust my fingers into his hair. The thickness of it teased my skin as he nibbled a slow circle on my breast. Then he sucked a hard bite against the curve of it and I swore it sent a bolt of pure lust through me that had me clamping down on his dick.

"Fuck," I whispered, the curse falling from my lips as he shoved it free with another rock of our hips. Oh, hell, he was lifting his hips and driving himself into me as he seemed to gorge on my breasts. I teased my nails over his scalp and just when I thought I might lose my mind, he hauled me back to him and kissed me.

An explosive moan escaped me as he increased the speed of our coming together. The friction of his cock hitting me deep and my breasts rubbing against his chest just amplified the dizzying tension spiraling through me. It was wanton and desperate, even as the way he teased at my lips took on a kind of heady sweetness.

"AB," I gasped out each letter in between kisses. But there was no evading the utter possession of his mouth as he locked me into place so he could drill upwards. Every strike seemed to press my pelvis into his and he moved a thumb down to add more pressure to my clit.

I was going to fly apart. It was almost too damn much. I lost the thread of what I was doing as my thoughts collapsed. We were nothing but sensation and straining bodies, hot breath, and frantic hearts, and more. The hunger was real, I wanted him so damn much.

Then the pressure splintered and the pleasure threatened to drown me. I couldn't escape his contact. The added pressure of his fingers as he pushed upward, filling me on every stroke ripped cry after cry from me.

"Too much," I strained to say, but his mouth swallowed every word. The world went white, and his hips stuttered before he swore. Heat spiraled through my belly as he came. Feeling his release just added another dimension to the impression of him.

Burned into my flesh, molded into my body, and filling me up. His shoulders were slippery when my hands fell to them and I sagged, damn near boneless as he grunted again, another half-jerk and his cum soaked between us as it slid down.

His heart seemed to be racing as fast as mine. His breathing was damn near as ragged. "When I said swim..." I managed to push out the single syllables between gasps of air. "I meant getting wet in the pool."

"Sure," he answered in an equally wrecked voice. "But I like being inside of you, where you're wet and you vise around my cock so goddamn sweetly."

A shudder raced up my spine and my nipples went taut even as my toes curled. I was still spasming around him, little aftershocks chasing through my system as he traced his fingers up my spine.

"We didn't actually get to the taking all our clothes off."

"You're right," he murmured, mouthing a kiss to my shoulder. "Give me a minute."

It was my turn to pat him. The sun spilled over us and it warmed my skin where it reached. Everything else was comfortably snug against him. I wasn't even sure what he meant. Honestly, I probably could have drifted off right there but a few minutes, or maybe it was a few hours later, he moved and lifted me with him.

One moment we were standing and then I was on my back on the sofa as he slipped free. He cupped my pussy and I whimpered. It was almost too sensitive for the heel of his hand to rub against my clit. Then he was pressing his cum back into me.

Another laugh escaped me as he spent a little time rubbing the excess around my clit. It sent starbursts to my vision and my hips bucked again almost of their own volition.

He bent over me and destroyed me with another drugging kiss. When he straightened, I sighed. He stood, gazing down at me like some blond god and all I wanted was to explore every inch of him.

"Stay there." Another kiss and then he strode away. I would push up on my elbows and look after him in a minute.

Just one more minute. I needed to put myself back together again. Find out where my own control went now that my muscles were all but dissolved.

A whisper of fabric roused me and I opened eyes I hadn't even realized had closed. Alphabet was back and he held out a water glass to me.

I managed to push up on an elbow and drank down about half of it thirstily as he peeled his jeans down. The movement revealed his legs to me. The thick ropey muscles of his thighs that tapered over his knee on the left and into his calf but disappeared on the right into the cap of the prosthetic that fit there.

The metal seemed almost insubstantial next to the rest of him. He toed off one shoe, but other stayed in place after he stripped the jeans away and tossed them back into the chair we'd abandoned.

I licked my lips as I studied him. Scars twisted up his

right thigh. Damage from the same injury that took his lower leg? Something else? It had a rough look to it, the skin seemed pitted and I wanted to touch, but even as I stretched out my hand, I glanced up at him for permission.

He drained the rest of the water and set the glass down before he moved closer. "You can touch me, Gracie-girl."

With care, I traced my fingertips over the memory of damage etched into his flesh. It was smoother in some places than others. There were striations in the scars that seemed to deepen over the thicker muscles in his right quadriceps.

He was built, but I hadn't been wrong about his swimmer's build. Or how really beautiful he was. His cock was semi-hard, jutting out. The redness of the tip promising me it was already flushing with blood again. I gave into the desire to stroke my hand upward and give him a couple of pumps before I explored his left thigh with the same devotion I paid to the right.

"If you want to know," he said. "I'll tell you."

That pulled my attention back up to his eyes and I laid back and held out my hand to him. He set his phone down next to the empty glass and then lowered himself until he draped me.

He was even bigger this way, a muscled and masculine blanket that had me wrapping my legs around him and propping my feet against the backs of his thighs. The weight of cock against my pussy just added to the connection.

"Tell me only what you want to tell me. Am I curious?" Oh look, I found my words again. My breathing wasn't quite even yet. "Yes, absolutely. I want to know. But I don't want to hurt you in any way."

What did I know about injuries like this?

One corner of his mouth curved upward as he studied me. "It's not a pretty story, but it's not all that special either. We were on a mission, special forces, Army. We were deep into territory we had no business being in, but the mission demanded it. It was fine until it wasn't."

He traced the lines of my face, teasing around the curve of my jaw with the gentlest of fingers. The deep blue of his eyes was so dark, it was like night fell over them.

"Bombs are definitely *not* fine. Mines are even worse. IEDs… they are the worst of all. The best ones are the ones you don't even see coming. The explosion didn't take the whole of it, but the damage…"

With a shake of his head, he nipped a kiss to my lower lip.

"There's a point where the pain is so much, you forget you're feeling it at all. It's probably endorphins from the agony, or maybe it's the shock. Doc came after me. He got burned really fucking bad trying to get me out. Then the guys were there and they were hauling us both out. Took a long time to get back to safety, but they didn't leave either of us."

A sigh left him and he ghosted another kiss over my lips.

"When I woke up, I was in a medical ward and the leg from below the knee was gone. They tried to repair it. Surgery has come a long way, but there was already infection and the bone was shattered." He waved his other hand as if nudging it all away.

"It feels like a million years ago. Doc was getting sent back to the States. The burn care was going to take a long time. They wanted to send me back too… I needed therapy and recovery and all the things you never think you might need some day."

The light shrug of his shoulders, an acceptance that humbled me even as tears filmed my eyes.

"I couldn't change any of it. It was done. I had to heal. Went to a place down in Texas, it was founded by a Marine —former one anyway. They built up this great rehab with psychiatrists and physical therapists and prosthetic technicians... pretty much anything you think you might need and some you don't."

Another kiss whispered over my lips.

"Eventually, the guys came back, helped pull my head out of my ass. Pushed me with the therapy. So did the guys there... I learned how to move again. I can do pretty much everything I could before with the prosthesis. Well, almost everything... going skinny dipping takes an extra minute cause I need to take it off so the sleeve doesn't get wet."

"That's... but you're okay, now? Right? You said therapy?" I couldn't imagine it. My body and my looks were my living, but that seemed so shallow compared to him.

"We all have good days and bad, Gracie-girl. I do okay most of the time and when I don't... Well, I have Goblin. He helps."

"I can see that." I stroked the hair away from his face. His phone buzzed and he stretched over to pick it up.

"One sec."

He eased upward again and I was suddenly a lot chillier without him. He didn't go far, just shifted to sit on the coffee table, phone in hand. His thumbs flew over the screen. Answering a message, clearly. Then he hit send and there was a little boop of it going.

A moment later another sound indicated a new message. He answered that, and I rolled onto my side to watch him as he went back and forth with the guys—one of them, all of them, did it matter?—for a few minutes.

Another flicker of a smile then he set the phone aside and looked back at me. "They are in place and have eyes on the target."

Fresh tension coiled in my stomach. "It's still daytime though."

"Yep, they'll be several hours yet. So we have time. They want to see if he leaves the house before I work on cracking his security. So we have another hour—maybe two before I have to work."

I licked my lips. "We can do a lot in a couple of hours."

"Gracie-girl," he said, a slow grin lighting him up. "You read my mind."

I don't know which of us reached for the other first, but his mouth was on mine and I was wrapped around him. We had time.

We were going to take it.

THIRTY-TWO

VOODOO

The warm breeze carried the teasing scents of the Mediterranean: salt, sand, and sun. The brightness reflected off the white buildings around us and seemed to add an intense glare to everything, so I kept my sunglasses in place as I strolled the neighborhood.

There were plenty of people, from older ladies to dog walkers to families out walking their pets, from little powder poof purse puppies to the proud, if pampered, standard poodles and everything in between. We'd tracked Gallo all day. He spent most of the day secure behind the walls of his villa.

The billionaire had a tight net of security with a half-dozen guards on the property. Every single one moved like they were military or former military. His driver was a part of the security force.

He also had easily twice as many women frolicking on the estate as well. I doubted there was a single one over the age of twenty playing in and around his pool. The idea this schmuck wanted Grace to be another plaything for his amusement grated more and more as the day passed.

Each hour served as another reminder that this man actually kept upping his offer into seven figures to get Grace to come to him. Was he paying for all those girls in his pool? And was he paying them or someone else?

I didn't like judging anyone's circumstances, but those kids deserved a lot better than that dick.

A *hell* of a lot better.

"Housekeeper is on the move," Lunchbox said over comms from where he was seated at a cafe just down the road from the market. He'd followed her when she left the villa.

"Cars are arriving," Alphabet said. "I have four, looks like two for security, a decoy, and a vehicle for the target."

That was pretty standard.

"Some of the girls are also leaving," Alphabet continued. "I've got four, no five, heading out the side gate on foot. They've got a couple of the security guards going along with them."

"Let them go," Bones ordered. "If he has cars coming, he may be preparing to depart."

That was my thinking. Particularly after we tracked the crew preparing his yacht. "Better to take him from outside the secure perimeter."

"Agreed," Alphabet said. "Gracie says that Gallo generally travels with at least one bodyguard in his vehicle with him—regardless of what company is also with him." That tracked with what we'd already learned. I checked my watch.

"Give him another hour, keep an eye on those vehicles." With that, I continued my slow stroll down the street as the vehicles in question drove right past me.

One hour turned into two and they seemed to drag as we maintained our positions. The vehicles had arrived on property. Security presented a very visible and armed presence. More of his girls left via a limo, so that whittled down more of the civilians around him.

At sundown, activity in the compound increased. Luggage was carried from the house down to the vehicles. That fit with what we knew. I checked my watch again.

Once he was out in the open, we would be free to move.

"Thirty minutes." With two words, Bones had us moving. "Get in position. Alphabet, lock on to his car. I want our target painted before they leave the compound."

"Done," Alphabet said in acknowledgment and our conversational chatter ended. As operations went, this one was more of a walk in the park than a challenge. I took the route back toward town.

Music drifted on the air from the clubs and restaurants. A number of the cafes and eateries had their outdoor seating open. Plenty were packed with customers and the scents of food, wine, cologne, and sweat perfumed the air before the breezes swept them away.

At the twenty-nine minutes and thirty seconds, I was at the cross street where they would turn to head down to the port.

"Marked," Alphabet said. "They are on the move."

I'd traded out my sunglasses for an entirely different pair of glasses calibrated to let me see electronic tagging. They weren't perfect, and had a short range. But all I needed them for was to see which vehicle I wanted.

Traffic increased slowly, but steadily. Two beeps in my ear told me the little caravan we were waiting for closed in on my position. I pulled out the bag of 1 inch triangle spikes. Timing my stumble for being near the curve of the traffic circle heading to the port, I released twenty-five or so to scatter over the road just as the first security car arrived.

More than half were picked up by its tires and the second car snared almost the rest. They weren't even a quarter of a mile down before the first car's tires began to blow.

Delayed reaction was the best. I slowed down the painted target by hitting the crossing button and jogging right into the street. The third car, wearing the painted target, hit their brakes hard.

Oops.

Still grinning, I continued east. "Cleaned out some of the debris. Still need to sack up the last one."

"I got you," Lunchbox practically hummed. "Pick you up in five."

"Good, I'd kill for a beer."

"Great," Lunchbox muttered. "Now I will too."

Chuckling, I canted my head at the sound of squealing tires followed by a blaring horn, then crunches of metal before tires spun out again.

"Oops," Alphabet said. "They missed their turn."

"Well," Lunchbox drawled. "Tag, I'm it."

With that, I went from jog to loping run. I'd just made it to the rendezvous when the painted SUV pulled up. Lunchbox winked at me from the driver's seat as I yanked open the rear passenger door, and slid inside with the pressure injector in my palm.

The bodyguard in the back lunged at me. Very nice of him to reach out. I broke the wrist of the hand with the gun and hit him in the side of the neck with the tranq even as I slid into the car.

The privacy partition was closed. Maurizio Gallo was all the way on the far side of the car trying to open the other door. Not that it was working for him. I knocked on the partition as I closed the door.

"What the hell do you want?" The man asked in a heavy accent, his eyes were wild and showing a great deal of white as they wheeled around searching for his escape.

"An ice cold beer, some good tunes, and maybe a meal with a beautiful woman. You?" I stripped down the gun to its component parts before I emptied the bullets from the magazine. Pretty sure this was an illegal weapon here in France, but then I wasn't going to judge.

"You're insane," Gallo muttered, sweat beading his spray-tanned face. It definitely made him look like an over-ripe melon on the way to going bad.

"Nope, I'm just Voodoo." I waited for the vehicle to slow to a stop again and opened the rear passenger door to shove the unconscious guard out. The rear driver's side door opened, and I swore that Gallo squealed as Bones slid in.

"Who are you?" The overweight man let out a vicious gasp as he tried to retreat. But the only place he had to go brought him straight to me and he ended up trapped in the middle. Bones and I closed the doors at the same moment, then Bones knocked on the partition.

"Any lingering concerns?" Bones directed his attention toward me and ignored the man.

"Not at the moment." I was definitely hungry. The wandering hadn't leant itself to eating much and I didn't really like snacking on a mission.

Bones flicked a look to Gallo, who raked a hand through his hair and shifted his hairpiece subtly. The sweat rolling off him stank up the car, particularly because it made for a vile combo with his cologne and spray-tan product.

I'd smelled better off men who'd been sweating in a

hole in the desert for the better part of a week. Did the man drown himself in product?

"You have no idea who I am," Gallo said. "Or the mistakes you have made."

I spared him a look, then glanced at the window. Lunchbox was taking us a roundabout way out of town. *This* vehicle was not going anywhere near our villa. It took us twenty minutes to reach the swap spot.

"Mr. Gallo, we can do this one of two ways. You can get out of this vehicle and get into the other one without complaint or incident," Bones informed him in a cool, impersonal voice as we stopped.

"Or what?" Gallo seemed to find some courage even if spittle flew from his lips as he tried to glare at Bones. I could have told the overstuffed piece of shift to give it up, but this was a little more entertaining.

"Or it will not end well for you." That was putting it succinctly. "Your choice?"

The silence extended, populated only by the man's harsh breathing. A knock on the roof told me Lunchbox was ready.

"Fuck you," Gallo snarled, actually snarled, and attempted to sound more like a wolf than the pampered pet he was.

Right.

Without rolling my eyes, I opened my side and slid out, then closed the door behind me. Lunchbox eyed me briefly, eyebrows raised.

"He chose poorly."

A grin flashed over Lunchbox's face. The yelp from inside was a little rewarding, but only a little. Then Bones stepped out on the far side.

"He's ready," he said but I was already opening my side

and reaching in to drag the unconscious man out. There were three mangled fingers on the guy's right hand.

Yeah. That had to hurt.

Lunchbox grabbed Gallo's other arm as we hoisted him out, then we dragged him over to our vehicle and loaded him into the back. Once he was secured and covered, Lunchbox spent another minute on the other car before he joined us and we were leaving Gallo's vehicle behind.

Five minutes after we left, it would burst into flames and that would take care of any trace evidence. The drive back to the villa took a little longer as we followed the least monitored route and let Alphabet blank out our progress.

By the time his people caught up to where we left the car, we would be secure.

"Incoming," Bones said over the comms.

"Already got you," Alphabet said. "Gracie put on the coffee."

Gracie.

I rubbed at my jaw then gave myself a careful sniff. Definitely needed a shower before we went to bed tonight. It took a little over an hour after we left Gallo's vehicle to drive through the gates at the villa. We pulled right up into the portico and parked, then turned off all the lights so we could unload.

Alphabet and Goblin met us at the door.

"Secure?" Lunchbox asked. I wasn't the only one making sure Gracie didn't have to see us carry in the sack of shit.

"She's in the kitchen. I asked her to let us put him in the wine cellar *before* she comes out."

Bones grunted, but if he didn't care for Alphabet's choice, he didn't say anything else. The man seemed even heavier after the short ride, or maybe it was just the dead weight.

We hauled him downstairs where a chair, a makeshift cell, and some tools already waited for us. It didn't take long to strip the man out of his clothes or secure him in place. The stench of him was even worse out of his sweat-soaked clothing than it had been before.

Once Lunchbox had his ankles and wrists lashed, I went for the banana bag and IV kits. I got the port in so he was ready for when it was necessary. The chair was set up on a clear plastic liner. Easier for cleanup.

By the time he started showing signs of waking up, we were done. I checked my watch again. "Start tonight or wait for morning?"

We could do it either way. Sometimes, spending a night alone in the dark, cold, unable to move, and unsure of who or what was listening to you could soften someone up a lot faster than heaping abuse on them.

Course, if it didn't work, abuse was next.

"Leave him," Bones said. "Showers. Food. Rest. Give him until dawn."

Worked for me.

Upstairs, the scent of sex was unmistakable even after being smothered in Gallo's funk. Grace stood in the archway separating the dining room from the living area and she studied us as we came up.

Alphabet stood slightly in front of her with Goblin parked between them. The dog was relaxed, but Alphabet seemed a little warier.

Then again, she looked worried as well. Right.

They'd had sex.

"Hungry?" Lunchbox asked, breaking the impasse.

Behind me, I could have sworn Bones cursed, but I ignored him.

"I'm gonna shower," I said taking the handoff easily and flashed a grin at Grace and Alphabet. "Give me fifteen and I'll happily eat and we can debrief."

"You guys are all okay?" Grace pushed forward a couple of steps.

"All good, Gracie," Lunchbox said. "Be back in five." Then he was jogging up to his room.

"Not a scratch," I told Grace. "Gallo is secure. You good?"

Her cheeks seemed to pinken. Was that a blush? That could have been the light, but the faint smirk on Alphabet's face said otherwise. It was utterly charming on her.

"I'm fine," she said. "We had a good day."

"Good. Be right back." I winked and yep, there was relief flickering over her face. Right, we needed to tackle that. If the guys wanted her, I had no problem with that, as long as she wanted it too.

Shower. Eat. Debrief. Put Grace's mind at ease. Sleep.

Tomorrow, we would crack Gallo like an egg and find out what the fuck he had to do with all of this.

Excellent plan.

THIRTY-THREE

GRACE

Dinner was grilled burgers and fast fried potatoes with rosemary. Lunchbox was back before Bones or Voodoo reappeared. When I slipped into the kitchen to offer to help, he wrapped an arm around me and dragged me close.

"You can give me a kiss," he'd murmured and I swore the knot of emotions inside of me twisted me up even tighter. Then his lips grazed over mine, more like miming a kiss than committing to it.

The whisper of his breath on my skin was even headier than the hint of a kiss itself. Shivers eddied over my skin as he lifted his head. "You are so damn dangerous."

"Never to you," he promised, then rubbed his thumb over my lower lip. "You okay?" The intensity in his eyes made them seem far darker than the blue they were normally. It was almost like they were a dark navy with hints of gray. Or maybe that was my imagination.

I sucked in a deep breath of him, the fresh and clean

scent of his soap tickled my nostrils. There were hints of sandalwood around him but the cooking burgers and frying potatoes threatened to drown out the crisper notes.

Despite how short his shower was, he'd taken the time to shave and the lines of his jaw were sharp and angular. There was something innately beautiful about the shape of his features.

He could have been a model. The combination of his height and long, rangy body with his athletic build made for a potent combination. The t-shirt he wore fit him so well it might as well have been tailored, and hid nothing of his muscular shoulders. At the same time, the contrast of soft cotton with the harder body beneath made me want to lean into him.

"Grace?" Lunchbox leaned back to study me, before he shifted to flip the burgers while still keeping an arm around me. The ease in the fluid motion was so damn natural.

"I'm fine," I said, stumbling a little mentally. I'd almost forgotten he asked me a question. Then I gave into the desire to just lean against him.

"Tired?" A hint of worry coated the word.

"She napped," Alphabet said as he came to my rescue. "We're all clear out there. His security is looking, but they haven't even tracked the abandoned car yet."

"Good," Lunchbox said, glancing past me to Alphabet, then to the food. "If you're tired, we call it and debrief in the morning."

"I don't want to call it," I said before they could start making decisions for me. Was I tired? Yes, but I was also... "I am tired, I can admit that. It's been a long day. But we did nap and I don't want to go to sleep without debriefing about what happened and what comes next."

"Good girl," Alphabet whispered as he traced a finger

along my shoulder before he eased past us to open the fridge and pull out the water and juice he'd stored in there earlier.

Pleasure flash fired through me at the comment. "I'm trying," I said, embarrassment creeping through me.

"You don't have to try, Firecracker," Voodoo said as he strolled in and I swore, he looked so damn supple and lithe with each step. It was like he glided, more catlike than human. "Just say whatever it is or do what you need to do."

One by one, the burgers were coming off the grilling pan, but Lunchbox still had his arm around me. The weight of his hand on my hip was both comforting and grounding. If he needed his arm, he wasn't acting like it.

"What he said," Lunchbox continued, as if picking up on the same thread. "You don't have to do anything more than you already are. I just don't want you to exhaust your-self. Even if you have the right to make the call for yourself."

Even if...

I turned that over in my head as he pressed another brief kiss to the top of my head and gave me a squeeze before releasing me. "Need to swap out the potatoes."

Scooting out of his way, I backed up right into Voodoo who looped an arm around my chest at shoulder height and glanced down at me. Heat scorched my face all over again at the knowing look in his dark eyes.

I didn't think Alphabet said anything to them and Voodoo had said earlier he didn't mind if Lunchbox was kissing me. At the same time...

"Stop worrying," Voodoo murmured, folding around me like a cloak that wrapped me up in him. The teasing pres-sure of his lips against my ear sent another wave of sensa-tion through me, especially since the softness of his beard tickled. "Seriously, Firecracker, don't worry so much. It's all good, okay?"

The reassurance helped, to a point, but also...

I tilted my head back and searched his face. Did he know...?

"Do I mean it?" Not one ounce of sarcasm marred the question. "Yes, I do." He flicked a look from me to where Alphabet leaned against the counter.

When my gaze collided with his, Alphabet just lifted his chin. He'd said the same things earlier. If anything, he seemed even more confident now than he had then.

"Did you enjoy yourself?" Voodoo's second question pulled me back to him again. Playfulness reflected in his eyes, then he winked. The heat in my face seemed to bloom to a full-on sunburn before my stomach bottomed out then clenched.

He definitely knew or he was guessing.

"Yes," was my answer. Because I really had enjoyed it. I'd enjoyed Alphabet and being with him. I'd enjoyed the closeness and the intimacy.

"Good." The emphasis in that single syllable dared me to disbelieve him and that cracked the dam of worry inside me. Relief spilled through the openings and I thought I might have fallen if he hadn't been holding me close.

"Food," Lunchbox said, and he cut a glance toward me. "Voodoo is right. As long as you enjoyed yourself, we're good."

Then he shot a look at Alphabet I couldn't quite interpret, but Alphabet just grinned at me and held out his hand. "C'mon Gracie-girl, let them feed us. We put in a lot of work today."

"Is *that* what we're calling it these days?" Bones desert

dry observation was so deadpan it splintered the last of my reserve.

I laughed, which drew Bones' far more irritated gaze in my direction. That just made me laugh harder.

"Food," Lunchbox said, mouth quirking as he cut between me and Bones. Voodoo tugged me over to the breakfast bar and the counter stools spread there. They only had four, but Voodoo just parked himself next to my seat and Alphabet climbed onto the one next to me. That put Lunchbox and Bones the furthest away—well Bones got the very other end of the counter.

It was kind of funny how swiftly they prepped everything. Lunchbox had apparently pre-prepared stuff before they left. There were slices of tomato, onions, lettuce, bacon, and peppers. The potatoes were the absolute perfect form of crispy and the rosemary just added a hint of spice.

The guys built enormous burgers and I took the beef patty, but skipped the bun and I added some sliced tomatoes and even though the potatoes smelled fantastic, I limited it to just a few.

I should probably have skipped those and just went with the lettuce and the onions, but I wasn't as big a fan of the onions. Voodoo grabbed me a knife and fork without me even asking.

"Thank you," I said.

"You sure you don't want more?" Lunchbox asked. The guys had also limited how much they'd taken.

"No, I had lunch."

"Like nine hours ago," Alphabet argued.

"We also had sandwiches at six." Or maybe it was five. I cut into the patty.

"We?" Alphabet countered, pointing one of the crispy

potatoes at me. "I had a sandwich, then finished yours because you didn't want that much."

I wrinkled my nose. "I wasn't that hungry then."

"Enough," Bones said abruptly. "As fascinating as the food conversation is, she's an adult. She can decide what she wants. We have other issues to debrief on that don't involve what Miss Black did or didn't eat."

Bones' interruption landed with a hard thud in the middle of the meal and the guys switched their focus from me to him. I frowned, and made myself take a bite of the burger.

What appetite I'd managed fled in the face of the rising temperature. Voodoo straightened. "If we're boring you, feel free to go to bed, Bones. We can debrief without you."

The two men just *glared* at each other and I chewed until I could manage to swallow the meat. The taste had gone to ash.

"Really?" Bones seemed to just dare him. "Pack it away, based on how it smells down here, you won't be scoring any points in her bed tonight anyway."

"Hey," Alphabet snapped as he pushed back from the counter abruptly. "Watch it."

"Woah," Lunchbox rose to get between them and I choked down that bit of beef. It got stuck in my throat and it seemed to just scrape its way down my esophagus. I went for a glass of water.

"Guys, this isn't helping anyone," Voodoo said and despite his relaxed posture, there was a core of steel in his voice.

My heart slammed against my ribs. The tension in the room seemed to wrap in ever tightening coils of barbed wire and violence.

Blowing out a breath, Bones raised his own glass. "Apologies, Miss Black. My opinions notwithstanding, you didn't deserve the comment."

The ballooning strain popped abruptly and Alphabet glanced at me. A muscle ticked in his jaw, even if some of the scruff hid it. I summoned a smile, I might not be feeling it at the moment but I knew how to put on a show. If he needed me to be okay with this to let it go, then I would be okay.

Frown deepening, Alphabet brushed his knuckles against the back of my hand before he took his seat again. This time when he met my gaze, the smile wasn't as challenging.

I licked my lips then said, "Apology accepted, Boney Boy. It's been a long day."

That sent the last of the anxiety encircling the room down the drain and Lunchbox chuckled.

"Wait, I should have said Mr. Boy, since we're being formal and stuff." That earned me more laughter from the guys and a bland look from the *"boy"* in question.

"Debrief," Bones said, then continued without waiting for any of us to add anything. "The snatch went clean with no injuries."

"Oh, there was at least one," Voodoo said. "The bodyguard has at least a broken wrist."

"Two," Lunchbox volunteered. "The driver wasn't all that willing to part with the vehicle. Pretty sure I dislocated his jaw when he argued." He shrugged with a small smile that just said, "oops" without saying a word.

"Fine, negligible injuries," Bones resumed. "We were able to divert the target from his security, then take him into custody with minimal damage."

It was so weird to hear them talk about it like that. "He's downstairs?"

"He is," Bones said, turning his icy gray gaze toward me. It was like looking into the face of a winter storm. "Where he will remain until we begin questioning tomorrow morning. We go back to working sleep shifts tonight. We need someone on guard at all times. Everyone sleeps with a weapon."

Before I could let my inner smart ass out to play, I took another drink of water.

"Miss Black, do you wish to be present for the questioning?"

Did I? That was a fair question. I put the glass down and reclaimed my fork to move some of the food around on the plate.

"Yes," I answered, without looking at any of them. I didn't want to see rough sympathy or doubt in their gazes. Honestly, I didn't want the encouragement right now. "I am assuming questioning will involve some kind of torture. Not sure I'm one hundred percent comfortable with that, but I'm not opposed to it either."

"You don't have to stay for that part," Voodoo offered.

"Yes, I do," I countered as I cut a tomato slice into quarters. "You're questioning him about me and about Amorette. I want to be there for his answers."

All of them.

"We won't keep anything from you," Lunchbox offered, and I glanced from Voodoo to him to Alphabet. All three of them were reaching out in their own ways.

Weirdly though, it was the absolute lack of anything resembling sympathy or objection in Bones' flat-eyed gaze that boosted me. "I know," I said, speaking directly to him. "But this is about me, I should be there. For one, I've dealt with him before. For another, I'm the one he was offering so much money to see."

If he had anything to do with Eleanor's death, then I wanted to know.

"I have to know." That was what it came down to.

"Then get some sleep tonight," Bones told me. "Dawn will come early."

CHAPTER

THIRTY-FOUR

BONES

Grace Black was in the kitchen drinking coffee when I entered. Dawn ribboned across the eastern sky and the whole team was up and present, save for Alphabet who was out with Goblin but would return shortly.

Five hours of sleep was usually enough for me. Today was no different, except I *felt* like I was on edge, sleep deprived, and tense. All three of my men were in different stages of a decaying orbit as they fell in toward Grace.

The model didn't seem to have to do anything but exist to be a colossal distraction. Whether she was in shorts and a tank top, or an oversized sweatshirt and leggings, she stood out against the rest of us.

Far too damn delicate, fragile, and small. I doubted she'd ever held a weapon or had a self-defense class. The image of her wounded eyes when we'd first begun placing or helping the former captives return to their own homes left an indelible impression.

No doubt existed within me that she had been hurt, likely raped. The attempts of a few to reacquire her had kept her in our custody. Taking her to base, however, had been my choice.

That was a command decision I had to live with, and I would. At the sound of the door opening, I downed the last of my coffee. "Ten minutes. Then we get started. Make sure Miss Black has something to cover her mouth and nose."

After rinsing the cup and leaving it next to the sink, I went to retrieve my gear. Every interrogation was different. Enhanced methods might get answers, but they didn't always get accurate ones or even particularly truthful ones.

A person would say just about anything to avoid pain—especially after they were in tremendous amounts of it. Pain could be compartmentalized, but survival could overcome resistance. You just had to know what you were willing to suffer.

Interrogation should be tailored to the subject. It really wasn't one size fits all, as most things in life weren't. I'd spent the past week learning about Maurizio Gallo from his likes and dislikes to his personal preferences, history, and habits.

More, I'd learned about his family. An abusive, authoritarian father and an emotionally aloof and distant mother fostered poor self-esteem in young Maurizio, along with a difficulty in regulating his emotions.

He struggled in school, his father's wealth often buying his son out of trouble. Based on observed behaviors and three ex-wives, Gallo struggled in social situations unless he was totally in control.

While there were no reports of physical abuse where his previous spouses were concerned, all three detailed his emotional unavailability and hostile home environments.

With his wealth, he could pay off his ex-spouses and detractors, essentially "erasing" their complaints.

The combination of traits and historical behavior made him the ideal candidate for human trafficking. He preferred to pay for his companionship, to own it, to detail what they could do, think, and feel. When he tired of them, he discarded them like a used-up toy.

Spoiled. Vain. Damaged.

This was the man who wanted to purchase Grace Black's presence and time. The amount suggested he wanted far more and he was willing to pay any cost. He was involved in the labyrinthine conspiracy surrounding her kidnapping and the disappearance of her sister.

How involved?

I opened the door to the wine cellar, flipped on the light switch to flood the darkness, and then descended the steps. The others were behind me. Maurizio Gallo squinted painfully against the sudden brightness.

The skin at his wrists was raw from his struggles with the restraints. His feet were swollen, likely from sitting in the uncomfortable chair. The sallow color of his skin under the spray tan looked even more ill. He was pudgy in several spots, a man used to soft living, rich foods, and too much alcohol.

Gallo glared at me even as he teared up from the light. Then he looked past me to the others as they ranged out. I said nothing, not yet. Let him get a good look at who we were and where he was.

The moment his gaze latched onto Grace, it reflected in his eyes. Shock rippled over his face, his mouth opened and he tried to wet his lips. He shifted against the hard wood of the chair and his shriveled little cock twitched.

"Come—" The word came out hoarse as though he'd

turned his throat raw from yelling. Or maybe it was just dry from lack of water. The dried yellow stain of urine on the plastic liner we'd spread out on the floor below him said he wasn't *that* dehydrated yet.

Gallo coughed.

The dry hack was as unattractive as the rest of him.

"Grace," he finally managed to wheeze out, though he added some reverence and lust to his rough voice. "Come closer."

"Get a grip, Floppy." I set the foldable tool bag down on the counter and unrolled it. "She's not even here."

"She's right—" He choked off the rest of his statement when Voodoo just stepped forward, blocking his view. The man had a gift for looming when he so desired. Gallo's eyes widened and he tried to retreat into the chair, but he couldn't really go anywhere.

"As I was saying," I continued, as I made a point of examining the tools I had with me. This wasn't the full measure of them, just some that might come in handy—the ball peen hammer for example. "Get a grip, Floppy. We're not here to answer your questions."

Lunchbox shifted and moved to stand right behind Gallo now. Yes, the guys understood exactly what we were doing. They didn't say anything or touch him. They were just there. From the corner of my eye, I caught Gallo beginning to tremble. Whether from cold or fear it didn't really matter.

"Then why—" The man's accented voice was a record scratch. The hints of Italian was nowhere near as profound as some I'd heard. Still, it was there.

"You're here to answer our questions," I informed him.

"Then you let me go?" Yeah, the man desperately needed a drink. *That* would be a reward, if he was good.

"That depends entirely on you," I said, drifting my fingers over to an ice pick. "Fuck around, and you'll find out." I pulled out the snippers. A tried and trusted tool.

Pivoting, I faced him and just tapped the device against my palm.

"What questions?" He jerked his gaze from me to Voodoo then tried to look back at Lunchbox before he flicked a glance to where Grace stood. I didn't turn or say anything. Alphabet hadn't closed in yet. He took guard position for now.

That worked.

Grace wanted to be here for this and she expected torture. Still, until you were face to face with someone else's suffering, you had no idea how you would react. Alphabet could pull her out if this got bad.

I took one step and Gallo *shrieked* like I'd stabbed him. Even prepared for a reaction, the sound ripped through me like nails dragged over a chalkboard.

Lunchbox made a face behind our *guest* and shook his head.

"What questions?" Gallo demanded. "What? You haven't *asked* me anything!" His eyes were wild, I swore they were rolling around so hard it was like seeing balls struck in a game of pool. He couldn't seem to decide where to look. "Grace, *cara mia*, we are friends, yes? I am always generous. Yes?"

Voodoo slapped the man with the back of his hand. An open palm slap was pretty damn insulting. The back of the hand was almost as bad. "Don't talk to her. Talk to us."

Gallo cringed. "Then ask me something?" It was as much a demand as it was a plea.

The stink of urine accompanied the trickling sound of

fluid. Yeah, whatever force he was trying to imbue into his words was lost with that response.

Fight or flight.

Maurizio Gallo had no fight.

Maybe he only had it when he paid for everything and had his lapdogs around him.

How sad for him.

Oh well, moving on.

"Explain your million dollar offer for Miss Black."

Gallo snapped his attention back to me. "It was at almost three million... I raised it."

That was an unexpected answer. "Excuse me?"

A soft scrape of shoe told me Grace was moving, but she didn't close in, so hopefully Alphabet stopped her.

I nudged Gallo with a toe of my boot and he flinched so hard, he nearly toppled his chair. Lunchbox had to brace it to keep him from going down.

"Three million?" I prompted when Gallo wrenched his focus back to me once again.

"The auction site... after the manager—after she say no *again*. I went to the auction and there she was, cara mia, the beautiful—" He hesitated to say her name. Smart. It was about time. "She was there. Opening bid, one million... I was in the lead. It was over three when they put it on hold and now waits in pending."

"Website?" Voodoo asked even as Lunchbox said, "Auction?"

The silence behind me reverberated with all her hopes, fears, and questions. Good girl, don't say anything to him. We hadn't discussed this part, but he *wanted* her attention. Denying him that was another tool in our arsenal.

"The website... The procurers, they find the best, the

most valuable. The coveted. Art. Beauty." Gallo licked at his dry lips.

"People?" I spit the word out.

"Yes," the man said and then he tried to shrug, but grimaced because his wrists were bound tightly to the chair arms. "The beautiful Grace was there, I will outbid anyone to have her."

They had an *auction* website. Rage crashed through me like a thunderclap.

Auction.

For people.

I tapped the snippers against my palm again keeping everything still. "Website address?"

"You have her, you have it." Gallo stared at me like I'd sprouted a second head. I could feel Lunchbox and Voodoo exchanging glances. I didn't check with them. I kept my attention riveted on the sad sack of shit in front of me. "How much do you want?"

I blew out a long breath. Instead of relieving my temper, it just fanned the flames. Lunchbox lost all expression and his eyes went flat. I didn't have to check Voodoo to know that the man had basically just signed his death warrant with that question.

I had no problems with dealing it out when we were done.

With that in mind, I reached for one of his hands where they were secured and put the snippers to the tip of his finger. Gallo shrieked and struggled, the stink of ammonia increased and sweat began to bead along his body even in the chill of the cellar.

Yeah, fear could devour a man alive.

"Website address. Not asking again." I kept him pinned

with my gaze, snippers open and around his fingertip just above that knuckle.

With spittle flying from his lips, Gallo babbled out a string of letters and numbers. It was almost impressive, because he didn't stumble once.

"Got it." They were the first two words Alphabet had said since we got down here.

"One more question..." I straightened, vaguely dissatisfied that I didn't have to start removing his digits one knuckle at a time. At the rate we were going, we'd intimidate him into answers.

"What?" Gallo snapped, impatient as I considered exactly how to word it. The sharpness in his voice matched the hard-eyed look he'd found.

Unimpressed, I broke his index finger. He blanched, all the color leaching from his face. His mouth opened and his scream came out harsh and grating. Fat tears escaped his blurry eyes and began to roll down his face.

Pivoting, I focused on Grace then lifted my chin and nodded her toward the stairs. Questions stamped all over her face, but instead of arguing she nodded and headed upstairs, with Alphabet a half-step behind her. I followed them.

"Feel free to continue with him," I told them when I was at the top of the stairs. They could pull more teeth, literally or figuratively, I didn't care much. Right now, I needed a conversation with Grace without her guardians on point.

We also needed more on this website. At the top of the stairs, I closed the door to the cellar before following Alphabet and Grace into the living room.

"What's up?" Alphabet's neutral voice betrayed none of the ferocity burning in his eyes.

"I need to speak with Miss Black for a few minutes—

alone," I stressed before he could object. "I need you to check that website. If there is some auction site that lists her, it's a good starting point to track it back to the source."

That would give us a target. Gallo was just the start. Frankly, I didn't get "mastermind" off him in the slightest. He was a wealthy, spoiled man used to getting his way without giving a single fuck for a consequence. I doubted he knew much more than he was saying, but we had time to get the rest of it out of him.

Frowning, Alphabet glanced at Grace. "Are you fine with talking to him? I can be just in the dining room."

"Your faith moves me," I told him, then looked at Grace again. "I'd rather take Miss Black for a walk." Away from all three of them. I needed answers and I was fairly certain she could give them to me if they weren't all trying to shield her constantly.

As it was, she stood there with her arms folded and her eyes huge. While she was pale, I thought that had more to do with the contrast of her dark hair and bright eyes than anything else. She was also shivering. It was faint, but it was present. "Is 'take me for a walk' code for take me out behind the wood shed or dispose of me?"

There was the barest hint of sarcasm underscoring her humor.

Barest hint.

"I seem to have misplaced my sap," I told her drily. "You'll be fine. We're going to take a walk, warm you back up, and I have a couple of questions I want to ask *without* you worrying about someone else listening or throwing in their two cents." The last I gave Alphabet a hard look before looking back at her.

For his part, Alphabet sighed. "You probably could use the air."

She chewed her lower lip then looked from him to me then to where Goblin watched us from the sofa. He'd been snoring when we got up here, but now he was in wait and watch mode.

That was good. It meant despite Alphabet's tightly fisted temper, he wasn't struggling.

"Okay," she said. "Let me get my shoes."

"Get sunglasses too."

"Take mine," Alphabet told her as he diverted to the dining room. I didn't miss how he made sure to tuck her phone into the back pocket of her shorts.

Keeping her trackable was a solid idea. Fortunately, he didn't make our leaving an issue. I guided her out the back door then toward the gate that separated the pool from the garden proper. After that, we descended steps to another gate that was tucked into a wall and hidden by overgrown flowers.

"This is kind of neat," she said as I held the gate open for her. The sun was high, and the breeze strong. It was barely ten in the morning. We hadn't been down there that long or at least it hadn't felt like it.

I scanned the area before I secured the gate then motioned to the right. "If we go this way, we'll take the long way around but we'll be back at the villa. Fifteen minutes. Probably less."

She studied me for a beat, or at least I thought she did. The sunglasses hid her eyes. With a nod, she turned to walk in the direction I indicated ,while using both hands to gather her hair up into a ponytail that she secured with a band she had around her wrist.

The heat felt good.

I let her set the pace. If I did, she'd have to take two steps for every one of mine and we'd be back a lot faster.

"You wanted to ask me questions?" The prompt was as unexpected to hear as it was to actually need it.

"I do," I said, getting my thoughts in order. "You haven't been a fan of our choices so far."

"I haven't been a fan of you just deciding everything for me without involving me." There was an edge to the words, almost like she wanted to rap my knuckles with a ruler for daring to say otherwise. "That said, you guys have all gone out of your way to protect me. I know I haven't exactly been easy."

"That's an understatement," I muttered the words and she stopped dead to stare at me. "What? You are difficult, sometimes childish, incredibly fragile, dangerously vulnerable, and you don't want to listen."

Oh, I could *see* the virtual steam rising from her ears.

"Before you get angry," I said, holding up a hand. "I accept that you have improved and that I could also learn to listen better."

It was a concession.

Her mouth fell open. Whether she was merely speechless for a few seconds or just preparing to launch into a tirade, I shifted to nudge her back into walking. The affluent area had homes scattered all over the hillside. But it was still better to not linger too long in one space.

"You're not wrong," she finally said on a huff of breath. Well, maybe we could get to detente. "I'm working on it."

"So am I," I said firmly.

"Fine, so ask whatever the questions you have are and I will try not to just jump to some wild conclusion."

"Very kind." Yes, I deadpanned the words particularly since she sounded like she was doing me a favor.

"I can be." Despite the catty little rebellion in her tone, she didn't stick her tongue out at me.

"Miss Black..." I sighed now.

"Mr. Boy?" She gave me a pointed look.

"Maurizio Gallo is not your problem." Better to start with the facts. "Did he wish to purchase you? Yes. Though he is more of the customer than the supplier."

"That's a horrible thought," she admitted.

"Agreed. Alphabet will deal with the website. We can use it to track back to whomever the suppliers were that were listing you there." While that might be an effective next step...

"He never mentioned Amorette." No. The man had not. "Maurizio didn't know about my sister before. I never talked about her. But down there, he was saying a lot but he never mentioned her."

"No." I kept my head on a swivel. There was a mother out for a walk with a stroller. Cars rolled by. The sounds of town a few short blocks down the hill carried upward. "He mentioned your auction as pending. Also, that he wanted to be the top bidder."

"Because he likes beautiful things."

"Yes."

"Amorette and I are identical." Her sigh was so deep, I wanted to offer her comfort but I had none at the moment. "He didn't include her in this."

"No, either she was sold separately or she is being held in abeyance for a future auction."

"Or it's that second group that took her." She let out a low groan. "I hate this."

"I know. I wish I could offer you some type of reassurance. This is merely the first mission. We gathered more information. We may yet gather more. If nothing else, we will shut down the website and its owners. We will eliminate that problem."

I could promise her that.

"But if they weren't involved with Amorette then we are no closer to her than when I came off that truck."

"No. The more time that passes. The more likely it is what trail there might have been will go cold. We don't know who the other parties are. Competitors? Allies? Until we do, we can't act on it."

She paused under the shade of a huge tree that seemed to drape over another garden wall like a lover. "You want me to give up on finding her."

I paused, facing her. "What I want is irrelevant. What I want to ask is how long do you want to devote to this task? We can do everything we can, but if we have an indeterminate timeline, at what point do you accept that we may never find her?"

At what point did she let her sister go.

"It hasn't been that long yet."

"No, it hasn't. We have actionable intel. We may turn up more. As we find it, we will act. But we cannot stay in this state indefinitely, particularly if all leads dry up."

This was why I wanted to talk to her alone. The guys were not reasonable where she was concerned. They were making more and more choices around her and for her, not for any plans we might have had or future mission objectives.

That was dangerous for all of us.

"Consider this, Miss Black, how long do you want to take? How much time will be enough? How far are you willing to go?" I held up a hand. "You don't have to tell me, you don't even have to know. Eventually, we will need to answer these questions. For you."

For them.

I needed solid metrics to plan around.

"I hate that you're asking me this," she said in a half-whisper that carried no anger, just sadness. That sadness scraped away at some of my irritation with her.

Rather than offer her any platitudes, I cupped her elbow and set us off again. We would be back at the villa soon enough.

We'd just turned the corner toward the gates that opened up to the drive for the villa when the first popping sounds reached me. Muffled gunfire, but definitely gunfire.

"The gates are open..." Confusion filled her voice. "Are they watching for us?"

No. The gates shouldn't be open. At the gate themselves, I tugged her back toward me and nearer to the wall. There was more gunfire. It was unmistakably the sound of a weapon's discharge. Semi automatic.

"We need to go," I told her, wrapping a hand around her biceps.

"What?" She looked up at me. "The guys..."

Yes. My guys were up there. "I'm aware, Miss Black." I pulled her with me. She wasn't armed and I wasn't taking her into that situation. Our current strategy called for whoever was closest to her to exfil with her immediately in case of assault or conflict.

She was my problem now.

"Bones," she argued as I increased our pace and she half-jogged to keep up with me. "We can't just leave them."

"We can," I told her. We were almost to the backup vehicle. We all had keys for it. "We will." When she would have dug in her heels, I just picked her up. "Listen to me, Miss Black. You fighting me and arguing right now just slows me down. We need to secure you *then* I can get them out, if they haven't already done it themselves. The longer it takes me to secure you, the longer it takes to get to them."

I kept everything as even and neutral as possible. Air whooshed out of her and she stopped struggling. "Fine."

Good girl. At the escape car, I unlocked it and pointed her inside. For once, she just obeyed. In the driver's seat, I started the car and kept an eye on the rearview.

In a perfect situation, the guys would have cleaned up the problem and would call us for a rendezvous within thirty minutes. That would be ideal.

When I got the car turned around, Grace let out a horrified gasp. Goblin raced toward us down the street. The closer he came to us, the clearer it was that he was covered in blood.

This was definitely not an ideal situation.

Goddammit.

****

The story will continue in OWN, Book 3 of the BLOOD Brothers.

AFTERWORD

Thank you so much for reading., we'll return to the chaos very soon. The preorder says August, but I have every intention of getting it out much sooner! If you enjoyed the read, be sure to leave a review and head over to the pack, we'd love to have you!

xoxo
Heather

Website:
heatherlong.net
Reader group:
facebook.com/groups/heatherspack
Spoiler group:
facebook.com/groups/teammadatheather

OWN

The closer I get to the truth, the further away it feels. Every step I take is met with resistance—not just from the monsters still chasing me, but from the very men who have sworn to protect me. Especially Bones.

Cold. Controlled. Ruthless.

He watches me like I'm the problem he's been ordered to solve, not the woman desperate to find her missing sister. And maybe I *am* the problem—because I won't stop. Not for him. Not for anyone.

But when a lead surfaces, one so risky even I can't believe I'm willing to chase it, he doesn't shut me down.

He should. Especially when the others are so violently opposed.

Instead, he offers help. Conditions attached. Motives unclear.

For once, Bones and I are on the same page, even if that page is stained with blood. Maybe he wants me to fail. Maybe he wants me gone. Or maybe, somewhere under all that armor, he understands what it means to lose someone and not be able to let go.

Either way, I'm taking the chance. Because this might be my last shot at finding Amorette before she disappears forever.

And if I have to break every rule—and every heart—to get to her, then so be it.

About Heather Long

I *love* books. Not just a little bit, but a lot. Books were my best friends when I was growing up. Books didn't care if I was new to a town or to a class. They were always there, my trustiest of companions. Until they turned on me and said I had to write them.

I can tell you that my own personal happily ever after included writing books. I've always said that an HEA is a work in progress. It's true in my marriage, my friendships, and in my career. I am constantly nurturing my muse as we dive into new tales, new tropes, new characters and more.

After seventeen years in Texas, we relocated to the Pacific Northwest in search of seasons, new experiences, and new geography. I can't wait to discover what life (and my muse) have in store for me.

Maybe writing was always my destiny and romance my fate. After all, my grandmother wasn't a fan of picture books and used to read me her Harlequin Romance novels.

Follow Heather & Sign up for her newsletter:
www.heatherlong.net
TikTok

Also by Heather Long

82nd Street Vandals

Savage Vandal

Vicious Rebel

Ruthless Traitor

Dirty Devil

Shamelessly Loyal (Novella)

Brutal Fighter

Dangerous Renegade

Merciless Spy

Reckless Thief

Fierce Dancer

Dirty Dancer

Bay Ridge Royals

Shamelessly Loyal (Novella)

Battle Lines

Deceptive Truce

Wicked Surrender

Violent Chaos

Desperate Victory

BLOOD Brothers

Burn

Lure

Blue Ivy Prep

Problem Child

Mad Boys

Party Crashers

Money Shot

Bravo Team Wolf

When Danger Bites

Bitten Under Fire

Cardinal Sins

Kill Song

First Chorus

High Note

Last Word

Chance Monroe

Earth Witches Aren't Easy

Plan Witch from Out of Town

Bad Witch Rising

Fevered Hearts

Marshal of Hel Dorado

Brave are the Lonely

Micah & Mrs. Miller

A Fistful of Dreams

Raising Kane

Wanted: Fevered or Alive

Wild and Fevered

The Quick & The Fevered

A Man Called Wyatt

Heart of the Nebula

Queenmaker

Deal Breaker

Throne Taker

Lone Star Leathernecks

Semper Fi Cowboy

As You Were, Cowboy

Shackled Souls

Succubus Chained

Succubus Unchained

Succubus Blessed

Shackled Souls (Omnibus)

STANDALONES

Kiss of Fate (w/Blake Blessing)

Taste of Karma (w/Blake Blessing)

I'll Be Home... (w/Tate James)

Overexposed (w/Tate James)

Switchboard Duet

Talk to Me

Don't Let Go

Untouchable

Rules and Roses

Changes and Chocolates

Keys and Kisses

Whispers and Wishes

Hangovers and Holidays

Brazen and Breathless

Trials and Tiaras

Graduation and Gifts

Defiance and Dedication

Songs and Sweethearts

Legacy and Lovers

Farewells and Forever

Hellos and Happily Ever Afters

Wolves of Willow Bend

Wolf at Law

Wolf Bite

Caged Wolf

Wolf Claim

Wolf Next Door

Rogue Wolf

Bayou Wolf

Untamed Wolf

Wolf with Benefits

River Wolf

Single Wicked Wolf

Desert Wolf

Snow Wolf

Wolf on Board

Holly Jolly Wolf

Shadow Wolf

His Moonstruck Wolf

Thunder Wolf

Ghost Wolf

Outlaw Wolves

Wolf Unleashed